THE CLAIRVOYANT'S GLASSES

Volume 4

Helen Goltz

Atlas Productions

The Clairvoyant's Glasses Volume 4

PUBLISHED BY: Atlas Productions

First published 2023.

Cover design by Karri Klawiter, Art by Karri.

PLEASE NOTE: This book is written in British-Australian English.

Dedicated to you, dear reader.

I only intended to write the first book as I had a quirky idea about glasses being cursed, but thank you for inviting me to make it a series.

PROLOGUE – WHAT CAME BEFORE...

A LONG TIME AGO, in the 16th century, a man named Samuel Rayne believed himself to be the most fortunate man alive. He won the hand of a beautiful woman, Issbelle, and they were blessed with a daughter, Elsopeth. Until one day, he heard men speak of an ugly old hag as they glanced towards his wife. Samuel dismissed the thought; his wife was a silver-haired beauty. Again, when passing through a village with his family, he saw men look away and the fear on the faces of the women. Had he been bewitched to see his wife in a form only he could see? Samuel knew her to have strong powers that she used for healing, but was she capable of this deception?

Tragedy struck, and young Elsopeth took sick. Despite all the healing Issbelle had offered to so many, she could not save their half-human, half-witch daughter. Samuel raged. Angry, bitter, and broken-hearted, he demanded the truth. Was he bewitched? Was his wife not whom he perceived?

On learning it to be so, Samuel Rayne deserted his wife, denouncing all witchcraft and denying the half-spirit child his wife brought back from the dead and proclaimed was Elsopeth. Falling into neglect, he was taken by fever, and the village healer, Saghani, brought him back to good health. There was no gratitude to be had; Samuel proclaimed her a witch. He wanted to die and join his daughter, but now he was alive with his grief.

Despite many years of separation from his childhood friend, Bran, on finding out that Saghani was Bran's wife, he did not relent. Instead, Samuel believed he was doing his friend a service and wished the same honesty had been shown to himself when in love with Issbelle. Saghani was sentenced and hanged as a witch, leaving behind her husband and children – Hadley and Harley.

Before she died, she cursed Samuel for claiming she had the vision when she had helped and healed so many. She cursed his glasses and that of a principal Rayne descendant for eternity so they would have visions and be tormented by the futures of all their loved ones, knowing what would happen to them without the power to change or help.

Saghani's son, Harley, was an angry young man who ensured the Raven side of their bloodline tormented the accursed for all time. Saghani's daughter, Hadley, was a peacemaker and the dove of the family, forgiving and protecting. Throughout time, their descendants fulfilled these roles. Many of the modern-day accursed learned to live with their visions, even making successful careers from their clairvoyance skills.

And so it is we have reached the current century. But a rare occurrence has eventuated – the cursed descendant of Samuel Rayne – Daphne Shelby – has died without bearing a child, and Saghani's curse has passed to Daphne's niece, a budding actress – the very same niece who also descends from Samuel Rayne and Issbelle's daughter, Elsopeth. For the first time in history, the accursed is a witch. Her name is Sophie Carell.

CHAPTER 1

THE OCCASIONAL SOUND IN the room reached him as he lay motionless, drifting in and out of consciousness. The beep of a machine was a constant, steady friend.

'Murdoch, open your eyes; come back to us.'

He knew the sound of his brother's voice, and he had told him to leave and go home to his family. Did the words reach Allanon? He felt the scrape of a razor across his face, methodically, words spoken in conversation by his brother as he completed the chore. He didn't want to be shaved, but Murdoch could not tell him that; perhaps it gave Allanon something to do other than stare at a brother he should forget.

A whisper, someone making a hushing sound, a child's voice, a gruff voice, medical opinions, his brother again – a cycle of small sounds filtering through his consciousness. But none of them her. Sophie.

He could feel himself falling, fast, the fear, wings beating, heart thumping. No, he wanted to fall, and then there was darkness again.

'Murdoch, it's time to come back.' His brother again. The same message over and over and over.

'Leave me, Allanon. Return to your family.' Murdoch didn't know if he was saying the words or thinking them.

'No change,' the doctor said.

Is he talking to me?

'Thank you, Doctor,' his brother said.

Still here. Go home, Allanon. Go back to your wife and children, and forget about me.

'I am not giving up on you, Murdoch.'

Did he hear me?

'You are my only brother, my only sibling, and I cannot be without you, don't leave me.'

You don't need me. Go home, Allanon.

He heard his brother sigh and rise and his footsteps as he departed. As Murdoch wished.

The sun hit the leadlight windows of the boutique *Optical Illusion* store at one-thirty p.m., making passers-by shield their eyes from rays of reflecting light. It was a welcome and constant cycle in winter, and septuagenarian Alfred Lens liked that which was constant – not much was in his world. The glass and giftware store was not easy to find, but customers were loyal and sought out the small store, no more than four meters wide at the front and neatly placed between the *Perfect Slice* cake store and *Just the Thing* gift store. A wider backroom could not be seen from the street. On closer inspection, the small diamond-shaped glass panels in the front window were framed by leadlight. Each featured little treasures on mahogany shelves – a pair of glasses, a small clock, a crystal glass, or a figurine – and by magic, they never needed dusting.

Lukas Lens entered, the quaint silver bell tinkled above his head, and he relaxed in the familiar surrounds, making his way to the counter where he worked as a master clocksmith on the timepieces that he serviced and repaired. He could hear them ticking above all else in the room, syncing with his heartbeat if the owner was nearby.

'Ah, you're back, thank goodness, lad.'

'Why? What's wrong?' Lukas asked, glancing around. The glass was intact, peace prevailed, and all seemed in order.

'Sophie is on her way.'

Lukas sighed and moved behind the counter, throwing his keys on a shelf below. 'I wish I could still sense her.'

'I know you regret giving up the role of her protector, but maybe it is for the best. Lucy is gone, but it might have impacted your relationship with Venetia.'

Lukas scoffed. 'Venetia's no fan of Lucy but seems relaxed about Sophie.'

'Fortunately, they are not competing for the Raven's affection, not like Sophie's namesake – Elsopeth – and Venetia did in the past. That is a relief.'

Orli entered from the back room where she had been working on optical orders and added, 'Elsopeth was a great beauty, wasn't she? The Raven and the shapeshifter pursued her if memory serves.' The ethereal, silver-haired beauty was a close friend of shapeshifter and accountant Nikolas Saggers, who stepped up when Lukas stepped down to be Sophie's protector and looked after the books for Sophie's clairvoyance business and community house.

'She was indeed beautiful. But we can't say anything about those relationships until Sophie finds out or raises the subject. It may distort how she views her current-day associations,' Alfred said. 'It's getting harder and harder to keep history in order.'

Lukas groaned. 'Tell me about it. Have we heard any more about the Raven?'

'I called Allanon last evening,' Orli said. 'He appreciated our concern and was at the hospital when we spoke. There has been no change.'

'It was a hell of a fall.' Lukas said. 'Why did you save him?' he asked his grandfather directly.

'Because I could,' Alfred said, surprised. 'Murdoch is a good young man and has always been fair with Daphne and with us before Sophie took the role of the cursed. How could I let him perish?'

Lukas grimaced. 'He is the enemy.'

'It would make no difference in our universe,' Orli reminded Lukas. 'If Murdoch is gone, someone else will become the Raven and the enemy. Maybe Allanon, although I can't imagine it, or someone else in their kin, like one of the twin nephews.'

'And that could be much worse,' Alfred reminded his grandson. 'Imagine if a power-hungry young Raven took up the mantle. Sophie could be harassed, and Nikolas would have his work cut out for him and be in danger.'

Lukas nodded, conceding the point. 'Fair enough. It's instinctive not to like him,' he defended his stance. 'Like cats and dogs.'

'Or ravens and doves,' Orli said. 'She is here.'

Moments later, Sophie could be seen exiting her car across the road and heading towards them. She was casual in jeans, white runners, and a white fitted top, her hair loose and wavy.

'Did she say what she wanted, Grandpa?' Lukas asked, studying Sophie as she waited to cross the road.

'No. She just rang to ask if she could come by. I told her she never needed to call, but she wanted to talk with us, not read the books this time.'

The door swung open, and all three witches welcomed Sophie, who her Great Aunt Daphne predicted would be the strongest witch of her time.

CHAPTER 2

S OPHIE FELT INSTANTLY CALM when she saw the *optical illusion* store, as if she were with kin, and in a sense, she was in the company of the Lens family. The customers didn't see what lay behind the locked cupboard doors of this ancient shop founded by Alfred Lens' father and then handed down to Alfred, who started his apprenticeship at age 10.

Now, it was in the hands of Lukas and Orli – cousins and descendants of Hadley, the peaceful line of the family. Alfred stayed on at Lukas and Orli's bequest and was happy to do so. It was his life's work, the customers loved him, and he was the holder of the key to Sophie's legacy – the journals.

Hidden from sight, secured in the cupboards, were diaries written by Sophie's ancestors, including her Great Aunt Daphne's volume and now Sophie's voice would be added to the collection. They went back to the first of the accursed – Samuel in 1582. The current generation had been very relaxed about the curse, as if it were an ancient fairy tale that did not fit into modern society.

As a young detective and the current Raven, Murdoch had worked harmoniously with the cursed, Sophie's Great Aunt Daphne, and with Alfred, who had been Daphne's protector. The relationship had been respectful and cautious. That relationship was now in danger.

The new generation was different, with Daphne gone and Alfred retired from his protector role. There was passion at stake, and for the first time in the history of the glasses, the cursed was a descendant of a powerful witch. There was another complication, rather a major one as Alfred would say – the Raven loved Sophie. Her enemy loved her. The peace that had prevailed was teetering.

Sophie entered the small store, the bell announcing her arrival.

'Hello, welcome dear, and you've come bearing gifts,' Alfred teased, noticing a tin in Sophie's hand.

'This must be important,' Lukas joked.

She laughed. 'Thank you, Alfred. Good morning to you all! You know Miss Sharpe would not let me leave the office without bearing a treat – today, her upside-down apple cake.'

'My favourite!' Orli announced, clapping her hands together.

'I am surprised you are not all spoilt being next door to the *Perfect Slice* cake store,' Sophie said, and Orli grimaced.

'They are not a patch on Miss Sharpe's cooking,' Orli said in a hushed voice as if the walls had ears.

'Shall we lock the store and have tea and cake then?' Alfred asked.

'Oh, there is no need to lose business; my request to talk is not that important. Well, it is, but it is not traffic-stopping,' Sophie said and followed them into a deceivingly large back room where they could sit around a table together. One might be correct in assuming a bit of magic added to its dimensions.

Orli and Lukas prepared morning tea while Sophie took a seat opposite Alfred.

'Is there any word on Murdoch?' she asked, and Alfred shook his head. 'Orli spoke with Allanon last night, and there is no change.'

'I want to see him.'

'I know, my dear; I am sure it is very painful for you,' Alfred said sympathetically.

'But best you don't,' Lukas said bluntly, dropping down into the seat beside her now that he had distributed tea and coffee.

'Have you tried to enter his thoughts?' Orli asked, joining them.

Sophie looked guilty and gave a slight nod. 'I can't reach him.'

'That may be something to do with his injury rather than him blocking you,' Alfred suggested, easing her pain.

'I hope so.' Sophie sighed, lifting her coffee cup. 'What a mess.'

That sat silently for a moment, anticipating Sophie's reason for coming, when she asked Alfred, 'How did you know he was in trouble and needed rescuing, if you don't mind me asking?'

'Of course not,' Alfred assured her. 'Murdoch and I are the most powerful of our line – the eldest and most powerful, even if I am no longer working as a protector. Thus, we can sense each other in extremes.'

'Wow, I didn't know that,' Lukas said. 'Can Nik sense the Raven since he's Sophie's protector now?'

'Only if he is nearby or Sophie is in peril,' Alfred said. 'It is not something either Detective Ashcroft – Murdoch – or I desire, but it has always been that way.'

'Have you heard from his partner, Detective Oakley?' Orli asked Sophie.

'Yes, I called Gerard, and he is coming by in a day or so.' She smiled. 'He is a few weeks from retirement and cranky that he has been partnered with a young female detective in Murdoch's absence. He was looking forward to an easy exit.'

'Let's hope Murdoch is back with him before he departs,' Alfred said. 'May we ask what happened that night, but do not tell us if it is too private. I ask as I hold myself responsible – I told Murdoch I would find a way for him to speak with you safely, in your dreams.'

Sophie's eyes widened. 'He didn't tell me that.'

'No. I imagine he wouldn't; a matter of discretion,' Alfred said. 'I believe he was distressed that the curse prevented him from managing his anger when talking with you, thus putting you at risk. Entering your dreams allowed him to talk it through with you and try and find a way to co-exist.'

'He has been waiting patiently for you in this generation, and now the curse is preventing you from being together,' Orli said, her voice laced with sadness.

'When he appeared to me, we were back in the past. I was my former self – Elsopeth,' Sophie started recalling Murdoch coming to her in her dream. 'He had just reached me through this long corridor of my mind; it was a ballroom setting. I said his name by way of greeting, and then Nik snapped me back to the present. Nik said I called out the Raven's name, and that's why he arrived as my protector.'

'Of course,' Alfred said.

Sophie saw Lukas and Orli exchange a glance. 'What are you both thinking? What does that look mean?' she asked, but before they could answer, there was a crash against the back door, making them all jump, except Alfred, who appeared at his age to be well used to shocks of all sorts.

Lukas arced up, and Alfred waved him down. 'Relax, lad; it's Nikolas.'

Orli tried to hide her smile as she stood and opened the door to him. 'I'm so sorry, Nik. I reinstated my protection spells with all the tension of late.'

'I noticed,' he grumbled and leant to kiss her on the cheek as he always had.

'I was sure I told you. Come in.'

'Hmm. Good morning, Alfred,' he said politely, acknowledging the most powerful amongst them. 'And you lot,' he added, joking.

'Good morning, Nikolas. Come in, have a coffee and join us,' Alfred welcomed him.

'Am I interrupting something?' he asked, looking at the group gathered. Regardless, he took the chair that Lukas had pulled out for him. 'My mind was buzzing,' he said, looking at Sophie. 'You mention the Raven's name and mine. Is everything okay?'

'Well, nothing has changed,' Sophie said and welcomed him. 'I wanted to talk about the Raven but didn't call you... I figured you had a life.'

'What's happened?' Nikolas asked.

'We don't know yet,' Lukas ribbed him. 'You interrupted with your grand entrance before Sophie told us anything.'

He shook his head and ignored their smiles. 'I'll go back to entering the conventional way.'

'A Harley and a biker out the front of our store will at least create some interest,' Lukas said.

'You are just in time, Nikolas. Sophie, how can we help?' Alfred cut to the chase and sat back, looking well-groomed in his usual dark suit and thin silver-rimmed spectacles.

'I have been reading my namesake's book, Elsopeth's diary.' She blushed slightly. 'I know about the... well, let's call it a love triangle between the Raven and the Shapeshifter.'

'Ah.' Nikolas sat back in his chair, now understanding why he was not invited to the gathering.

Lukas read the awkwardness of the moment. 'That doesn't mean you have to like him in this generation, Sophie,' he said with a wry look to Nikolas. 'Every generation is different, isn't it, Grandpa?'

'Maybe so, but I am so much more than a shapeshifter,' Nikolas smirked. 'I'm good-looking, have a good job, and—'

'Run howling when the full moon is out,' Orli added and smiled, 'that's a good thing, I'm sure.'

'You are all very cavalier today while the Raven lays immobilised, but I guess even if he is related to you, he means little to you,' Sophie said in a small voice, saddened by the situation.

'You knew we wouldn't be upset,' Lukas ribbed her.

'I thought you might be a little concerned on his behalf,' Sophie said, giving him a wry look when he huffed.

'They are indeed cavalier, Sophie. I suggest you ignore them and we shall speak,' Alfred said, with a raised eyebrow at Lucas, Orli and Nikolas and a pretend scolding look that had them grinning worse than before.

'I feel like we are about to be sent from the room without dinner,' Lukas said.

'If that would work, I might try it,' Alfred said. 'But in answer to my grandson's question, whoever we love in one generation isn't automatically our love interest in the next. Sophie, you may end up loving someone who has not crossed your path yet.'

'Except you don't want to,' Orli sensed her sadness and touched Sophie's hand. Sophie was sure Nikolas bristled beside her.

Lukas lightened the mood. 'So, if we take Lucy, for example. She has no magical powers, so most likely, she wasn't in my life before this one or may never feature again. I'll look on the positive side of that,' he said, embittered by her betrayal.

'I did not say that,' Alfred clarified. 'I said you may love someone entirely different. We all travel together in different guises in each generation. Lucy may have come in and out of your life many times, even if she is not magical. She has had a role to play.'

'We know she has been in your life before,' Sophie said and looked to Alfred, who had read all the diaries over the years and translated many to modern speak for ease of reading.

'We do,' Alfred confirmed.

'You're kidding?' Lukas looked from his grandfather to Sophie. 'Who was she back then?'

Alfred nodded to Sophie to tell the story.

'She wasn't a witch or had any powers if I'm correct, but she was a woman in your life who loved you, was jealous of you and lost you.' Sophie tried a bite of Miss Sharpe's cake now that she was feeling a little better in the present company.

'How did you come across her?' Lukas asked.

'Are you making this about you again?' Nikolas asked, and Lukas gave him a grimace.

Sophie grinned at the two old sparring partners.

'Yes,' Lukas said, 'I'm one of the most interesting people in the room, so why not?'

Orli laughed and then pretended it was a cough. 'You are Lukas; please, go ahead, Sophie.'

Sophie grinned, and it felt good to do so. Since the Raven's crash, her heart had been heavy and poor Miss Sharpe had done her best to lift Sophie's spirits by keeping her busy and providing baking gifts.

Sophie continued, 'Well, I was reading Elsopeth's diary of her first entry to society when she was at a dance and was introduced to some of the ladies making their debuts. She became firm friends with a lady named Lucia, apparently. Even then, girls whispered about Elsopeth and said she was half-human, half-spirit. But to get to the most important part related to Lukas,' she teased, 'Elsopeth accepted a dance from your former self – the duke – and she wrote how this young woman named Lucia glared daggers at her and thought Elsopeth had designs on her man. Lucia withdrew her friendship, even though Elsopeth explained it would have been rude not to accept the duke and that she had no fascination for you.'

'I was a duke? Excellent. Why didn't she fancy me?' Lukas exclaimed, and Sophie rolled her eyes as the small party laughed at Lukas's self-indulgence.

'How many girls did you want to win over?' Sophie retorted.

'All of them, of course,' Lukas joked. He turned to his grandfather. 'I thought I was a younger soul than you all.'

Alfred shook his head slightly. 'Only because you have chosen not to remember your history yet. A little like Sophie. She had no knowledge of this life until she accepted it.'

'Is there any point in me looking back?' Lukas asked, and Sophie's shocked expression mirrored everyone else's looks.

'That is entirely up to you, lad,' Alfred responded. 'So, Sophie, you know of the enduring love between Elsopeth and the Raven, and between Elsopeth and the shapeshifter. What did you want to discuss, and can you do it in Nik's company now that we've established you need not love him in this life?'

'I'm loveable,' he assured her in jest.

Sophie patted his arm. 'That you are. But I have been going over and over the same thoughts: when there's so much at stake – the curse, the danger to Murdoch, Nikolas and me if the Raven and I were together, not to mention the roll-on effect to all of you – maybe a sacrifice is required.'

'Do you think that is what Murdoch was thinking when he... fell?' Nikolas diplomatically asked Alfred.

'I could not say,' Alfred responded. 'He was not capable of speaking when I came upon him.'

'How long had he been lying injured?' Orli asked.

'I recovered him immediately when he fell into the water; he would not have survived otherwise,' Alfred said. 'I felt him falling.'

'How awful.' Sophie grimaced. 'Was he flying over the sea for that reason?'

'He wasn't out to sea,' Alfred answered honestly. 'He may have known he was weakening and flew over the water.' Alfred hesitated. 'He had been flying until he fell with exhaustion.'

Sophie groaned, and her hand went to her heart. 'How long had he been flying before he dropped from the sky?'

'A raven can fly up to one hundred miles in a day, but I found him closer than that,' Alfred said.

Nikolas – who was good with figures – quickly did a calculation and said, 'One hundred and sixty kilometres.' The group nodded, understanding the distance better.

Sophie looked at her hands. 'I tried to get back to him after Nikolas woke me that evening, but it took me a long time to get to sleep. In the early hours, I was back in the ballroom in my mind, but he wasn't there.' She turned to Alfred. 'I need to find a solution, a way that we can be together. We can't even work together at the moment because he fears he will harm me.'

Alfred nodded. 'I have been undergoing some research.'

Sophie sighed with relief. 'I knew you would be; thank you, Alfred.'

He held up his hands, not making any promises. 'I am not sure a solution can be found, but we'll cover every angle.'

'Is it the first time such a problem exists in the history of the glasses and the curse?' Orli asked.

Alfred thought before answering. 'There is nothing in history like this modern-day scenario because of Sophie's pedigree. No accursed ever had been a witch or a descendant from a powerful one. But...'

All eyes turned to him. 'Once, in the 1940s, a Raven did fall in love with his enemy the accursed – she was not a witch – but regardless, it was unprecedented.'

'What happened?' Sophie hurriedly asked.

'It did not end well.'

Lukas waited impatiently for Sophie and Nikolas to leave; only his grandfather could feel his tension. No sooner had they left, he asked Alfred, 'Do you believe Nik? That he heard Sophie call out and came thinking she was in distress? I think there's more at play here, and Nik needs to come clean.'

Alfred departed the back room, and Lukas and Orli followed him to the front of the store, ready to resume their duties.

'What I believe doesn't matter,' Alfred said. 'But it is complex. I asked Nikolas to let Sophie know Murdoch would try and reach her that evening in her dreams, as he has done before – it was a safe option.'

'And Nik didn't, I bet,' Lukas said. 'He came to so-call save her the moment the Raven appeared.'

'Well, we don't know that for sure, but I suspect Nikolas has his reasons,' Alfred said diplomatically.

'I believe he has feelings for Sophie and wants to rekindle them in this generation,' Orli said, loitering near the counter and straightening several glass ornaments.

Suddenly, Lukas braced. His eyes flared yellow, and glass shattered.

'Lukas!' Orli screamed, raising her hands to prevent the glass windows from shattering. A figurine crashed from the top shelf, shattering; others tottered.

'What is going on?' Alfred looked around, trying to sense the danger that Lukas was seeing.

Lukas's lips thinned in a grimace. 'The Raven is here.'

'He can't be; he isn't. Steady yourself, lad,' Alfred assured him.

'I can feel his presence,' Lukas hissed.

'Ah... I see,' Alfred said, calm in the storm.

'What is it?' Orli asked, panicked.

'Raven clan – Murdoch's nephews, the twins. Calm yourself, Lukas; I believe they come in peace.'

'What do they want?' Lukas glared out the shop windows, keeping them in his sights; his eyes were still dangerously yellow.

'I will meet them outside and find out,' Alfred said, heading to the door. 'No, stay here please, Lukas,' he answered the question he heard Lukas thinking.

Lukas's eyes returned to their usual pale blue colour, but he focused completely on Alfred as his grandfather departed the shop to greet the two young men. The larger twin looked like he had spent too long at the gym. He wore jeans, runners, and a white T-shirt that showed the bulk of his arms. The smaller twin looked more studious with his thin steel-rimmed glasses, dark grey suit, and conservative haircut. There was no mistaking that they were twins, and from the Raven side of the family, with their dark features, Lukas could sense their power.

'They mean no harm,' Orli said, 'they are radiating peace.'

Lukas grunted; he trusted no one on the Raven side of their kin. He felt a message from his grandfather tap into his mind. 'Steady lad, all is fine', but Lukas's eyes narrowed, watching them.

Alfred accepted each of their extended hands and shook. They spoke for a few moments, and the men departed. The bell tinkered happily over the door as Alfred entered the store as if nothing happened – certainly not the meeting of two enemy sides of the family.

'What did they want?' Lukas asked, watching the twins until they drove off in a black sports car.

'To thank me for saving their uncle. I told them we have always held Murdoch in high regard, and deference has flown both ways. It was respectful of Jordan and Joshua to come by.'

Lukas reined in his emotions and exhaled.

'Thank you, lad,' his grandfather said.

'What for?' Lukas turned to look at him. 'Losing my cool again and smashing up the shop?'

'For being protective of your old grandfather.'

Lukas smiled. 'Old? You may be senior, but you could lay us all low.'

'I'm not inclined to, though,' Alfred teased. 'Only one figurine broken?'

Lukas looked sheepish as Orli nodded. 'Lucky it was not one of our favourites, Uncle,' she teased and waved her hand, restoring the pieces together and returning it to the top shelf.

'If the Raven – Murdoch – cannot return to his role, one of them will take the position, won't they?' Lukas asked.

'It remains to be seen,' Alfred said, 'but my guess would be one of the twins, possibly Jordan, the eldest. The curse would bypass Allanon; it doesn't like its holders to be too passive.'

'That's unfortunate.' Orli sighed. 'I could almost see the curse dissolving if it were you, Uncle Alfred, and Allanon, as the holders.'

'If only it were that simple,' Alfred agreed. 'I believe the curse ends when no more descendants walk the earth. I hope I am wrong; nothing is written in stone.'

'And yet here we go again,' Lukas said, 'the Raven loves Elsopeth, or rather he loves Sophie, and so does the shapeshifter.'

Orli snapped to look at Lukas. 'Do you think it is love?' she asked.

'If not, it is the competition between two old rivals to win Sophie's affection,' Lukas suggested.

'Time will tell,' Alfred said. 'Time will tell.'

CHAPTER 3

T HE PACKAGE SAT ON the kitchen bench, wrapped in
brown paper and tied with string; it looked like an
old-fashioned gift.

'What is that? Anything exciting?' Sophie's flatmate, Melino
Karta, squealed as she often did when excited, and her joy of
life found her excited often. She eyed the package as she and
Sophie cooked dinner together.

Sophie was grateful to Mel, who came into her life at the
perfect time after her friendship breakup with Lucy. Mel once
worked in the *Sport for Every Girl* community office on the
premises – just one of the community groups that benefited
from the subsidised rental Sophie's aunt, now Sophie, offered
in one of the mansion's wings. Mel had breezed into Sophie's
office with her infectious smile, bright clothes and a pink streak
in her fringe and suggested she become Sophie's flatmate. The
ladies renovated the bedrooms in Sophie's newly inherited
mansion with a bit of help from Nikolas, and just recently,

Mel was able to leave the community group and, using one of the spare rooms – and there were many – developed her own potions business. She could sense when those gifted with powers were on the premises because her nose and fingers would twitch on their arrival. Her Tongan grandmother and great-grandmother before her were healers, and Mel had the gift and the family's book of healing spells as well. No one who met Mel forgot her.

Sophie glanced at the wrapped parcel. 'That, my dear flatmate, is a copy of the diary pages of Aircraftwoman Margaret Dillon, who served in our air force.'

'Oh my,' Mel's eyes widened. 'Does she know you have it?'

'She's passed. Margaret served in World War II and has been gone for about forty years.

'Goodo then, I think you're safe to read it. Is she an ancestor?' Mel tried a carrot from their tofu stir-fry and declared the dish ready.

Sophie pushed the two bowls forward for filling. 'She is. On the paternal side of the family... the cursed. She was an inheritor of the glasses and the only person we've found so far who fell in love with the Raven, her enemy.'

'Ooh! It's kind of weird, don't you think that in all those centuries, only one of the accursed fell in love with a Raven?'

'They probably didn't get close enough to form an attachment,' Sophie said as they made their way to the table and sat for dinner. 'If Murdoch wasn't a cop or working with Aunt Daphne, I don't know how our paths would have crossed; he'd probably be stalking me from afar or flapping his wings near my window every night,' she joked. 'Elsopeth, who wasn't cursed but one of my ancestors, met the Raven when she tripped in front of him, and he caught her.'

'How romantic.' Mel sighed.

'Or clumsy,' Sophie joked. 'She was half-witch, half-human and not the accursed, so she was free to love the Raven, even though her father brought the curse upon the family.' Sophie frowned. 'It all sounds so ridiculous in a modern world, like some weirdo Grimms' Fairy Tale.'

'That's what I love about it!' Mel exclaimed.

'There's a lot more cases of the cursed falling in love with their protector than falling in love with the Raven.'

'I can understand that,' Mel said. 'It's so dreamy to have a protector, and Nikolas is gorgeous.' She lowered her voice like he was listening.

'If you like the tall, dark, handsome and caring kind,' Sophie teased, and Mel chuckled.

'And do you know what happened to the Air Force lady, the Raven and their love affair?'

'Not until I read that,' Sophie said with a nod to the package, 'but Alfred did imply it didn't end well.'

Mel grimaced. 'I hope the poor lady didn't die an awful death.'

'Me too, but I have to know. I've learnt from Alfred to breathe, slow down, and don't immediately react. Alfred always says time has a shadow, and we just have to wait sometimes for it to pass over us as the day is long.'

They both had a bite of their stir-fry while thinking about that.

'You are being very strong about all this, Sophie,' Mel said, 'but I am an empath.... I can sense you are quite grief-stricken about Murdoch, but you are masking it as best you can. You don't have to with me.' Mel rubbed her heart as if she was carrying some of Sophie's pain and hoped to massage it away.

Sophie gave her a grateful smile. 'Oh, Mel, thank you. I'm so glad we discovered each other, and you came to live here. But I don't want to drive you away with my dramatics.'

'It all goes around,' Mel said. 'When Jack and I fall in love, I am bound to be annoyingly melodramatic.'

'Oh well, in that case.' Sophie chuckled and then sobered. 'It hasn't been easy; I toss and turn and see nearly every hour, and then I wake up in surprise when I do sleep. But then, usually I've dreamt about him, so there's no rest. I'm staying as busy as I can.'

'The house is spotless,' Mel said with a small smile.

Sophie gave a small laugh. 'That was Saturday morning. Poor Bette Davis hid for fear she'd be polished! Murdoch has it easy being comatose,' Sophie said in jest. 'It's weird because we have nothing but hope and promise so far... everything has been in a dream, but yet the feelings I've developed are so real and strong.'

'Maybe because it has always been him, you know, in the past, and you can feel that,' Mel said.

'Maybe. So, tell me what is happening in your world.'

'Well, I made a potion today for a woman who wanted to have the courage to tell her twin she didn't want to wear identical clothes anymore,' Mel said.

Sophie looked surprised and then laughed. 'Oh wow, people's problems come in all shapes and sizes.'

'Do you think a potion might help Murdoch?' Mel asked. 'I did look through Grandma's book, and there are a couple that can assist with quick healing.' She bit her lip and then teased Sophie lightly, 'Nothing that says if you fall from the sky as a bird and come back to being a human, this will mend you.'

Sophie chuckled. 'It's bizarre. Thanks for looking, though.'

'What if Miss Sharpe could tell us who is the most powerful existing witch we know, and we could ask them to do something to help him.'

'That's kind of interesting,' Sophie said, looking sheepish.

'Oh my God, it's you!'

'It's Alfred, but technically it's me. It's just that I'm only discovering my powers as I read about them or accidentally call them into action. Like when I stilled the storm that afternoon when I was cranky having to pick a protector, and when I faded out of sight when it got stressful. Nik's worried I'll get in a bad situation and my powers will return to me all at once and obliterate everyone around me, including me.'

Sophie realised she might have said too much as Mel's eyes widened with shock, and she was uncharacteristically speechless. Sophie scoffed. 'Don't worry about it; I'm sure Nik exaggerates.'

'Okay.' Mel drew in a sudden breath and looked around. She pinched her nose.

'What is it?' Sophie stilled.

'There's a witch here. They could be friendly... wow, they're strong.' Mel held her fingers out in front of her and stretched them. 'Super strong tingles,' she said by way of explanation. 'Are you expecting anyone?'

'No.' Sophie stood and hurriedly moved to the windows, looking out on the dark garden. The lamps were lit, but no one was there. One flickered, and she turned her gaze towards it, but still, no one appeared. She rushed to the front door and checked it was locked before realising that it would be useless against a witch's powers.

'It's growing stronger, Sophie,' Mel said, rising and holding out her hands. 'My fingers on both hands are full of pins and needles.'

'I should call Nik, but it's not the Raven… I don't think Nik is supposed to protect me from witch intruders.'

'You could ask?'

'It might put him in danger.' Sophie bit her lip, thinking. And then she unlocked the front door, thrust it open and went outside.

CHAPTER 4

Nikolas Saggers needed to let off some steam. The Raven was not the only one waiting for Sophie to inherit her destiny. He had loved Elsopeth – Sophie's former self – with a passion that was not earthly. In all truth, he had hoped he didn't feel the same when reincarnated in this new life. He hoped to fall in love with someone mortal or a fellow shapeshifter who could run with him. But the desire for her was carnal, and knowing the Raven wanted her only made it worse. The Raven wasn't good for her in this generation, now that Sophie was also the accursed. If the Raven truly loved her, he would leave her, Nikolas thought angrily, but he knew he would not give up on her if the situation were reversed, if there was any chance they could find a way to be together.

If only Alfred had not saved the Raven, there would be a new inheritor with no interest in Sophie other than as her enemy, and he would protect her.

'You will be the death of me, Sophie,' he whispered. 'Like last time.' Although he conceded it was not completely Elsopeth's fault. In this generation, there had been no time to discuss romance or foster feelings with Sophie. She had only recently claimed her true self and inheritance of power. Lukas was her protector until recently and Nikolas's own exposure to her had been brief at best. Yet it was cruel how instinctive his love and protectiveness of her felt, so achingly familiar that the pain was not welcome, not again.

How much did she know of us?

How much has she read?

He recalled how dismissive she was of their past at the Lens' store as if it didn't have to be repeated, as if he were off the hook. If they had been alone, he might have declared his interest or made light of it but suggested she consider him and gauged her reaction. The thought of her with the Raven made him involuntarily grind his teeth, and his jaw lock – time to shift.

It was dark and cool outside, and Nikolas shrugged off his clothing – stripping off his corporate layers – shoes and socks, his shirt and suit pants and boxer underwear – and laid them over the railing. His dogs sensed what was coming and waited, keen to run with him. It was why he lived on the forest's edge, so he could run unhindered, feel his bones stretch, and feel depleted in the hope of sleeping at night. His body was toned and tight; the nightly running ensured that.

He began with a slow jog, the dogs at his side, and by the time he reached his gate, down the long driveway he was sprinting. He felt his body change. It felt better when it changed in motion – more fluid and less painful. Moments later, he was looking through the eyes of his beast, racing into the forest, hearing the creatures scatter as he entered with his dogs astride. Nikolas's mind was distracted by rustling, the noises of the woods, the vision of night, all diversions to give him some peace from thinking about Sophie. Maybe he should hand over her work accounts to someone else in his accounting office and step back a little. It was enough that he was her protector. But then he would have no reason to visit, which would be worse. Out of sight, out of mind.

He ran through the woods, up the rise, further and further, until he reached the top of the hill where he could pace, cool down, and see his house from afar. He sat and remembered their first meeting in the 18th century.

Extract from the journals of Nikolas Charles Saggers

August 12, 1744

My future wife

The last thing I wanted to do was go to the Trevington's ball, and my uncle knew that, hence his insistence. I am of age to wed as he keeps reminding me, and as his heir, it is my responsibility to bring a son into the world. I have been managing his estates for a year now and he is satisfied with my progress but threatens to disinherit me and choose another successor if I am not married within a year.

My saving grace is that I do not care to become the fifth duke in our family line, nor will I be accepting an invitation to join the cabinet, and my uncle knows this, so his threats never take their full form. He is worried if he pushes me too far, I will renege on my duty. My life goal is not to manage estates, staff, and books, although I am pleased with his country estate and would be happy to reside there. I cannot see myself using the town residence too often. I would be happy with a humble existence, a piece of land to work and nature surrounding me so I can run when I need to let my transformation take over. But I accept my family duty, and family always comes first. Besides, Uncle Charles is ailing and time is of the essence. Thus, duty calls.

I dressed, allowing my valet to fuss with my grooming until I could bear it no more, and he declared me ready and bound to appeal to the ladies. Regardless of my appeal, the title would achieve that; I had several friends wed to great beauties that they would never have snared with their appearances if they were not titled. My valet's concern was not as much for my turnout but his standing if I did not look adequately presented – pride and reputation exist at every level of society, which I believe is good and makes us all strive to be better.

Uncle Charles was ready and waiting, insisting on accompanying me to ensure I attended and did not stray to a card game or a drinking venue. After arrival, he departed to his card tables, leaving me to work the room. I had no intention of seeking a wife tonight, but I would do what was expected and dance with a few ladies, flatter where necessary, and depart as soon as possible.

I fronted, smiled, and bowed as the young ladies preened, keen to be a future duke's wife. Some were pushed forth by their mothers, whose duty it was to see them married; all were at their best advantage. I was pleased to see a few friends scattered on the dance floor or drinking and socialising in the corner of the room, and I joined the latter group hoping to bide my time there.

Then I saw Miss Elsopeth Rayne. I knew the Rayne name, of course. In these diaries written by my ancestors, you can read of the curse bestowed on Samuel Rayne, and of his powerful witch wife, Issbelle, and how we have served the Rayne family in matters of business advice. And this was their descendant from that mighty bloodline, the beauty Elsopeth. Oh, and she was a beauty.

I cannot say what made me sense her amongst all the other young ladies of similar gowns and appearance in a room full of perfume and desire, but her scent reached me from across the room. We both appeared to turn and see each other at the same time. If she were like me, I might explain it as primal – the animal instinct within me from my other half and the ancient need to mate. But she was not like me. Despite my urges, my human side was discerning and controlled the animal half of me to some degree. Trust me, I did not feel this urge for every pretty young thing presented to me; quite the opposite, and I found many of their scents overwhelming and not in an alluring way.

Why did Elsopeth Rayne have the same reaction that she would turn and study me simultaneously? She was a witch, of that there was no doubt, it was strong in her. Maybe she sensed a threat. To ensure I did not cause her alarm, I smiled and gave her a small bow, which she reciprocated with a smile that made her more beautiful, if that were possible. She glanced away shyly, asking a question of the lady beside her, who glanced at me and also dropped her gaze. Did Miss Rayne not know who I was? That would be refreshing as most of the young ladies researched the most eligible gentlemen to approach before attending the evening.

I could not look away, and neither could she; even when her companion took her elbow and guided her across the floor, she glanced back at me several times. My friend, Edward, nudged me.

'Lost your heart already, Nikolas?' he asked.

I laughed at such a notion and asked, 'That is Miss Elsopeth Rayne, is it not?'

'Yes,' he confirmed. 'I believe she has captured the eye of another.'

'But yet here she is without him.' I stated the obvious, which was to my advantage.

'Indeed,' Edward agreed.

I glanced her way again and she caught my eye once more and looked away. She was not being demure or coy, rather, I felt it to be curiosity. My breathing grew shallower, which was most disconcerting. I did not come here to do my uncle's bidding and form an attachment. But I knew I could not leave without making her acquaintance and asking for a dance, and with hurriedness, in case the man who has her affection should arrive and I lose my chance.

'Do you know her to introduce us?' I asked Edward.

'No. But I know her companion who will do the introductions. Come then,' he said generously, and I was relieved to move towards her finally. But before the introduction was made, before Edward had even announced my name, she gave me a small curtsy and said in a low voice, 'I am sorry for the pain I will cause you.'

She could not have shocked me more, and I remembered my manners enough to offer a quick bow before I turned and departed with haste.

Nikolas felt his body cooling; he needed to run again and get home before he changed form. His memory was as strong today as it was then. He would be best to avoid Elsopeth and have nothing to do with her reincarnation – Sophie – unless it was a professional relationship. He put his head back and howled; the release was just what he needed, and then he ran, his dogs trailing behind him.

CHAPTER 5

FEAR COURSED THROUGH HER, but Sophie walked out the front door, ready to face the threat head-on. She heard Mel call her name, but she didn't stop.

'Hello?' She immediately regretted her bravado, sensing something menacing was nearby. A dark premonition seemed to take her by the shoulders and warn her to run. The air moved around her, cold and hostile. There was no doubt the presence was foe, not friend.

'Show yourself,' she hissed, 'unless you fear to face me.' A challenge issued... someone was watching her; Sophie sensed a presence nearby with malicious intent.

She felt a breath against her face, the movement of her hair, a nudge on the shoulder and a stirring of the air again near her face.

She held up her hands and yelled, 'Begone!'

It was as if she had created a tidal wave of the air; a current pushed her back, whirling, angry, tumbling in front of her, pushing out into the garden, sending leaves and dust flying.

Sophie stepped back towards the mansion; she heard hissing and murmuring... male voices, and turned sharply at a presence behind her; it was Mel watching in the doorway.

'Go inside, quick, lock yourself in,' she warned, but Mel remained steadfast. Sophie stepped back slowly, away from the noise and currents in the air, and the air stilled.

'It's gone; the presence is gone,' Mel said, looking at her hands. 'I feel nothing.'

'Me either,' Sophie said, gasping as the dust and leaves settled, and she saw what lay before her.

Nikolas appeared beside her, half-dressed in his suit pants, no shirt. 'What the hell happened here?' he asked. 'I felt your rising fear.'

The ground was littered with feathers. Black raven feathers. Three or four dead ravens lay nearby. Both ladies were talking at once, over each other.

'I killed them,' Sophie gasped. 'I don't know how, I just said begone in anger, and this wave thing rolled out.'

'It was sinister; whatever was here meant harm,' Mel told Nikolas.

'Why didn't you call me?' he demanded.

'I didn't know it was a Raven presence, given he's in a hospital bed. Do you think it was him here in spirit form? I thought it was just... well, something not welcome.'

He threw his hands up in the air. 'I'm your protector. I protect you from everything... Ravens, ghosts, idiots.'

Sophie couldn't help but smile at that, and then, calming herself, she studied Nikolas. 'Did we interrupt something?' She ran her eyes with appreciation over his toned physique.

'Exercise, a run,' he added in case Sophie's definition of exercise differed from his own. 'Are you both okay?'

'I am, but I didn't run out for the fight,' Mel giggled.

'I'm fine too, and you should have locked yourself in, Mel,' she scolded her flatmate.

Nikolas shook his head at the pair of them. 'I arrive, and you are both standing out here, so neither of you is getting out of a lecture. Let's go inside. Do you have any idea who it was?'

Sophie shook her head and looked at Mel.

'No,' Mel said as they moved indoors, closing and locking the front door behind them. 'It was strong, though. And, there were two of them.'

Sophie's eyes widened, and she snapped to look at Nikolas. 'The twins,' she whispered. 'Why didn't you sense my danger?'

'I sensed your fear because it was strong. I couldn't sense your danger because the twins, or whoever it was, was not the Raven; I could only sense his presence near you. But if you call my name, I will come anytime. And now, we need to call on Alfred.'

'Tonight?'

Nikolas glanced at the clock in Sophie's living room; it was nearing nine p.m. 'I guess it can wait until tomorrow. I doubt the menace will be back tonight, but just in case, do you both want to come and stay at my place?'

Sophie shook her head. 'As keen as I am to see your abode,' she teased, 'we should be safe. Orli has protection spells around the house; they might have worked tonight if I hadn't acted first. Is that okay?' she asked Mel.

'Sure.'

'Then don't go out again into the bloody garden,' Nikolas stated the obvious.

Mel hid a smile, and Sophie exhaled. 'I'll do my best to stay indoors, but you've got to admit I was stronger. Whatever it was, twins or another force, they've been plucked.'

Mel laughed, and Nikolas couldn't help but smile.

'Or,' he became grave, 'they came unprepared this time.'

Sophie sobered and nodded.

'And call me, even if you are just spooked,' he added. 'I'll return in the morning and get rid of the birds.'

'The predators will come in and get them tonight,' Sophie said.

The three stilled at the thought.

'Odd if it were the twins,' Nikolas mused. 'I heard they called on Alfred to thank him for saving the Raven. What's going on in their heads?'

'They've called on me to have their revenge. They think I drove the Raven to despair.'

'Then they need to be set straight,' Nikolas said, and Sophie could have sworn she heard him growl.

After Nikolas disappeared and Mel turned in, Sophie nestled in bed, making herself comfortable. She liked to read in bed in case she fell asleep, and then she didn't have to drag herself up the stairs and change. She had never been allowed to bring a journal home before as it had to be read in the surroundings of the *Optical Illusion* store, but Orli had magically produced a copy for her that supposedly vanished if anyone but Sophie touched it. Why she could not do this before for Sophie was a mystery; perhaps Alfred was softening his rules and allowing Orli and Sophie some leeway.

Opening the diary wrapped in paper and string, she threw aside the wrapping. She allowed herself a moment to enjoy the antiquity feel of the book, the beautiful penmanship, and the old leather binding. As a copy, it was wonderfully authentic.

She began to turn the pages, treating them with reverence. Sophie scanned the index Alfred Lens had placed at the start of the book, finding the lady in question – Miss Margaret Dillon – and flipped to the start of her pages. She was on a mission to find out how Margaret met the Raven and spent long enough time with him to fall in love. She also wanted to know what the outcome was for both.

She began to scan the pages, looking for his name to glean as much as she could. The Raven had been a Murdoch throughout time, an old family name, yet she had not been an Elsopeth through every generation. Perhaps her family had found the name too cumbersome. Sophie hoped one day she could read through all the volumes of books at leisure and know all about her ancestors' journeys, including the diaries of the other families – the Saggers and maybe even the Raven clan. If she had only accepted Aunt Daphne's prediction that she would be the strongest witch of her time and had started studying years ago, Sophie sighed and began scanning...

'Raven, Raven, wherefore art thou, Raven?' She murmured, remembering Juliet's romantic line from Shakespeare's *Romeo and Juliet* and being melodramatic as she searched for the Raven's name in the diary. It seemed like a million years ago when acting had been her calling, and there were no regrets for throwing in the actor's life of auditioning, learning lines and always trying to be the next best thing. Sophie admitted she had enjoyed middling success at best, and her profile since taking up her calling as a clairvoyant was much higher. Not to mention, she had actually done some good in the world working with the detectives.

As she searched for the Raven's name in Margaret's diary, Sophie mused how Juliet's situation was not so different to her own. Juliet wanted Romeo, who belonged to an enemy family; they could be together if they both denied their names. She recalled the following line and whispered it; 'Deny thy father and refuse thy name, Raven. Or if thou wilt not, be but sworn my love, And I'll no longer be a Capulet or rather a Carell.'

'I'm here, Sophie.'

Sophie jumped and lowered the book, looking around the room in trepidation.

Murdoch?

She put the diary down, threw off her bedding, and went to the window to peek through the curtain. She could see the shape of the dead birds on the grass, but there was no one in the garden under the lights or on "their bench" where she and Murdoch had sat in previous lifetimes while he wooed her.

Had she imagined it? She scoffed at herself and returned to bed, evening out the sheets and gathering the diary to her again. After another glance around the room to ensure she was alone, she debated whether to call for the Raven again or keep scanning the diary. The answer was simple. Sophie placed the diary on the pillow beside her, leaned back and closed her eyes. Thinking of Murdoch, she whispered, 'Raven, Raven, wherefore art thou, Raven?' And she waited.

The voice came through again, clearer this time.

'I'm here, Sophie. I'm here.'

Her voice broke – all the fear for him and anxiety of separation hit her. 'Murdoch, is it you?' Sophie did not dare open her eyes, scared he would disappear from her mind, and the connection would break.

'Yes. Where are you?'

'In my bed, thinking of you. Hoping to see you. I need to see you.'

There was silence, and she waited. 'Murdoch?'

'I'm here.'

'I'm frightened of what's happening between us.'

'I know.'

'Where are you?' Sophie asked.

'Somewhere, in between worlds. Not with you, not on the other side.'

'Can you come back to me, to us?'

There was no reply. Sophie waited, tears choking her throat, but she kept her eyes closed, her motions stilled for fear the connection would be gone. She stayed that way for the longest time, but not another word was spoken.

CHAPTER 6

AFTER MIDNIGHT, SOPHIE KNEW the Raven was not returning and that sleep would elude her. She had called him softly numerous times, not wanting to rouse Nikolas or have him appear as he did last time, breaking her link with the Raven. Her dismissal of Murdoch after their fight was never meant to end like this; it was a lovers' tiff at best. But then he couldn't come back to her. His Raven powers would not allow a Raven to be dismissed by an accursed, and somehow, her actions had driven them apart. She ruined it out of ignorance, and now they were separated, and it consumed her every thought, all day, every day. If only she could have that time over again, if only, if only... she felt like she was always stuck between the past and the present of late.

Sophie had never been so grateful to have work and her team to spend time with daily, or she was sure she might go insane. Still, now, his words haunted her:

In-between...

Where is he?

In a state of limbo?

Stuck between heaven and hell?

The thought terrified her, and unable to sleep, Sophie resumed her original task and propped herself up, reopening Margaret's diary. It must have been an amazing time to live through the war, she thought as she read extracts of Margaret's life – signing up for duty, being assigned a work area, and sharing a room with five other girls on the base. Extracts told of Margaret's fears and excitement in uncertain times.

> 'Today, I drove the General to the 12th Station Hospital to visit the wounded soldiers. Driving around the top brass was very exciting; he was a kind and considerate man. As I waited for him, I could not help but put on my glasses and see his future. He is one of the lucky ones to survive the war and return to his wife and daughters. He has no sons; that must be a relief in a time of war.'

So, she was using her glasses, Sophie thought, moving on and looking for references to the Raven. Now and then, she paused, hearing a noise. She was not frightened by the prospect of the twins or whoever the presence was before, returning. In truth, she was pumped by her powers. But her hope that every noise was the Raven coming to her or trying to reach her failed to eventuate. Sophie read on, the clocking ticking over to two a.m. She stopped at another paragraph that boasted good news.

'A great outcome today. While using my glasses, I was able to see a spy amongst us. It was thrilling and frightening. I went to my superior officer, and I didn't think she would believe me – of course, I didn't tell her about the curse or the glasses, but I informed her I had witnessed suspicious behaviour. She acted immediately, which was very gratifying, and came back to tell me hours afterwards that I was right and the spy had been arrested! For king and country, I felt very proud to have served today.'

Sophie smiled, delighted that the glasses were doing good as well as causing poor Margaret distress, as the next extract illustrated:

'I had a very sad incident today after I dropped some of our recovered soldiers at the train station on their way back to war to re-join their regiments. They were handsome and lovely, and I shouldn't have looked, but I couldn't help it. I was to wait for the new commanding officer and return him to the base – our previous commanding office was commissioned elsewhere. So, while I waited, I put on the glasses. My heart fell – only one of the three would come home. What a terrible, terrible waste of such beautiful lives. I vowed not to look again; it was heartbreaking and did me no good.'

'Aagh, I can imagine, Margaret,' Sophie whispered. 'That is so tragic.' She studied the black and white photograph that Alfred had clipped to the page. Margaret was beautiful. She had a cute smile with dimples and was gorgeous in her uniform, with her hair done in the style of the 1940 screen icons. Sophie could imagine all the soldiers at the base falling madly in love with her. And then, at last, the Raven's name appeared in Margaret's writings! Sophie's breath hitched as she read in anticipation:

'... an unexpected encounter. I was to wait for our new commander and I did not make the connection with his name! I could not believe what I was seeing. I hurriedly grabbed my paperwork as a tall soldier, looking resplendent in his uniform and powerful in his presence, started towards me, recognising the official vehicle I was in no doubt. Several soldiers saluted him as he passed. It was true... it was him. My paperwork read Wing Commander M. Ashcroft, the twenty-eight-year-old Commanding Officer of Number 72 Squadron. My squadron.

Words cannot express my shock or horror – Wing Commander M. Ashcroft was Murdoch Ashcroft, my enemy, the Raven. How could it be that we are put together? Is fate truly so cruel that of all the men at the commanding officer level, it must be him assigned to the same squadron as me? And then he saw me and needed no introduction. He stopped in his tracks and his eyes narrowed seeing me behind the wheel. What to do?

He started walking again, confidently now like a hunter towards its prey, and opening the car door, slipped into the back seat. His eyes were almost black.

'Wing Commander,' I said with a small nod of acknowledgement.

'Miss?'

'Aircraftwoman Margaret Dillon, Sir.'

He did not know my rank or could see it from my Women's Auxiliary Air Force uniform, so I drove, and his eyes never left me. I glanced back in the rear-view mirror several times, and he stared back at me. He was broody and handsome without a shadow of a doubt; he was also my very powerful enemy. The Raven could eliminate me in a heartbeat, and here I was in the car with him, alone. I knew that standing, I would barely come to his shoulders; I was as fair as he was dark, as slight as he was strong. It was a terrifying drive from the station to the barracks, and I would be assigned to him day in and day out.

He did not say a word for the entire drive, but there was no doubt he knew who I was – the cursed.

Sophie moved ahead through the diary. The next few encounters were the same... the Raven driving with Margaret, staring, saying nothing, always watchful. It must have been stressful and terrifying for her; Sophie sympathised and, as expected, came across a few lines where Margaret considered leaving.

I have thought of putting in for a transfer, but I am happy here, aside from the Raven, and I love the girls with whom I share the dorm and our daily ups and downs. My protector has also said the Raven may follow me to wherever I transfer just because he can. We did not know if fate brought him here or if he requested it, desiring to be closer to the woman he could torment as was his destiny.

Sophie had not thought of it that way, that she was the Raven's destiny in this generation. What if he chose to ignore that destiny, she wondered. I must ask Alfred if there was ever a Raven who held no interest in being so. Continuing, Sophie looked for the time when the wheel turned, and things changed. Then she found it, several months ahead of the last entry.

Today while I was driving the Wing Commander, we were stopped at a roadblock. That was not uncommon in high-security areas. We were about three cars from the checkpoint, and I could sense his impatience as he was always busy. Of course, he said nothing.

Then there was a terrifying explosion; I screamed in fright as an enormous fireball appeared in front of us, my ears were ringing, and the air was full of dust and grit. Pockets of fire broke out everywhere and the smoke was thick; several guards had been flung with the impact. One was on the roof of the car in front of us; he was not moving. Another I could see lying on the ground was also still.

Our roof was gone, the car two places in front of us was on fire, the car before that was a black shell... blown up, the driver incinerated. I had never seen or experienced such a thing; the shock of it! My ears were ringing, and I looked behind in the back seat and the Wing Commander lay trapped, unconscious; the roof of our car and other debris was pinning him down.

I pushed open my car door, relieved it would open, and ran around to his side, and then the front of our car lit up with hot fiery flames. The car in front was almost a burnt-out wreck, but someone had managed to drag the soldier from it before it finally exploded into a fireball. It was all happening so fast, and yet it seemed to be in slow motion, I can't explain.

People were calling for help. They sounded so far away, but my ears still suffered from the explosion. I heard myself scream for someone to help us, but there was no one able. Then he was conscious again.

'Get out, run,' he yelled at me. The fire in the front of our car was licking forward towards us.

'No.' I pulled away the metal trapping him, lifting it as best I could and cutting my hands on the sharp protruding bits. I threw the bits and pieces that I could lift off him. The roof had cut into his leg. He must have some powers as the Raven, but he didn't use them; I don't know why. He grimaced in pain, the smell of the petrol and the heat bearing down on us.

'That's an order, ACW Dillon. Get out now!'

I ignored his order without thinking, I couldn't walk away, and my back was to the burning so I didn't see the threat, but I could feel the heat singeing my clothes. I kept going until it was impossible, and then just when I could barely see for the smoke and my eyes watering, the heat pushing me away and the burning from the smoke in my throat, I had him free. He pushed up and staggered out, then saved me in return.

As the car was consumed in flames, blowing up with an enormous burst of firepower, he picked me up and leapt, landing far enough away from the vehicle not to be burnt and his whole body covered mine. The flying metal and glass hit the Wing Commander, and I was cocooned below him. I don't know how long we stayed like that but when the noise died down, he rolled off me.

We were covered in dirt and soot, our breathing laboured, our uniforms singed and torn. He ran a hand through his dark hair.

'Do you make a habit of disobeying orders?' he asked, an eyebrow quirked in my direction.

'It's the first time I can recall doing so, Sir, but better not test me in battle,' I told him in all seriousness, and he smiled. Then he chuckled, and I couldn't help but do the same. It was the first words we had spoken to each other that weren't a direction or location that I had to drive him to, and my return acquiescence to acknowledge the order. Looking around us, we sobered at the scene before us. The Wing Commander – the Raven – glanced at me.

'Thank you.'

'Thank you, too,' I said to him.

He staggered to his feet and assisted in pulling me up.

'You were fearless,' he said as soldiers arrived on the scene, and we heard the wails of ambulances and military vehicles approaching.

I wasn't. I was doing what had to be done, but as I began to calm down, I became emotional. I shook my head and told the Raven, 'No, I was terrified.' I quickly wiped a couple of tears that threatened to make me look even less professional, not realising they left a trail in the soot on my face and were quite evident. Then, he did the weirdest thing. He pulled me to him and held me until I stopped shaking.

And something shifted in both of us.

Sophie sighed. 'Margaret, I know the feeling,' she said. 'So what happened to your love for the tall, dark, handsome Raven? Was it reciprocated? Why couldn't he call on his powers?' Sophie thought of "her" Murdoch. Had she ever seen his powers, or was his anger just implied? She couldn't recall a time when he transformed, but he could obviously become a raven, given that was the reason for his current predicament when he fell from the sky. But why didn't the Raven save himself from the fire that day? Would he have saved Margaret if he could get out and she was the one trapped? She read on, expecting Margaret to ask him the same question if she were brave enough.

I woke looking forward to getting to my job and seeing him. His smile told me he felt the same. We spent hours each day driving around together, and when I looked in the rear-view mirror, his smile was warm, his eyes teasing; it was all I lived for, day in, day out. But it wasn't that simple. My protector was torn between concern and anger. The Raven and I didn't know where to take our feelings or what they could mean.

I loved him. I loved the Raven. But something else had changed, something neither I nor my protector understood. I still had visions when I wore the glasses, but the Raven told me he no longer felt the fire inside him that warned him I was the enemy. We didn't know what to make of it. By saving the Raven, had the curse become nullified? I know from reading my history that Samuel Rayne could have saved Saghani, but instead, he persecuted her to her death. Because I saved a Raven, am I exempt from the curse? Are all future generations now or just me in my lifetime? We do not know as this seems unprecedented, and the Lens' men cannot tell me.

Wow, Sophie mused, stopping to absorb this information. She smiled at the thought of the Lens' men helping Margaret and realised it was Alfred's father and that a young Alfred might have been involved too, or maybe he was just a babe in arms. She realised that if only she had saved Murdoch instead of Alfred, they might have been able to live together happily ever after, well, in this lifetime at least. In her mind, Sophie saw Nikolas's face as she said that; he was always so good to her. She sighed, recognising Elsopeth's feelings of being torn. Sophie did not intend to let her feelings towards Nikolas go that far.

But the question Margaret asked was answered – Sophie was living proof that the curse continued and had only ceased for Margaret. Aunt Daphne was most likely the next recipient, and then Sophie herself, she mused. Sophie turned the page and read the next entry.

Tragedy has struck. Murdoch invited me to his room last evening as we had been getting closer and desperately wanted privacy and intimacy. He had a private room, of course, as the commanding officer of our squadron. It was later in the evening, after dinner, and I was nervous. Would I look like a tainted woman slipping into his room at night? We dined together in the hall but had not made our affections public to anyone on the base. My protector did not want me to go, he thought it was a trap, but I could not believe that of Murdoch, not after the hours we'd spent in each other's company alone in the car and the happiness we were creating.

But when I knocked on his door, it wasn't the Raven who answered. My protector arrived behind me.

'Leave,' the man in the doorway snapped at me, and I stepped backward, turning and then running down the stairs. I heard his laughter following me. I knew from his features that he was one of the Raven's kin, although I did not know him by name. He was arrogant and evil and looked like he would strike me down if given a chance. All night I expected to be summonsed to speak with the commanding officer, and Murdoch would be there to explain. But it didn't happen.

The next morning, I arrived for work and was greeted by the second in charge. He said Murdoch had died overnight from injuries due to a fire. One of the petrol reserves had exploded when he was supervising their delivery. I didn't believe it. He was attacked by his own for loving me, it's the only explanation I could think of, and I am distraught. I have no will to live; I wish I could enlist for action on the front line, run away, be reckless, and fight with wild abandon. Murdoch was such a powerful man that he must have loved and trusted his kin and been caught unaware.

The new Raven did not appear, and I didn't know who it was, but my protector found out. It was not the man I suspected killed Murdoch – that was a distant relative who was angry at the Raven's love for me and took matters into his own hands to honour Harley, or so we were informed. The Raven mantle had gone to Murdoch's brother, who was serving overseas. I was safe for now. Safe and heartbroken. I had lost my first love at war.

Sophie closed the book. *Murdered*. The Raven was murdered, and his brother took up the mantle. Was it Allanon then in some form? A gentle, kind soul. Regardless, someone on that side of the family took the curse very seriously. To her surprise, Sophie drifted to sleep. When she woke a few hours later in the early light of morning, her first thoughts were to see the Lens family as soon as she could get away and visit them, get word on "her" Raven, and find out why Margaret's Raven did not, or could not, save himself from the fire.

CHAPTER 7

ALLANON ASHCROFT HAD A restless night, as he did every night for the past week since his brother was found and hospitalised. He was grateful beyond all measure to Alfred Lens. They were related, but neither man claimed the connection as Allanon was from Harley's line of descendants and Alfred from Hadley's line. But he had always liked the gentleman and held him in high regard. Everyone did, and it wasn't fear-based, as Alfred could extinguish them all in a heartbeat.

Allanon's only brother would be dead if not for Alfred Lens. He would be forever indebted, making Allanon an uninspiring enemy if a new Raven had to step up. Only the holder of the curse – Murdoch – knew the inheritor, and he had never said. Allanon believed the twins to be too young for the responsibility, and the eldest was too in love with power and dominance. Allanon was determined to bring his brother back, believing Murdoch could hear him when he spoke. Why would he not return? It was only a matter of weeks since Murdoch had told Allanon about his state of despair, but Allanon had no idea his brother would take it this far, that he would shift to his raven form and fly until exhaustion caused him to fall from the sky.

Allanon pulled into the car park of Sophie's inherited mansion and the community offices, parking under one of the large trees in the shade. He looked at the shoe box on the seat beside him, sighed, and, picking it up, alighted and locked the car. He admired the gardens – a small oasis in a busy suburb, like a private park with small paths weaving around hedges, old-fashioned lamp towers, and seats scattered throughout the grounds.

'Landed on your feet, young lady,' he said with a small smile even though he was of similar age to Sophie. The mansion she inherited from her great aunt, the famous clairvoyant Daphne Shelby, was grand and gothic. The estate was enormous and had been divided into a separate residence wing and offices for community groups.

But Allanon was on a mission; he needed help, and it wasn't from Sophie. He needed to bring his brother back into consciousness to stop him from dwelling in the space between living and not existing, and the grifter, Jack Eabe, was the man to help him.

Before Allanon had taken the turn into the car park of Sophie's estate, Miss Sharpe appeared in the front room where Sophie and Jack sat opposite each other, with a view of the garden through the large floor-to-ceiling glass windows.

'Murdoch's brother, Allanon, is here,' she said, glancing outside.

Sophie and Jack looked to the car park; there was no sign of him, and then his car turned in.

'I hope there is no bad news,' Sophie said, rising.

'I don't feel that,' Miss Sharpe said with a hand on her heart. She was very intuitive, and Sophie could never work out how she knew most things in advance but claimed not to have any powers.

Tallish, thin and wiry like her glasses frame, Miss Sharpe had been with the "glasses" a long time now and was loyal to their service and that of its beholders, including Sophie's great aunt and, on her passing, Sophie. For Miss Sharpe, it had all begun at the age of seventeen. On receipt of her typing certificate from *Mrs O'Grady's Professional Typing Academy for Young Ladies*, an ambitious Miss Valerie Sharpe had presented herself at the *Optical Illusion* store to begin her profession as a typist with Alfred's father, Mr Bertram Lens. Miss Sharpe learned about lenses, and in time, she was told of the curse – although it was often thought she was drawn there because of it – and became an indispensable team member.

That changed. It was no secret that the son of Bertram, the dapper Alfred Lens – ten years her senior – had fallen in love with Miss Sharpe. But that would not do. Miss Sharpe was a professional young woman, and rejecting his advances, Alfred went on to marry a lovely homemaker. Miss Sharpe dedicated herself to the services of Mr Bertram Lens for the next twenty-five years until he dropped dead one day while signing a cheque.

Alfred stepped into his father's shoes. Naturally, Miss Sharpe could not become his office manager as that would be most inappropriate, so she remained in the employ of the glasses and became the personal assistant of clairvoyant and the curse beholder, Daphne Shelby. There, she worked for seventeen years, and with the passing of Daphne Shelby, Miss Sharpe decided to retire and join a bridge club. She was unsure she could work with the brash niece, Sophie, but agreed to stay to see her into the role. Unexpectedly, Sophie grew into the position, and the two rubbed along nicely. Again, Miss Sharpe was indispensable, but she did negotiate to work part-time to join her bridge club.

Months earlier, she had brought a new employee on board to assist with the bookings and media requests as Sophie's fame grew, and Jack Eabes joined the team. In his thirties, he was a giant man with huge tattooed arms, wavy shoulder-length hair, and a gentle and jovial temperament that nicely added to the office atmosphere. He also wore glasses for reading and work, but his skills were not "glass" related. Jack was a grifter, which he explained to Sophie on his first meeting was a being 'only known to magical and spiritual folk, and that's the way we like it. We accept a gift, provide a protection spell or blessing and return it. Hence the name grifter, so it's gifter with an "r" in there because the gift gets returned,' he said. From what Allanon was carrying, Jack was likely to be asked for help.

'He doesn't look too upset,' Sophie agreed as Allanon alighted from the car and took the garden steps to the building. She would not need to call Alfred now for an update on Murdoch, but she was still curious as to why Margaret's Raven couldn't save himself. She noticed the box. 'What's he carrying?'

'A shoebox of sorts,' Jack said, squinting as they watched Allanon until he disappeared into their building and could be heard walking down the hallway toward their office.

'Miss Sharpe,' he said on entering, and smiling, they embraced.

'You must be terribly distressed, Allanon,' she said sympathetically.

'My brother is always causing me trouble,' he said in good humour. 'Sophie, Jack.'

Jack moved to shake Allanon's hand and encompassed him in a bear hug instead; Allanon put the shoebox down just in time to avoid it getting crushed. 'He'll be right; he's the strong, silent type,' Jack said.

'Thanks, Jack.'

Sophie moved to embrace Allanon as well, and they hugged briefly.

'I got your message,' he said, 'but I was coming over and thought I would speak to you in person.'

Sophie nodded. 'Murdoch spoke to me last night.'

Her words stilled the room as all eyes turned to Sophie.

'Let's sit down,' Miss Sharpe suggested, and Jack sat at his desk, the remaining three in scattered chairs.

'I was reading the diary of Margaret Dillon, who fell in love with the Raven in her time, in the 1940s, and before I started, I desperately called to him, not expecting a reply,' Sophie explained.

'How did he communicate with you?' Allanon asked, frustrated, running a hand through his hair and exhaling deeply. 'Nothing I do is bringing him back to me.'

'There was an incident before then...' Sophie told of the presence in the garden, Mel thinking it was two people, Nikolas thinking it might be the twins.

Allanon's jaw tightened, and his eyes narrowed with anger. 'No! They had no right to frighten you. Murdoch will be very angry. I'm sorry, Sophie.'

'It's okay; it might not have been them,' she said. 'I can understand why they are angry at me.'

'They are loyal,' Miss Sharpe said, 'but no one could foresee the force of the curse and how it would have impacted Murdoch and Sophie.'

'I would do everything differently if I knew,' Sophie said emotionally.

Allanon held up his hand in a peaceful gesture. 'You both would. I will talk to the twins. What came next?'

'I was looking down on the garden from my bedroom window, and I could see the black feathers on the ground, and I got a bit sentimental,' she said, a little embarrassed. She bit her lower lip and then finished the story. 'I went to bed, and as I lay there feeling sorry for myself, I said "Raven, Raven, wherefore art thou Raven?" because I felt like we were being denied because of our names, you know, like Romeo and Juliet were because they were Montagues and Capulets.'

'And he answered?' Allanon asked.

'He said, "*I'm here, Sophie*", and I freaked out and looked around, but he was nowhere to be seen. I got up and looked out over the garden as well. He didn't appear or say anything more, so I closed my eyes and tried again, saying the same words. He responded louder and clearer this time, but I didn't risk opening my eyes in case I lost him. I asked where he was, and he said, "Somewhere, in between worlds," and I asked if he could come back, and he didn't answer.' Sophie wiped tears from her face. 'I waited for hours, but he didn't utter another word.'

Allanon nodded, clearly emotional. 'Thanks for trying.'

'I want him back,' Sophie said.

'We all do,' Miss Sharpe agreed supportively. 'Allanon, what can we do?'

'Thank you, Miss Sharpe,' Allanon sobered. 'I've come to ask for Jack's help.'

'Anything,' Jack said.

'I'll make us all tea,' Miss Sharpe suggested, but Allanon declined.

'I'll head straight back to the hospital once I've secured Jack's help, but thanks, Miss Sharpe.' He retrieved the box he brought and took the offered seat in front of Jack's desk while Miss Sharpe and Sophie moved closer to sit on the couch nearby and watch. Sophie had only seen Jack in action as a grifter a couple of times and found the whole concept fascinating. She didn't put her glasses on like she had the last few times to see the before and after results of Jack's work. Fortunately, the cursed could not read the Raven in this case, so there was no pressure on her to reveal an outcome, good or bad, to his brother.

'How can I help?' Jack asked.

Allanon put the box in front of him. 'Murdoch is not or will not come out of his state of unconsciousness, but I know he's there.' He looked at Sophie. 'We know that now for sure.' He returned his attention to Jack. 'I need him to come back. I've brought these branches from home. Growing up, we had the same trees at our childhood homestead, and he'd recognise the smell. I thought it might bring him home, so to speak.'

'Excellent,' Jack said. 'Let's do this. Please ask your request.'

Allanon nodded, and Sophie watched on fascinated as Allanon said: 'I wish to bring my brother home, and therefore, please let me gift this to you.'

'Thank you. I will take your gift,' Jack said, accepting the box with both hands and placing it firmly on the desk before him. He opened the lid and put his hands on the branches. The beautiful fragrance of cedar and pine wafted around them. Jack closed his eyes, and after a short while, he started to say a small verse which Sophie and Miss Sharpe leant forward to hear:

'On this day you will cease to roam

And return to your ancestral home
Stronger be you since the fall,
Harken when your brother calls.'

Jack stopped, waited a moment, and then looked up and said, 'Allanon, please accept this gift from me.' Jack put the lid on the box, rose and regifted it and its contents to Murdoch's brother, who wrapped his hands around the box, securing it.

'Thank you. I accept your generous gift,' Allanon said, offering his sincere thanks. 'Thank you for the strengthening blessing too.'

'We all want him recovered,' Jack assured Allanon. 'When you arrive at his bedside, open the box, place it near him and call his name; tell him to come to you now.'

Looking slightly emotional, Allanon swallowed and said, 'I will, thanks, Jack. Forgive me for rushing off, Sophie, Miss Sharpe.'

'Of course,' Sophie said, 'will you let us know—' her voice trailed off.

'Straight away,' he assured her, and with that, he was gone, the box tucked under his arm and the three of them hopeful of his success.

CHAPTER 8

D ETECTIVE GERARD OAKLEY'S WEEK started badly, and the responsibility rested solely with his partner, Detective Murdoch Ashcroft. Gerard had four weeks until he officially retired. Four weeks. All Murdoch had to do was go the distance, but no, Gerard fumed. Murdoch took up some stupid extreme sport, according to his brother, and fell while climbing, hitting the water hard. He's never been interested in climbing before; couldn't he have waited until Gerard retired? He'd be angrier if he weren't a little suspicious. Gerard was prepared to buy the story for the Ashcroft family's sake, but the truth would be coming out if he got a one-on-one with his partner.

Extreme sport my arse, he muttered.

'What was that, Oakley?'

'Talking to myself, Fletcher, old people do that,' he said, making her grin. For some reason, he and his new partner had fallen into calling each other by their surnames from day one.

He considered the young woman – his new partner – who would be Murdoch's partner when Gerard retired with a wave, gold watch, and a fishing rod in hand. Gerard conceded it could be worse; she was alright, and they surprisingly got along well enough. He put it down to the recent opportunity to work with clairvoyant Sophie Carell. It gave him some first-hand experience working with strong, young females. He'd been sceptical about anything that Sophie could bring to the table, but Murdoch wasn't, and then Sophie helped him solve a cold case – one of his first as a young detective, the death of a beauty queen. Gerard gave credit where credit was due; she had some talent that young clairvoyant. He could retire happy with his oldest case put to bed.

Yeah, Detective Rachel Fletcher was alright, he conceded. Fit, ambitious, could take a joke and accepted his apology because he was sure he was going to offend her on so many levels – culturally because she had Indian roots, or because she was female, or young, and he wasn't sure about all that non-binary stuff, which may or may not apply to her.

'Apology accepted in advance. I'll give you a crash course over the next four weeks,' she had said to him with a wink and a laugh.

He liked the fact that she liked her food as well. They could talk over a burger and chips at lunch or a hot curry she'd select for them, unlike some women who only ate lettuce or even Murdoch, who wanted healthy bloody sandwiches every second day. Now, they had their first case – a young woman missing after a night out with friends – very out of character, apparently. His new partner sat at Murdoch's desk and studied the whiteboard in front of them where they'd written up some notes and pinned the missing woman's photo with a magnet. She wore her dark shoulder-length hair tied back with a black band, and he watched as her brown eyes ran over the information on the board, squinting while thinking.

'Where are you, Hope Yardley?' she said more to herself than Gerard.

'Let's take stock. What have we got?' Gerard rose and came to join her, taking the chair in front of her desk where they could both see the whiteboard.

'From the top,' Rachel said and began, 'Hope Yardley, eighteen. She has a Filipino mum, an Australian dad, and two younger siblings, and she still lives in the family home on the south side. Hope just started nursing studies at university. Her friends say she is a good person and doesn't do drugs, hitch, smoke, drink to excess, party hard or play around. She's academically good and did well at school,' Rachel sighed.

'She disappears well, too,' Gerard added, and Rachel suppressed a laugh.

'So inappropriate.'

'Well, I wouldn't say that to her folks, obviously,' Gerard joked. 'She's a pretty little thing. I hope this has a happy ending,' he said, studying the whiteboard.

'Maybe she's gone on her first bender or is staying over with someone her parents wouldn't approve of, but I'm not confident.'

'Yeah, my gut says the same.'

Rachel continued, 'I spoke with her three best friends who were at the hotel with her that night. It was an 18th birthday party for one of them. She left first and with a football player.'

'Not so innocent then.'

'Men can be very persuasive,' Rachel said, 'and this was no ordinary football player.'

Gerard looked at the photo on the board of Matt Sutton, captain of the Vikings, one of the state rugby league football teams. 'Yeah, women like a bit of power. I imagine the captain of a winning football team would be a good catch.' He raised an eyebrow, waiting for her bite.

'I imagine a pretty young virgin would be a good catch, too,' she paraphrased him. 'For these guys, it's always on tap.'

'But he put her in a cab, and we know that. I spoke with the cabbie, and he confirmed he picked Hope up. She asked to be dropped off at the hotel where her friends might still be.'

Rachel nodded. 'Yeah, the footy player was okay, respectful. It's what happened after the cab rides that's sketchy.'

'Given time is of the essence in a missing person case, I reckon we should see Sophie, the clairvoyant, and cut to the chase. Besides, I've only got a few weeks left, and we want this one cleaned up before Murdoch returns,' Gerard suggested.

'You surprise me, Oakley,' Rachel said, swaying in the chair and studying him. 'You'd be the last person on earth I'd pick as open to all that other world spiritual and tarot reading stuff.'

'Surprised me too, but Sophie is one of the real ones. Murdoch has used her a fair bit, so she'll be part of your team. May as well get to know her now.'

'Sophie Carell. I saw the story in the newspaper. She's good; truth be known, we haven't got much to go on.'

'Or it could be fun just to knuckle down and do some good old-fashioned police work together,' he tested her, waiting for a reaction.

'Let's do that and see the clairvoyant as well.'

'If we could drag it out and solve it in my last week, that'd be better,' he said, half in jest and half serious.

'Oh wow, this could be the last case of your career, and you are working it with me!' she said, hand on heart and with great reverence. Rachel grinned.

'Lord help me,' he muttered, glancing at her.

'I think we need lunch first. We could talk about the missing girl over a burger and then go and see the clairvoyant if she's free.'

'Now you're talking,' Gerard agreed and rose. 'Lead on, Fletcher.'

'Do you think she'll know we're coming?'

'No doubt, or Miss Sharpe, her assistant, will,' he said and prepared himself for a barrage of questions about that.

Imogen Harper was the queen of the WAGs – the wives and girlfriends of the Vikings rugby league team – and it was not luck that got her there. Slim, fit, sexy and blonde, she was engaged to the team's captain, Matt Sutton, and her most important job, as she saw it, was to keep him satisfied so that her profile continued to grow. At twenty-six, she wasn't the youngest or the eldest WAG, but she was the highest-profile partner and that took a lot of work to maintain.

Imogen had her big break at twenty-two. She was so desperate for stardom that she could taste it, and if it had to come from infamy, she was not opposed to the idea. Whatever the trend was, Imogen had set about emulating it, mostly with limited success. As a beautician, she made videos offering make-up advice, produced fan content, entered modelling competitions, took acting classes and went to auditions, sending out her photos to the agents she had researched and followed online. Her dad had said men liked a woman with something to grab onto, but the modelling agencies weren't interested in her full figure, honey-coloured hair and glamorous look – a glut of her type, one of them told her. Imogen kept a list of those agents and event organisers who shunned her, every name meticulously documented in a spreadsheet, so that when she made it – and that was now – she would be sure not to give them the time of day. The satisfaction was its own reward.

She tried the starving waif look, but that hadn't worked for Imogen. So, she reinvented herself – the curves were gone, replaced by a super-fit body that begged to be seen. Every piece of her fitted lycra featured her assets to her best advantage. Now, on the arm of the captain and with several sponsors, including beauty companies and leisure wear paying for her to wear their products on her social media feeds to inspire her 764,000 followers, Imogen Harper, soon to be Imogen Harper-Sutton was at the top of her game.

The ride hadn't come cheap, even if she was in the money now. She had spent a fortune to get her look, investing in herself – bigger lips, longer lashes, smaller outfits. Plus, plenty of products provided through her beautician work found their way into or onto her body. It paid off.

Her father said she was the most beautiful girl he'd ever seen and any guy would be lucky to have her. Imogen's mother told her to go for the top shelf and not waste her time on the local mechanic who had asked her out or the salesman she met at a club. Aim high, and that's exactly what she had done. Imogen had checked out the WAGs and researched the players – she knew who was single and who wasn't and who might be swayed to cheat. The WAGs had their own followings; some were successful before hitching up with the players, but most of the ladies enjoyed their careers taking off when they started dating the guys.

It was all she could think about, and she was ruthless in her preparation, following the football stars, working out which bars and clubs they frequented, watching their social media feeds to try and be in the right place at the right time, and trying to catch the eye and win the heart of one of the players so she could be a WAG – and hang out with the wives and girlfriends.

And she picked a recruit, Matt Sutton. Sweet, tall, handsome, and starting with the club. It was a gamble, but he was the top pick of the recruits that year and had never attracted a glamorous girlfriend until now. And luckily, he wanted one. They were both twenty-two then, and by twenty-five, she was engaged. At twenty-six, Matt became captain. It was her best long-term investment yet. And if that tart he picked up at some trashy bar while he was celebrating at a boys-only event thought she was going to get her claws into him, she had a reality check coming her way.

CHAPTER 9

ALLANON ASHCROFT ENTERED HIS brother's hospital room with more hope than he had felt for the past week. His brother was as he left him – still, quiet, unawakened. Allanon partially closed the door and carried the box with reverence, placing it beside Murdoch on the white-sheeted bed. His breathing quickened, fast and shallow; what if this didn't work?

Why wouldn't it work?

Because the Raven is strong, maybe immune to a Grifter gift and blessing?

The doctors could not believe how quickly his brother was recovering; they wouldn't. Murdoch had the blood of Raven generations pumping through him, the power of Saghani – a healer and witch – from whom the Ashcroft and Lens families descended. If his recovery was hampered, it was because of Murdoch's spirit, his will, his peace of mind or lack thereof. In Murdoch's state of repose, Allanon rarely saw his brother looking so peaceful, and he did not like it as much as he thought he would. Murdoch was always mulling over a case, stewing about his partner's antics, restless, in and out of love, waiting... waiting for Sophie to become his Elsopeth of this generation.

Allanon envied women sometimes. His wife, Bree, had been distraught at the sight of Murdoch and shed her tears freely, as the women in his clinic and his patients often did with their own dramas. He wanted to cry, put his head back and yell to release his pain and fear. His only brother – they might not see each other often, but they had never lived more than a short drive away from each other, never not spent the big occasions together as a family. He could not conceive a life without Murdoch.

Get on with it, he told himself, and standing beside Murdoch, Allanon placed the box against his brother's side, removed the lid and allowed the scent of pine and cedar to waft into the room and reach their senses. The smell always calmed him and reminded him of a happy place. He just hoped to hell it had the same effect on Murdoch. Maybe Sophie or Elsopeth's perfume might have worked better.

Focus, he told himself, annoyed he allowed himself to be distracted by panic, or was he avoiding doing this in case it didn't work?

Taking a deep breath, Allanon did as the Grifter instructed and said aloud: 'Murdoch, come to me now!'

For a second, nothing happened as Allanon stared intently at his brother. And then Murdoch's eyes shot open. He gasped and sat upright. The box and pine branches flew off the bed and fell to the ground.

Allanon cried out in joy. 'You're okay. You're safe,' he assured Murdoch as his brother drew deep breaths. He grabbed Murdoch's shoulder. 'You're back.'

Murdoch turned his dark eyes to his brother. Gaunt and pale, he steadied his breathing. Allanon grabbed him in a hug that Murdoch did not return his arms staying by his side. Allanon released him.

'Where have you been?'

Murdoch swallowed. 'In-between.'

'You're back now, safe,' Allanon tried to keep him relaxed. 'Why didn't you return? I was sure you could hear me.'

'I couldn't find the path,' Murdoch said and leaned back, his eyes fluttering with weariness. Allanon pushed the pillows up behind him.

'Sophie?'

'Distraught. Alfred Lens saved you. Bree hasn't stopped crying; the twins even went to thank Mr Lens.'

That earned him a smile from Murdoch. 'I'm sorry. I didn't think it would matter.'

'Seriously?' Allanon huffed. His reaction quickly turned to anger and then raw emotion. 'I thought you had left me... for good,' his voice lowered as he choked and swallowed, clearing his throat.

Murdoch looked like he would say a thousand things and then grabbed Allanon's arm. 'Forgive me, Anon; it was selfish.'

'It was desperate,' Allanon said, looking at him with concern.

'I need to see her.'

Allanon's breath hitched. He expected the request but not so soon, and then the Raven's eyes flared dark, and the machines in his hospital room shut down, restarted and began to wail. Staff rushed in – two nurses, one pressing the button to summon a doctor while another quietened the machines.

'When did he wake?' the younger nurse asked.

'Just now,' Allanon said, not taking his eyes off Murdoch as the nurses checked his vital signs and asked questions of Murdoch, such as his age, if he knew his name and that of his brother, and what year it was currently.

The doctor entered and asked all the same questions. She was an older female and had seen Murdoch on the night he was brought in.

'Your recovery is amazing. I see no reason why you can't go home this afternoon. I'll begin the paperwork.'

Murdoch and Allanon thanked her and the nurses, and when alone again, Allanon lay down the law.

'You're coming back to my place to recover.'

'Thanks, Anon, but I'll be–'

Allanon cut him off. 'You may be the Raven and the eldest, but there is no discussion on this subject. You will stay with me until Bree and I deem you are well enough to leave. If you do not, we shall all come and stay with you.'

Murdoch grinned. 'Your dog will chase me.'

'That's why I only got a small one. Try not to swoop him, and he might let you be,' Allanon joked.

Murdoch became serious again. 'I tried to reach Sophie last night.'

'She told me.'

'She did?' He started to sit up.

'Relax, you're not getting out until this afternoon; sit back.' Allanon gently pushed his brother backward and stood beside him, arms folded across his chest.

'Are you the bed bouncer?' Murdoch smirked.

'If need be.'

Murdoch groaned. 'You've spoken to her? I have to see her.'

'Brother, I know it has been hard for you–'

'Anon, I have to see her.'

'How? We haven't found a way yet. If you can go to her in her dream state, we believe it's the safest way for now.'

'We? Who is the "we" you speak of? Are you trying to find a way to beat the curse?'

'I've been discussing it with Alfred Lens. He and Sophie are also searching the books to see if a Raven has ever loved an accursed in history and to find out what we can learn from it.'

'And?'

'There might be one possibility.' He saw that was enough to give his brother hope.

'I'm so tired,' Murdoch said, trying to keep his eyes open.

'You're recovering. Let them run their final tests and I will collect you this afternoon. Don't leave until I do. I mean it, Brother,' Allanon said in a firm voice that Murdoch had used on him many times over the years.

Murdoch nodded his agreement and tried to stay awake. 'Tell me the truth, Anon, is she with him, the shapeshifter?'

'No.'

Murdoch exhaled with relief and slipped into sleep.

Sophie's phone beeped, and she grabbed it, read the message, and exhaled.

'He's back,' she said, looking up at Jack and including Miss Sharpe, who had just entered the room. Sophie smiled. 'It worked, Murdoch's back. You're amazing, Jack.'

Jack shrugged and looked embarrassed. 'I've got to tell you I had my doubts; I thought the Raven might be too strong a force for me to bring back.'

'Now, Sophie, dear, you need to be very careful,' Miss Sharpe warned.

'I know. I will be, thank you, Miss Sharpe. I don't know whether to go and see him or if I should try and reach him through the mind, but I can't do that; he has to initiate it... or maybe I should wait to see what Allanon says. Maybe that is better,' she said, thinking out loud. Sophie looked up at them both. 'I keep going around in circles. I'm reading Elsopeth's diary and scanning through it so I can skip all their liaisons and the romance stuff and see if there is anything that might help our situation, but she wasn't the accursed when they were together; she was just a witch. So, I'm hoping Margaret Dillon's diary might help – which I'm also reading – but... I have to see him.'

She saw Jack and Miss Sharpe exchange looks – were they thinking she was raving and should be institutionalised? It would not have surprised Sophie. Miss Sharpe spoke up again. 'Detective Oakley is arriving.'

'Now?' Sophie frowned, glancing at the window.

'It's probably a good thing to stay busy,' Jack said as if he experienced his share of grief and knew being busy was the best way to outrun it, even short term.

'You're right, of course,' Sophie said and saw the detective – Murdoch's senior partner – pulling into the grounds in his old red Holden sedan with someone in the passenger seat beside him.

'I believe they need your help,' Miss Sharpe said.

'I best get my glasses,' Sophie said. Suddenly, Nikolas appeared beside her, causing her to yelp.

'Sorry, I didn't have time to come over on the bike,' he apologised and turned to Jack and Miss Sharpe, greeting them both.

'Thanks for dropping in last night,' Sophie said as she watched Detective Oakley and a young woman come up through the garden on the path.

'My pleasure. Just quickly,' he said, getting Sophie's attention, 'I've cleaned up the um... leftover birds and feathers or rather, Orli did a quick spell and got rid of them. I thought it might be a good time to practice some of those skills you are accidentally displaying.'

Sophie grinned. 'Like banishing dark and gloomy spirits?'

'Like that,' he smiled. 'It was a wonder you didn't fell the trees. I suggest you come to my place, and we can see what you can do while safely nestled in the forest.'

'That'd be great if you're up for a bit of danger?'

Nikolas laughed. 'Sure. Tonight? I'll collect you, your place at eight.' He started to fade.

Sophie called out, 'Wait up. We have news. The Raven is back.'

'Right,' Nikolas said, and with that, he was gone.

CHAPTER 10

S OPHIE SMILED, HER HEART at ease for the first time in a week, knowing Murdoch was back with them. It was as if a load had fallen off her shoulders, and a cage around her heart opened.

'Well, if it isn't my favourite retiring detective,' she greeted Detective Oakley.

'How many retiring detectives do you know?' he asked suspiciously with a twitch of a smile; he didn't wait for an answer. 'Gidday, Jack. Formal introductions then... Detective Rachel Fletcher meet Miss Sophie Carell and...'

Jack stood to introduce himself, his large hand engulfing Rachel's. 'Jack Eabe, assistant to Sophie and Miss Sharpe... the gatekeeper, you might say,' he said with a grin.

'Good to know and to meet you.' Rachel laughed. 'Hello, Sophie, I've heard and read much about you.'

'Rachel, welcome. Well, you've got your work cut out for you.' She glanced at Gerard, who laughed.

'The cheek,' he said. 'Can you spare us fifteen minutes.'

'She can,' Jack answered.

'I can, apparently,' Sophie agreed, 'always happy to help our police service.'

Miss Sharpe entered carrying a tray with a pot of tea, coffee, and biscuits as if she was anticipating the guests and had prepared the tray earlier – which she had. She greeted the senior detective and, allowing Jack to take the tray, clapped her hands in delight at seeing Rachel, who exclaimed, 'Miss Sharpe, it's great to see you again.'

'Rachel, dear, and you. Congratulations are in order, I believe – a detective now,' Miss Sharpe said, accepting a handshake from the young lady detective.

Sophie threw her hands up into the air. 'Seriously, is there anyone you do not know in the whole world, Miss Sharpe?'

'Oh, I'm sure there are a few people,' Miss Sharpe said in jest.

'You didn't tell me you knew Miss Sharpe,' Gerard said, looking at his partner.

'I would have, but I didn't get a chance,' Rachel said. 'Miss Sharpe and I met way back when I was a senior constable working on a prison skills program.'

'I was volunteering with several ladies to teach some of the prisoners new skills to assist them when released into society again,' Miss Sharpe explained. 'We taught several of the lads how to cook.'

'You are a dark horse, Miss Sharpe,' Sophie said. 'You never stop surprising me.'

'Have you seen any of them since they got out, Miss Sharpe?' Jack asked.

'Oh yes. One of the lads helped me carry my groceries to the car when I bumped into him at the supermarket a few years back.'

'He didn't run off with them?' Gerard asked.

'So tired and cynical,' Sophie teased him, and he grinned.

'No, I'm sure he didn't want my baking goods.' She laughed. 'I also saw another of the young men about six months ago while I was buying some sherry.' Miss Sharpe sighed. 'But I heard he robbed that bottle shop a few weeks later and was back in prison. Such a shame; he was a nice fellow.'

'The company you keep, hey? At least he can cook in prison, which is not a bad job for getting extra rations,' Gerard joked. 'Well to business.'

'If you'll excuse me, I've got to go to the post office,' Jack said.

'And I'm off to the bank,' Miss Sharpe said. 'Please sit, have tea and coffee, and Sophie dear, will you pour?'

'Of course, Miss Sharpe, thank you,' Sophie said.

Gerard and his partner sat around Sophie's small round table near the window with the garden view as the office staff departed.

'I've read about your cases, Sophie,' Rachel said, 'Oakley and Ashcroft landed on their feet when you agreed to help them.'

Sophie laughed. 'I love that you are on a last-name basis with them. Murdoch worked with my Great Aunt Daphne long before I came on board; I sort of inherited him. And Gerard was the icing on the cake.'

'That's how most people see me,' he agreed, and Rachel grinned and rolled her eyes.

'Shall I?' she asked Gerard, and he gave her the floor. Rachel filled Sophie in on what had happened, the little evidence they had, and that time was of the essence if the young girl – Hope Yardley – was alive and in trouble. 'So, nothing on CCTV from the hotel. We're waiting to speak to some bar staff who aren't rostered on until later today, the footy player is in the clear – well he's cheated on his girlfriend but that's not a crime, sadly – and her friends say she was there when they all left one by one at different times. She may have left with someone and will stumble home in a few days, but the family said that is very out of character.'

'And she's not answering her phone,' Gerard added. 'It's turned off and not trackable.'

'We checked CCTV footage in the street, it's limited. Hope returned to the hotel, the cab took off and she re-entered. There's no footage of her leaving, but cameras don't cover all the exits. The security guy on the door can't remember her leaving, but he saw hundreds of people that night,' Rachel said, talking fast with frustration.

'We're coming to you early in this case, I know, but in missing persons' cases, a day can make a difference,' Gerard said soberly.

'Of course. Is it worth me speaking with the footy player, or are you convinced she left him alive?'

Gerard nodded. 'Yeah, we're good with that. Hope returned after her liaison with Matt Sutton – the footy player – and her girlfriends saw her after that.'

'Matt Sutton? The captain of the Vikings?' Sophie asked, wide-eyed with surprise.

'That's him. Boyfriend of fitness influencer Imogen Harper! He'll want to keep this as quiet as possible,' Rachel said.

'Hell yeah,' Sophie agreed. She turned to Gerard. 'After your cold case and the lying girlfriends—'

'That was a fascinating outcome,' Rachel cut in.

'Didn't see it coming,' Gerard agreed, sitting back and exhaling. The frustration and the years of drama that case had caused him because the beauty queen's girlfriends collaborated in a lie, continued to provoke him despite the case being solved thanks to Sophie.

'So, do you trust what these girlfriends are saying?' Sophie asked.

'Fletcher spoke with them,' Gerard said, looking at her.

'They seemed genuine, but I'm still working through their alibis after they left the hotel. We might get further with the hotel staff rostered the night Hope disappeared.'

'Okay. What if you set up a time tomorrow for me to speak to any available staff and anyone you don't believe is telling the truth? The bartender on duty that night would also be handy; I might see something if he recalls seeing Hope. Morning is best – Jack leaves it free for me to do my own thing.'

'Perfect, thank you,' Rachel said. 'We could ask them all to come to the hotel and get the manager to open for us.'

'Excellent idea, Fletcher,' Gerard said.

Sophie turned to the senior detective. 'This could be your last case,' she said with a smile. 'Does it make you a bit melancholy?'

'Hell no,' he said in his usual gruff style. 'I can't wait to depart and leave it to Fletcher and her adventure-sports sidekick.' He scoffed at the thought. 'He couldn't wait four weeks.'

Sophie chuckled. 'He's going home today, well, back to his brother's place.'

'You've heard from him?' Gerard asked, surprised.

'No, Allanon told me.'

'Well, that's good news. The sooner he is better, the sooner I get to kill him myself,' Gerard said in jest.

It was nearing four p.m. when Lukas's breath hitched momentarily with the shock of his heart changing rhythm. His grandfather looked at him.

'Alright, lad?'

He nodded. 'Venetia is coming; I've just synced with her watch and heart.' He gave a small smile as he looked outside the window frames of the *Optical Illusion* store. A master clocksmith, Lukas often synced with the watches and clocks he was repairing and sometimes with the wearer, so he knew when they were nearby.

They watched the great beauty – once Raven's love in another time – as she crossed the street and came towards them. Her look was classic and timeless – light coffee skin, dark tresses, an ample figure and full lips, high cheekbones, and sea-green eyes. Today, she wore a fitted cream dress with matching shoes, and Lukas could not believe they had found each other and that she was with him. Venetia had been living in Europe, in Florence, but when Sophie was without a protector for a brief time, she could sense where the Raven was and came looking for her lost love. Knowing the Lens family would have the diaries of the cursed and expecting the cursed to go there, Venetia bid her time, hoping the Raven would be nearby as a consequence. She had no interest in the accursed – Sophie – she only wanted to find the Raven. She was unaware that the accursed and the woman whom the Raven had dropped her for in the past – Elsopeth – were one and the same.

Fortunately, she discovered the Lens's store and sought a service for a timepiece she had gifted the Raven centuries ago. Then, she and Lukas's hearts fell into a rhythm. When the Raven told her they would not be lovers in this generation, she turned her attention to Lukas, and they had been inseparable since.

The door swung open, and the small bell chimed above, announcing her entry.

'Mr Lens,' she greeted Alfred in her soft Italian accent and then turned to Lukas, 'amore mio.'

'My love,' Lukas reciprocated her greeting, a little embarrassed at the show of affection in front of his grandfather but too much in love not to return her term of endearment.

'Hello, Venetia dear, you look most beautiful today, as always,' Alfred greeted her.

She nodded her thanks and smiled. 'Thank you, Mr Lens, too kind. Please forgive the intrusion to your place of work.'

'You are always welcome,' he said. 'And you know to call me Alfred.'

'Maybe in time, but I wish to show you my respect,' she said.

Lukas knew Venetia was a capable witch, more so than himself, who had been slow to learn, but no one was as powerful as Alfred Lens, and that was only one of the many reasons he was respected. Orli appeared from the backroom.

'Venetia, how lovely to see you. Would you like a drink, a tea perhaps?' she asked.

'Will you have one?'

'Always, and Uncle Alfred needs no persuasion.'

'I am a tea-drinking English man from way back,' he agreed with a chuckle.

They moved between the rooms to have a tea break in the back room, which was beautiful in its lush antique feel and more spacious than one would believe looking in from the front. They sat at the table, Lukas joining them once the tea and shortbread were served, and Alfred positioned himself to see the front door should a customer enter.

'I have spent the day reading accounts of my family,' Venetia said, sipping her tea. She laughed. 'I have come to the conclusion my family consists of very boring witches.'

Orli grinned. 'That might be a good thing; I wish we had less drama in our ancestry.'

'Indeed,' Alfred agreed.

'Well, I am tempted to embellish my own accounts just to make them more interesting for future generations,' Venetia said in jest.

'I suspect with the glamorous life you have led thus far, they will make for fascinating reading,' Lukas said, taking her free hand. He turned to his grandfather and Orli. 'I know that Sophie and I are both slow to our history and have shown little interest in reading it, but that is why,' he said, agreeing with Venetia. 'Reading all those old diaries is like watching someone's home travel videos.'

Alfred – who had translated most of the diaries into modern speak – laughed at the notion, as did Orli.

'Yes, how boring reading about your relatives meeting the Brontë sisters or being executed because they told the king that he was to be exiled long before he was,' Orli teased.

'Or seeing a client was going to board the *Titanic* and knowing of their demise, or warning of the great plague of 1665 coming and being the only survivor in the village,' Alfred added.

'Or meeting Florence Nightingale and working with her to nurse the soldiers, or coming across villains like Hitler and knowing you could not change history. One of our ancestors wrote of meeting Elvis Presley, and she told him he would be a big star. But yes, so boring,' Orli agreed drily.

Lukas and Venetia grinned and exchanged looks.

'Fine then, you've made your point,' Lukas conceded.

'I came across your ex-fiancée in my reading today,' Venetia said demurely, and Lukas raised an eyebrow with mild curiosity. He had thought little of Lucy since her betrayal of Sophie when she told the newspaper Sophie was nothing without her glasses. She had also betrayed him by sleeping with her ex-boyfriend, Andes, the veterinarian. He could smell the deceit and betrayal on her. The only thought he had given to Lucy since their break-up was to mull over how different they were and wonder how they ever came together.

'Lucy is not a witch, but she has travelled with us for centuries,' Alfred said. 'Some people do, like manifestations of Miss Sharpe.'

'Thank goodness for Miss Sharpe. So, what was Lucy doing in your history, if I may ask?' Orli said.

'Of course,' Venetia said with a smile to Orli, her soft Italian accent always sounding like a gentle purr, which Lukas loved. 'She was doing what she has always done.' She gave a slight shrug and, glancing at Lukas, added, 'It does me no favours to tell you because you will assume I speak from jealousy.'

'Aren't you jealous at the thought of me with someone else?' Lukas teased.

'That is not love,' she assured him. 'I would never give you grounds to feel jealous of my affections.'

'So very true, Venetia,' Alfred agreed wholeheartedly, 'and mature,' he added, teasing his grandson, who rolled his eyes.

Lukas knew Venetia spoke the truth. One of his powerful skills, unique to him, was that he could smell emotion – and he could smell sincerity on Venetia – a rich, alluring scent – as strong as her perfume. However, he would trade this skill to have the ability to read minds like his grandfather, but he knew he could develop that if he worked harder.

'Tell me what she was up to then, I can only imagine,' Lukas said, his voice betraying that he didn't really care.

Orli cleared her throat lightly. 'Lucy has always been an aficionado of those with magical powers.'

'Yes, your cousin is most diplomatic,' Venetia nodded.

'An aficionado?' Lukas frowned. 'Meaning what?'

'I think these days, you young people call them groupies,' Alfred said, and Venetia laughed.

'Thank you, Mr Lens; I did not want to be so direct – a devotee, follower, fan, or maybe even a fanatic. Lucia or rather, Lucy, has always wanted to be around the magical and win their affection in the hope of becoming magical herself. I remember in one generation when I met Elsopeth at a dance, the Earl of Denbury requested a dance from her, and it would have been a great slight to have turned him down.'

Alfred nodded. 'Absolutely, one did not cut an Earl.'

Venetia agreed and continued. 'I have never seen such fury from a young lady as I witnessed from Lucia, in public too, mind you. She was visibly angry; it was most unbecoming. Apparently, Lucia had been working on gaining the Earl's affection for months. If Elsopeth had not been a witch and her mother, Issbelle, such a powerful witch, I might have been concerned for Elsopeth.'

Alfred frowned. 'Yes, and Elsopeth was quite naive then.'

'The Earl ended up marrying a non-witch but an heiress, so he did rather well for himself,' Venetia said.

'And how did Lucy feature in your family story today?' Lukas persisted.

'I was reading only about a century back, and she was in love with the shapeshifter.'

'Nikolas?' Orli asked, surprised. 'I had forgotten about that.'

'Nikolas's ancestor,' Venetia said. 'But I believe you have had that love triangle play out a few times?'

Lukas nodded but would say no more of his fiancée before Lucy, who met Nikolas at their engagement party and wanted to pursue him. 'I haven't read enough to say,' he concluded.

He knew his grandfather was reading the swirl of emotions in his mind as the hurt quickly surfaced.

Alfred stepped in, 'Well, we have had the pleasure of Lucy's company already this generation, so perhaps with the Raven intent on winning Sophie's hand and you two having found each other, Lucy might have fulfilled her role for this lifetime.'

'I would like to meet Sophie,' Venetia said of the woman who continued to steal the Raven's heart from her even if she professed to be happily in love with Lukas.

Lukas shot a quick message to his grandfather. *Thoughts?*

Alfred nodded and said aloud, 'I think that is a fine idea. One can never have too many friends.'

CHAPTER 11

J ORDAN ASHCROFT READ THE displeasure in his Uncle
Allanon's look. He knew his antics at Sophie's house
had been revealed, and he anticipated some fallout from the
family. But Jordan had ice in his veins and loyalty in his heart.
In all the generations that had lived and died since Saghani
cursed Samuel in 1582, there was never a descendant more
like Saghani's son, Harley, than Jordan Ashcroft. It was Harley
who refuted his twin sister, Hadley, and chose to avenge his
mother's death and uphold the curse as the first Raven, while
Hadley chose peace as the dove, and the family line had been
divided ever since.

If the curse was meant to be upheld in Harley's vision,
Jordan – dark and brooding –epitomised the perfect Raven
heir. Tall, powerful and menacing, he wore his black hair short
at the sides and longer – messy – on top; his face always sported
a few days' growth carefully groomed, and his tattoos took
away his prettiness and made him edgy. A small black feather

tattoo on the base of his neck at his collar line led to a full black raven tattooed on his side, his ribcage at the centre as if it were the backbone of the raven. His twin was identical but without the hard edge; Justin was best described as a gentleman – learned, quiet, calm – everything his brother could not profess to be.

And as much as Jordan loved his uncle, Murdoch, he knew he would be better at the Raven role. He knew Sophie would come to fear and respect him. She was only half-witch, as was he, so her power didn't frighten him. He might have liked her in another lifetime when she wasn't the accursed, but she was. It was bad luck for his uncle, but the curse and family honour came first.

'Was it you and Justin?' Allanon asked his nephew as they walked to the back of Allanon's property to sit under the stars.

Jordan grinned. 'We were just giving her a warning.' His eyes narrowed, seeing his uncle's displeasure. 'We didn't hurt the precious witch.'

'Sit. Let's talk before Murdoch and Justin arrive with the drinks,' Allanon said, glancing at the house where Bree and Justin's girlfriend were preparing dinner.

Jordan knew his twin had always hero-worshipped Murdoch and Allanon, but he didn't feel the same; his respect was more hard-earned. Nevertheless, he didn't think to disobey his uncle and followed as invited. He and Justin had been wards of Allanon and Bree since they were young boys since their mother – Allanon and Murdoch's only sister – had died; the boys' father was never on the scene.

Jordan dropped down onto the log opposite his uncle.

'Is Uncle Murdoch okay? Is he still the Raven?' he asked, his voice low.

'To the first part of the question, yes and no. Murdoch is reserved and does not let me in, but physically, he is better. As for the Raven question, you tell me?' Allanon asked. 'I am not the heir; if I am, I have not been informed. Are you not the heir?'

Jordan's eyes widened in surprise, and he leant forward, his elbows on his knees as they sat on logs around an unlit fire pit – the night was not cold enough yet.

'Uncle Murdoch has never declared that. I thought it might be you.'

'It's not something I want to think about or ask Murdoch about; he will tell us in his own good time,' Allanon said. 'I want him to be around for decades yet.'

Jordan understood. There were only the two brothers left. The thought of anything happening to his twin brother was too unbearable to contemplate.

'What you did was out of line and could have consequences,' Allanon said. 'Not just because Sophie is a powerful witch or is on her way to being so, but she is protected by the shapeshifter and the Lens family. It is not for you to act as the Raven.'

Jordan's jaw tightened. He was twenty-one, too old for a lecture, despite the fact he was still living under his uncle's roof.

'I wasn't assuming the role of the Raven,' he said.

'So you knocked on the door, introduced yourself, said you were unhappy about what happened to your uncle and wanted to talk about it?'

Jordan smirked. 'You know I didn't.'

'I heard from my sources that you were a dark presence in her garden. She had to come outside to see what was threatening her, and both Sophie and Mel – her flatmate – were frightened. Is that what we do now? Terrify young woman for a power rush?'

'I doubt she was frightened,' Jordan huffed.

'She clearly reacted to protect herself,' Allanon said and nodded to the bruising on Jordan's face.

'I didn't see her force field coming.'

'What did you expect?'

He shrugged.

'Fate will call soon enough, Jordan, but I suspect you have some maturing to do if you are chosen to take on the mantle of Raven.'

'That's because you assume it has to be peaceful and respectful,' Jordan straightened. He felt his uncle's scrutiny as he rarely challenged him.

'I've often thought about Saghani, our ancestral mother who cursed Sophie's ancestral father. I can't profess to know her, but I've read some of her writings. I think she would be appalled that her curse is still going to this day.'

Jordan considered this. 'But she's the one who established that... she could have just cursed Samuel Rayne, but she cursed his descendants. Saghani knew what she was doing.'

'Maybe, but she was acting out of fear and despair. She was going to be hanged and never see her husband again or watch her children grow up. I can't believe hundreds of years later, she would want to see Sophie bullied and threatened, especially when one of her descendants is in love with her.'

'We'll never know,' Jordan said and shrugged. 'But I'm upholding her memory and legacy as Harley would.'

'If you were upholding her legacy, you'd be a healer. That was what she did selfishly and did best.'

The two men sat silently before Jordan asked, 'Is that why you are a psychologist and why Uncle Murdoch is a cop?'

'I felt a natural calling for it; I can't speak for why your uncle chose his occupation. The fact our careers reflect on Saghani's life work is a bonus; we try to help people. I have clients as well who threaten and strike out at me. If one of them killed me, would you hunt them down and curse their family line forever?'

Jordan scoffed. 'I'd certainly hunt them down. I don't know about their family line... it's not really their fault.'

'Exactly.'

'But Sophie drove Murdoch to despair, here, now, today, in this lifetime,' he said, emphasising every word. 'She has to learn to respect the Raven.'

The conversation stopped as Murdoch and Justin approached with several beers for the group.

'I need to stay out here for a while,' Murdoch said to Allanon. 'Perhaps you best give me a sleeping bag.'

'Why? What has happened?' Allanon frowned, trying to imagine who Murdoch might have been short-tempered with now. He was testy when in pain and frustrated.

'Your dog won't come out from under the bed.'

Allanon chuckled, relieved. 'Poor Merlin.'

The men sat, and Murdoch looked at his aggressive young nephew.

'The thing with being the Raven is, I have sharper powers than you... when you are in my vicinity, I can hear you if I choose to do so,' Murdoch said, and Jordan's jaw dropped before he regathered himself.

'Nowhere near as good as the owl, though,' Justin said, 'they have amazing hearing abilities.' They all turned to look at Justin, and he gave a small shrug.

Murdoch continued, 'I love you boys, as I loved your mother, but understand this, Jordan, keep away from Sophie. She is mine to love and mine to punish.' His eyes flared black, and Allanon raised his hands hurriedly.

'He understands that. I've already spoken with Jordan about his visit; it's under control. Isn't it, Jordan?' Allanon asked.

Jordan gave a nod of his head and said nothing.

'You have raw energy coming off you in waves, Uncle,' Justin said, amazed. He grabbed a stick off the ground and threw it in his uncle's direction. As it neared Murdoch, it crackled, lit up, and fell to the ground extinguished. Justin huffed. 'Amazing!' He was the lighter of the twins in nature and fascinated by the history of the curse.

'She needs to know you are not to be menaced with Uncle,' Jordan said in a low voice. He knew his uncle was laid back by nature, but he did not expect the flare of anger from him.

Murdoch shot to his feet and grabbed his nephew, who was the same height but more solid. But Jordan's strength was nothing compared to his uncle's power when enraged.

'And you need to know not to question me. Do you understand?'

Jordan was gasping for breath, his eyes wide with surprise and fear at the strength of the man before him, and Jordan did not frighten easily. This was a strength he had never seen before.

Allanon pulled the men apart.

'Settle down, everyone, settle down,' Allanon said, adding a few exasperated swear words for good measure.

Jordan rubbed his throat and sat again. Murdoch did not.

'I'm leaving. Thank you, Brother, apologise to Bree for me.'

'You're not leaving. No one's leaving,' Allanon said, 'let's just chill. Please, sit down.'

'I'll pull my head in,' Jordan said to him as way of apology.

Murdoch turned to him and shook his head. 'Your loyalty is appreciated, Jordan, but your ambition overrides you. There's a balance of peace that you should not take lightly. Despite my powers, the role is not all about fear and intimidation.'

'But she's given you attitude and—' he saw his Uncle Allanon's look and shut up.

Murdoch sat again and gulped a mouthful of beer before answering, showing he could control himself despite the aggravation and his inner turmoil.

'Don't you think when I was your age that I wanted to burn up the place as you do? I was power-hungry, tripping on my success at being given the mantle of the Raven. Believing I'd be so great at it.'

'So what changed? You're so mellow you could be high,' Jordan said, and his brother smiled beside him. 'And don't say maturity. You've only got about fifteen years on us.'

Murdoch looked to Allanon, who gave a small nod as if approving of him to tell a shared story.

'I am not going into detail, but I destroyed someone... and their family line that was to follow. I never gave it a second thought until I came across their relatives and their raw grief. Shame overtook my satisfaction.'

'You knew them too, Uncle Allanon?' Justin asked.

Allanon nodded. 'He was a difficult man, but his wife and children... they loved him.'

'He wronged Anon, and that was enough for me.' Murdoch's eyes narrowed as he recalled the killing. 'He begged me to show mercy, as did Anon, but I was like you. Why should I? I'm the Raven; he hurt my brother, and I loved his fear and the power I felt. I can still feel that rush.'

Jordan nodded, keen to feel the same.

Murdoch continued, 'He was a lower-class witch who pushed me too far. But I should have held my power over him, made him fear me because of my mercy, not extinguished him. Do you get what I mean?'

Jordan nodded slowly, processing the Raven's words.

'Is that why you became a cop?' Justin asked, 'Because you wanted to make amends?'

'Partly,' Murdoch said. 'Trust me, I've got no problem getting rid of murderers, rapists, and anyone I deem to be a deviant, and I have, but at the end of the day, our power is over the accursed, and they have rarely been a problem. Daphne was a good old girl who helped many people in her time, and Sophie...' he hesitated and swallowed, containing his emotion and energy, 'Sophie is mine for better or worse.'

No one said anything for a moment, but Jordan was not convinced. He would have her begging for mercy if she was his, even if she loved him. The thought turned him on.

'Don't forget,' Murdoch added, talking more than he ever had about his role, 'the strongest amongst us could destroy us and all we love in a heartbeat.'

'Who?' Justin asked.

'Mr Lens,' Allanon said in a hushed voice.

'And you could reciprocate,' Jordan argued.

'What would be the point of that?' Allanon challenged his nephew.

'A war,' Justin said, thinking aloud. 'Who is your heir, Uncle?'

All eyes turned to Murdoch, who shook his head slightly. 'I will let you all know when he or she is ready to be trained.'

'But if you had died, how would we know?' Justin asked.

'And if it is me, I am ready to train,' Jordan added, pushing for an answer despite the weariness that overtook his recovering uncle.

Allanon lost his patience. 'Enough. Leave us, both of you, before I regret doing what I'm capable of as well. Please go see if Bree needs a hand.'

The twins exchanged looks, rose and began to walk away. Jordan heard Murdoch saying, 'I'm okay, but I need to be at my place, alone. I need to... recalibrate.'

'And you can do that next week, once you've recovered,' Allanon responded.

Their voices faded, and Justin looked at his brother. 'That was amazing,' he said as if he was writing a paper on a subject. 'Seeing all that power Uncle Murdoch was trying to contain was fascinating.'

'Hmm,' Jordan mused. 'I could do a lot with that.'

Justin's girlfriend called him, and Jordan went to make a phone call to his new partner before dinner, as he promised. She was amazing, a gorgeous model who had befriended him at the gym. He had his share of women, but he always got the girls with attitude. Never the pretty dolls; he liked them softer; it made him feel like the man. His new girlfriend was a little older, sexy in a glamorous way, he'd go so far as to say delicate, and she was interested in him when she could have had any guy at the gym; they were all watching her. But she chose Jordan. He'd never had a girlfriend like Lucy.

CHAPTER 12

S OPHIE LOOKED FOR SIGNS constantly. A hum of a light, a buzz in her mind, the sound of a crow... was it Murdoch trying to reach her? She vowed that later that evening, when she lay in bed alone, she would focus on Murdoch and open her mind to receiving him or trying to contact him. The accursed had no power to reach the Raven, but she was more than the accursed; in her own right, she was a powerful witch, allegedly, she thought with a small shrug. For now, it was a relief to have "training" with Nikolas just to rest her mind and distract her from being hyper-vigilant.

Bette Davis arced up, hissed and ran up the staircase to Sophie's bedroom.

Nikolas appeared. 'Sorry, Bette Davis,' he called after her and gave Sophie an apologetic look.

'Poor Bette Davis, between your dog and Murdoch's bird, it's a wonder she doesn't need a therapist.'

Nikolas laughed, and Sophie took a moment to admire him. She rarely saw him out of a suit, but tonight, he wore jeans, runners and a white T-shirt, and he wore it well. His defined arms were shown to best advantage. She quickly raised her eyes.

'Thank you for this,' she said. 'I'm guessing we're not going on your bike then?'

'No, it will be quicker if I just, you know, transport us. Is that okay?'

'Sure. Freaky but fine. Am I okay in this?' she asked, unsure what Nikolas had in mind, but she wore the same as him, only her black T-shirt.

'Perfect. Front or back?'

Sophie looked confused.

'Do you want to hug me front on, or turn and I'll wrap around you... for travelling purposes?'

'Oh, right.' She felt the colour rising in her face and tried to adopt a look that said, "*I am not at all phased about being pressed up against your muscly chest*". A challenge even with her acting skills. 'Whatever is best for getting all of me there. I don't want my right arm left behind.'

Nikolas grinned and shook his head. 'Fold your arms across your chest.' He didn't waste time on preparation but stood behind her, put his arms tightly around her, and they were gone.

Sophie spluttered as they arrived in a cool paddock moments later, and he released her.

'You get used to it.'

She shuddered and looked down, patting herself over and testing her bones. 'I'm all here?'

He rolled his eyes. 'You need to forget that film, *The Fly*. The worst that can happen is that we'll get mixed up.'

Her horrified expression had him laughing. 'I'm joking; that won't happen.'

She shivered. 'It's cool out here.'

'I love the chill,' Nikolas said, looking around, his house in the distance, the woods at his back. The sky was awash with stars, and the night air was crisp.

'So quiet,' she whispered and then realised they were standing in a wide circle of sorts, with a huge circumference nearly as big as a school sports oval.

'Orli set it up for us earlier,' Nikolas explained. 'It's a protection circle, so you can't wipe out the forest or my house.'

Sophie huffed. 'That would be a fair achievement. Sweet Orli, that was good of her. Do you see a lot of each other?' she fished.

'We've always been good friends. She likes to convert and fly sometimes, and it is safer out here... fewer hazards and air-born predators.'

Sophie studied him with curiosity. 'Birds don't usually like flying at night, do they?'

'Doves don't, but I'm not an expert on all bird species,' he said in jest. 'She comes after work at dusk or on the weekend.' He adopted the voice of a nature documentary host, making her laugh by saying, 'While the common dove does not normally fly at night, it will sometimes go too far and thus need somewhere to roost for the night. Thus, the humble abode of a shapeshifter.' He pointed to his house in the distance and dropped out of character, laughing along with Sophie.

'Good to know,' she said, finally sobering. 'I hate to think how you explain our friendship if that is the best you can do for you and Orli.'

Again, he adopted his biologist's voice and said in hushed tones, 'Look... a rare sighting of the witch clairvoyant without her glasses, thus making her as blind as a bat to all predictions, but her pesky shapeshift is nearby to protect her.'

She laughed and shook her head. 'You're a dill. Come on then, or you'll be stuck with me all night.'

'Right you are. The force field Orli has set up will let you throw things at it without them bouncing back or penetrating. What do you know of your powers?'

'Nothing! I'm reading every spare moment... words coming at me all the time, but I've found nothing that says, "You can do this and that". I'm going to write a manual for my descendant!'

'Oh? Planning to have kids any time soon?' he enquired with interest.

Sophie smirked at him. 'You'll be the first to know.'

'I hope so,' he said encouragingly, making Sophie redden slightly again.

She continued, 'Aunt Daphne didn't leave any notes because she was from the accursed line and not a half-witch like me. Issbelle left a diary, and I've been working through it, but it is more about her encounters, not her skills. She will occasionally say she did something by using her powers, but there are no tips or notes on how to call up those skills... it's so frustrating.'

'But Issbelle must have had a spell book or something like that.'

'If she did, I haven't discovered it yet... Duke.'

'Ah.' Nikolas grinned and toed the ground with his runner. 'You have discovered my history amongst yours then. I did wonder.'

'Don't tell me the ending; I haven't read much further than you and Elsopeth meeting.'

He looked up again. 'It would be interesting to read her take on our first meeting. It was rather abrupt.'

'That's her take, too,' Sophie agreed.

'Right,' he returned his attention to the job at hand but not before Sophie stopped him in his tracks again by revealing, 'I do know Elsopeth loved the duke and the Raven.'

Nikolas cleared his throat. 'And the duke was crazy for her, I believe.' Neither of them said anything for a moment as they spoke about their past in a removed fashion.

'At least she could pat you, unlike the Raven,' Sophie said and laughed. 'Did she run her hand through your mane?'

'I don't transform into a lion,' he joked, 'but I believe she used to love to run her hand through my predecessor's fur.'

'Oh, right, of course. I forgot we were talking about them, not us. So, are you more of a wolf or dog?'

He grimaced. 'A big furry loveable mutt... okay, I'm more wolf than dog.'

She grimaced.

'I'm not scary.'

'Did you ever attack her; did your predecessor, I mean?'

'Of course not,' Nikolas said and frowned at her. 'When we're animals, we are still half-human and conscious of right and wrong and who everyone is in our lives. My ancestor wasn't her protector back then, but he loved her.' She sensed Nikolas was uncomfortable with the subject as he looked around at their work area before looking back at her. 'Let's begin... tell me what you did the other night to scare away the unwelcomed force?'

'Nothing textbook. I could feel a threatening presence nearby, Mel alerted me to it, and it felt sinister. So, I held up my hands, said "Begone" or something like that, and made a pushing motion as if I were getting rid of them. I was pretty freaked out, so I said it with a fair bit of force. I don't know why I did that; nothing might have happened, and I could have looked like the biggest idiot, but...'

'It was instinctive?' Nikolas asked.

'Exactly. And it worked.'

Nikolas nodded. 'Perhaps that is how your magic works – it comes instinctively when needed.'

Sophie frowned. 'Maybe, but I'd like to have more control than that.'

'No doubt.'

'Will you transform for me? To your wolf.'

He stopped, surprised at the change in conversation. 'I don't know, maybe one day. Focussing on what you did the other night, try doing it again now. If we can harness it in here, we'll know what you are capable of doing and its forcefield.' He came to stand beside her, and she did the same motion but felt nothing. She shook her hands and did it again, yelling out forcefully, 'Begone'.

'As I suspected,' he said.

'What did you suspect? If it's instinctive, it should still come when I focus on it, shouldn't it?'

'I'd say your power comes when needed, not on demand, probably because you are only a half-witch. Elsopeth was the same.'

'Was she? You say it was your ancestor, but you have all his memories.'

'It's hard to explain,' he said, hands on hip and thinking for a moment. 'It was me, but this is a new me with all the influences of a modern time. It's like thinking back on a movie you watched and remembering some of the scenes.'

'Right.' Sophie nodded, thinking about his words.

'Elsopeth believed that her power source came when needed as a form of preservation, so she did not get overwhelmed and fade as you did at the crime scene a while back.'

'Then I don't know how I can be one of the strongest witches of my time, thanks, Aunty Daffy, if my power is not on tap.'

Nikolas chuckled. 'Daffy, huh?'

'Mum always said Aunty Daphne was a bit that way.'

'Well, maybe you are stronger than you think, and when your power comes, it is deadly in its force.' He studied her. 'I could convert, and you could try and ward me off if you want to see what control you have.'

Sophie's eyes widened in shock. 'No way. I can't control it. I might kill you; you might kill me.'

'I won't kill you; I know exactly my limits, but it would be good for you to know yours.'

'No. That's crazy. Imagine if I really did kill you?'

'Elsopeth did,' Nikolas said under his breath, and Sophie just heard his words as he turned away. Tempted to press him, she didn't get the chance before he added, 'Maybe you are not strong enough to harm me.'

Sophie grinned. 'Yeah, challenging me is not going to work. I'd have to live with the guilt of wiping you out, and I've got enough of a guilt load at the moment, thanks.'

'Okay, how about we try something else...'

'You know how it ended for Elsopeth, don't you? Tell me, Nik.'

The night was so still that Sophie could hear his sharp intake of breath at the abruptness of her question, as if it still pained him to speak of it.

He shook his head. 'I know how all of our ancestors lived and died, but you have to know them from the beginning. Know their life. That's what my Uncle Charles used to insist on,' Nikolas said. 'To only know their demise doesn't make them a whole person; it dismisses their life.'

'Wise words from Uncle Charles,' Sophie conceded, and she dropped the subject, given his reluctance to elaborate. 'I have an idea. Why don't you transform for me, and maybe the sight of a fearsome wolf might release my flight or fight powers? Just don't come at me, and I won't put you in danger,' she warned. 'I'd love to know that part of you.'

'My party trick? Why? What will you do in return?' Nikolas teased.

Sophie laughed and before she could answer, they saw headlights coming up the long road to Nikolas's place, so bright in an area with no streetlights or houses spilling their lights onto the streets. The closest neighbours were over the hill.

'Visitors?'

Nikolas waited until he could see the body of the car. 'It's Lukas. I wasn't expecting him.'

'And he's come the traditional way, not flown,' Sophie joked. 'Oh, that's right, doves don't like flying at night. Shall we head to the house?'

Nikolas bristled, sensing another presence. 'Venetia's with him. They don't know you're here. Perhaps I'd better take you back.'

'Oh, Venetia, as in the Raven's ex, his great love for centuries?' She watched the car advance with interest.

'That's her.'

'Before Elsopeth. Wow. I'd like to meet her,' Sophie said, her eyes narrowed as she thought. 'There's no need for us to be enemies in this generation now that she's with Lukas, is there?

There was probably never any need to be enemies, but from what I've read, she was rather territorial.'

'That's putting it mildly.'

'Besides, if I need protecting, you can transform and chase her to the car.'

Nicholas scoffed. 'Then it'll be a showdown between me and Lukas while he protects her. Do you never tire of men fighting over you?'

Sophie started like she had been slapped.

'I'm sorry. That was... I didn't mean to say that; it was just off the cuff.' Nikolas rubbed his jaw as if that would help take the words back.

'All those old movies playing in your head?' she asked. 'I think I should go. Can you take me home?'

'Sophie...' he looked remorseful.

'It's all good, we're all good.' She regarded him thoughtfully before adding, 'I've got so much reading to do and a solution to find.'

'Of course. How to live with and love the Raven,' he said testily. 'I wouldn't wish to keep you from that. Let's go.'

Now, it was Sophie's turn to give him an exasperated look.

'Is this how we were back then?' she asked.

'No.' He moved closer, she presumed to prepare for the journey home, but instead, he leant down so that his mouth was near her ear and whispered, 'This was how we were.'

His body was against her, his mouth near her cheek, his strong arms enveloping her, and in moments, they were in her living room.

'Thanks,' she said, catching her breath as he pulled away.

'Sure.' With that, he was gone, and Sophie exhaled – a long, slow breath of frustration.

So much for the men who want to be with me, yet here I am, alone.

CHAPTER 13

PERSONAL DIARY OF **Miss Elsopeth Rayne**

November 3, 1744

Torn

Sinfully handsome. There was no other way
to describe him. He entered the room and it
was as if he were the sun and all the women
were sunflowers; all eyes turned towards him.
His dark hair was tied back at his collar, and
the manly planes of his face and jaw had every
lady's heart aflutter.

Nikolas was now a duke; his uncle had passed, leaving his heir in possession of a great fortune and much power. He was also a single man of marriageable age, and his eyes searched the room until he found mine.

Our thoughtless, dangerous attraction has caused us both pain, and I should never have encouraged his suit. I was younger and silly when it started, flattered without thinking about the consequences. Yet, I had been waiting for him to arrive. Dreaming of the Raven, waiting for Nikolas, this anguish must end. I must end it, and I have made plans to do so.

I glanced around nervously because I was expecting Murdoch's arrival. Now too, Venetia entered the ballroom. Could there be any more tension in this room tonight? It would be impossible. I am so wearied by the affections of both men, by being pushed and pulled when I don't know where my heart belongs. My maid says I have lost weight, my dresses have all been adjusted, I don't sleep well, and I constantly test myself to imagine how I would feel without Nikolas or Murdoch in the hope my true feelings will reveal the man I most wish to be with for the rest of my days.

Both have requested an answer, and both deserve one. I asked for their patience and advised them they would know my answer the day after the ball.

I felt all eyes upon me now as if people were waiting to see how the drama before them might unfold. Why did I come this evening? I could have feigned an illness if it were not an obligation to a close family friend hosting the evening. No one would expect a lady to attend a ball if she were not feeling her best.

Nicholas made his way towards me, the guests parting, and when he arrived in front of me, he took my hand, leant over it, and placed a kiss appropriately before subtly turning my hand and kissing my palm.

'Miss me?' he teased.

'Not at all,' I answered with a small smile, and he did what he does so well; Nikolas romanced me.

'If I could plant a flower for every time I missed you, I would walk through my garden and never come to the end of it.'

I am sure I blushed like a debutante, but it was hard not to look into his dark eyes, believe his passion for me was real, and not be affected when my heart was aflutter.

A small ripple of noise from the guests made us both look in the direction they were all looking, the Raven had entered. The duke rose to full height and stiffened beside me. His eyes narrowed, as did Murdoch's the moment they saw each other. So, I did the only thing I could think of to get out of this situation – in reality, it was taken out of my hands – I faded.

I could still see everyone in the ballroom, but when all eyes turned back to me for my reaction, I was not there. Nikolas looked around and whispered my name, knowing what had happened – I had confided in him, and he had been witness to it once before. The Raven did not know of my penchant for fading when overwhelmed. A few people nearby looked confused; how could I have just disappeared? They were no doubt surprised to have found themselves so distracted that they did not notice me slipping out, and over the coming days there were bound to be whispers and rumours that the spirit girl had vanished, it was inevitable.

And with that, in my ghost-like state, I departed. The music continued, the dancing resumed, and I did not look back to see what became of the two men or Venetia. They were both too much. Two nights earlier, I received an enormous bouquet of red roses, so large I am sure the Duke of Montmount – Nikolas – deprived every other lady in the city of red roses. Attached was a note reading:

'There are limits to any man's powers of endurance. I cannot bear this. Please, release me or love me. You are trying me too far.'

And, only the evening prior, the Raven visited me for a stroll in my garden, and I could sense he was incensed; he had heard about or seen the flowers sent by Nikolas and he was not a man willing to play second best. We argued, and he demanded I make a choice or he would make it for me. I had never seen him so angry nor knew what that meant.

The Raven stormed off, and I received flowers and his visit the next day. I was not home to receive him, and when I arrived at my residence later, a letter arrived expressing his utmost and sincere apology for his behaviour. He promised it was out of character and would not be repeated and begged for my forgiveness and good favour. I responded immediately, saying:

My dear Sir,

The expression of your pain and acknowledgement of your misjudgement last evening as contained in the letter I have just received, does provide relief to my distressed heart and assures me of your honour.

I accept your feelings for me have not changed and your letter serves to convince me that my indecision caused you to sway from the sound judgement which is the usual guide of all your actions. My feelings for you are not changed; I hold you in high esteem, but in truth, I confess to some apprehension at your show of anger. I take responsibility for rousing this within your breast.

Let us not talk of this again and banish last night's visit as if it never happened. I will do as you requested and make my feelings clear to you and the Duke of Montmount with as much haste as I can administer. Forgive me for my role in your distress, dear Murdoch.

Yours, still sincerely,

Elsopeth.

I sealed the letter and returned it with one of his yellow roses. The despair and guilt that has overwhelmed me since receiving both of their demands has led me to undertake a course of action – I have made arrangements to go to my family's country estate first thing in the morning as the sun rises. There, away from the city, away from them both, and in nature, my emotions will be balanced, and I will be able to glean whom my heart pines for, and then, I shall write to ask if they will still have me. I will write to the other, offer my heartfelt thanks for loving me, and release them of any obligation. It is arranged.

With my plan and actions, I was ending this tomorrow for good.

'I totally get it, Elsopeth,' Sophie said, sitting on the couch with a cup of tea and stroking Bette Davis with her free hand. The room was lit with two lamps she had selected to fit the grand décor of Aunt Daphne's home, and the television was on in the background, the voices down low to provide just enough background noise not to feel alone. An old black and white movie played that she had found on the movie channel – on screen, Gregory Peck and Audrey Hepburn raced around Rome on a scooter, both so beautiful.

Sophie felt safer tonight; maybe it was because she discovered she could ward off danger capably on her own if needed. In a few hours, she would go to bed for the night and try to open her mind to Murdoch. Poor Elsopeth, torn and browbeaten – Nikolas, Murdoch and Venetia – not much has changed, but the roles are all a little different. Elsopeth was never the accursed and Venetia was now in love with Lukas.

So, who did Elsopeth choose, she mused, guessing from what Nikolas had implied that he had come out the loser. Sophie turned the page of Elsopeth's diary. She froze.

'Oh no, Elsopeth, what has happened?'

There were no other entries from the Elsopeth of the late 18th century, just the journal's blank pages. An old newspaper notice attached to the page and inserted by Alfred Lens read:

TRAGIC END.

Death of Miss Elsopeth Rayne

VERDICT OF SUICIDE.

"Everything is entirely my fault. God forgive me." Thus read a note left by the young beauty, Miss Elsopeth Rayne, whose body was found in her bed by her maid on Tuesday morning.

Today's evidence at the inquest showed that she had been worried about responding to the affections of two gentlemen who demanded she selects a suitor. The coroner, in returning a verdict of suicide while of unsound mind, said

Lady Elsopeth Rayne was anxious, resulting in insomnia which led to mental instability and the self-administrating of poison.

Sophie groaned and hurriedly reached for another news clipping below it. The newspaper was yellow with age, and she sat upright to read it.

SUICIDE BELIEVED TO BE MURDER

Police investigating

The suicide of Miss Elsopeth Rayne has come under review, with detectives believing the young lady may have been murdered. Several house staff claim to have heard a noise on the stairwell before and after the estimated time of Miss Rayne's death, and a person was seen loitering near Miss Rayne's townhouse in the early hours of the morning.

A most telling clue has also come to light – the finding of a torn-away section of the young lady's diary that aligns perfectly with the 'suicide note'. Detectives believe the note may have been the writings of a young woman in despair of love and not her suicide letter.

The investigation continues.

At that moment, everything changed for Sophie. Did one of the men who professed to love Elsopeth murder her in a fit of passion or jealousy? Crimes throughout the century have been committed as a result of love gone awry, as had wars been fought. Was Sophie in danger of history repeating? Is that what Nikolas meant when he said Elsopeth killed him? Was he hanged for her murder?

Suddenly, she no longer wanted to hear from the Raven or Nikolas until she got to the bottom of Elsopeth's murder. She would not allow her mind to wander tonight, to call Murdoch or think on him. She would not see Nikolas unless in the daytime, preferably in the office with Jack and Miss Sharpe nearby. Sophie needed to discover more, but no further insights would be found in Elsopeth's diary – the volume of her 18th-century life had ended. But Alfred would know.

Murdoch walked around the back of Allanon's property amongst the imposing trees, inhaling the crisp night air and feeling frustrated by everything in his life. He was comfortable in the dark and quiet, in the solitude. Everyone had gone to bed, but there was no sleep for him. He needed to return to work, he needed to get his life back on track, and he needed to let Sophie go.

He knew it, everyone knew it, and the reality was if he didn't, history might repeat itself. Although, he didn't truly believe that. Venetia had transferred her love – she had little to gain from threatening Sophie; the shapeshifter was still in love with Sophie, but he was her protector and unlikely to harm her, and even though she faded, she was not as delicate as her predecessor. Not as prone to emotional stress and not as easy to murder. He flinched at his thoughts and the agony endured at the time, the ripples still as real today as they were then. But it was the truth; Sophie was sassier than Elsopeth and had attitude and plenty of front to stand up for herself.

His Elsopeth was an innocent, a woman of her time, brought up by her witch mother and a protective non-witch father. He missed her; every generation he missed her, crazy but true. But he missed most of all the era when they first fell in love – it had its good and bad; he was a respected, wealthy and even feared Lord, his tenants were well looked after, and his family was close by, but his heart was hers from the moment he sighted Elsopeth. Some days, he wished they had never had that encounter when she fell into his arms, literally. How different his history would be.

He sat on one of the logs and lit the fire pit with a flick of his hand. It was enough to keep him warm and make it feel homely. Why was it that each generation of Elsopeth was fated to meet an early death? Just to torment him? She had died of illness as a young girl, then was brought back as a spirit by Issbelle. She had died young many times after, always before her time, and he was left to carry on.

That couldn't happen again; he had to protect his own heart and hers. He had to leave Sophie alone as best he could. He had stayed away from her until she accepted the role Daphne had bequeathed her; he could do it again. Murdoch knew he had to love another. Sophie was stronger, but she was cursed. And he was her greatest threat.

CHAPTER 14

THE SUNNY MORNING CHEERED her up as Sophie pulled into the hotel carpark where Hope Yardley was last seen and where Sophie was to meet Detectives Gerard Oakley and Rachel Fletcher. She was happy to have a busy day ahead and relieved and disappointed that Murdoch had not contacted her last night. Sophie wasn't sure if she successfully blocked him or if he didn't try. Either way, she felt odd about it... flat. But for now, she had to stop thinking about herself and try and help Hope and her family. Day three and no sign of the young woman... it did not bode well for Hope's future.

Sophie parked and approached, finding the young detective outside waiting for her.

'Hey, thanks for coming,' Rachel Fletcher said, giving her a welcoming smile. 'The premises are closed, but we've got the staff that worked that night inside, ready to be interviewed.'

'Great. No update on Hope then?'

'No,' Rachel sighed, 'dead end after dead end. Like she vanished into thin air.' She pushed open the door for Sophie. They both entered and Rachel locked it from the inside. Sophie allowed her eyes to adjust to the dimmer interior and gave a professional nod and smile to Gerard and the eight witnesses, who all looked like they were about to undergo the Spanish Inquisition. Sophie restrained a laugh and moved to a booth as directed. She sat and got her glasses out, pushing them up on her forehead until needed.

'They look like they're on death row,' Sophie said in a hushed voice to Gerard, who chuckled.

He looked at them and yelled, 'Buck up, everyone. It's a few questions about what you might have seen that night to help us find Hope. Then you can go. You're not facing a firing squad.'

There were laughs and eye-rolling, and Sophie shook her head at him. Rachel came and sat beside Sophie, ready to take notes.

'Ready?' Gerard asked.

'I am; I hope I can help,' Sophie said sobering. She glanced at Rachel and then began to work her way through the stream of people who came to sit opposite her. Gerard asked the questions, and Sophie gave a small shake of her head when there was nothing to be gained from the witness. Gerard thanked them and dismissed the staff when their interview was done.

Sophie watched as the images appeared above the witnesses – their futures laid out with the usual life milestones of love, marriage, career and family. She focussed on the immediate past – one side of the images that appeared to her, but occasionally, she drifted to the future. At one stage, Sophie stopped a young guy when he rose to leave. He seemed nervous, and she saw that he needed the job to support his partner and young baby. He looked all of twenty years old if that.

'Can I tell you some good news before you go, if you can keep it a secret?'

'Sure,' he said, looking from the detectives to Sophie.

'You're going to own this bar one day.'

He laughed, his eyes wide with surprise. 'Yeah?'

'Yeah. And it will be a huge success.'

'Thanks, thanks a lot,' he said and laughed again. He gave them a nod and left with a huge grin.

'Aren't you nice?' Gerard said.

'That I am,' Sophie agreed, joking with him. 'But there's nothing amongst them that can help your investigation. In the visions, I saw Hope a few times, being served at the bar or amongst her girlfriends, but what they saw does not include what happened to her.' Sophie sighed, pulling off the glasses and rubbing her nose. She wasn't used to wearing glasses and didn't need them except to tell people's future. One day, when she would need to wear them daily, she would be accosted by constant images of people's past and future – that was her curse to bear.

'It all helps,' Rachel said. 'It helps us move on and eliminate them.'

'One more,' Gerard said, 'the senior barman who was on that night and closed up.'

Sophie nodded and waited until he joined them and was introduced. She lowered her glasses and watched the images appear as he responded to the questions. He was telling the truth, and then her hand shot across the table to grab his arm.

'It's the truth,' he said as if she caught him out in a lie.

'I know, that's fine,' Sophie assured him. She could feel Gerard and Rachel's hope and anticipation as she studied the images.

'There's a girl with Hope who was not one of the friends at her party. You served them both a drink. Do you remember her?' Sophie asked.

He gave a small shrug. 'I couldn't tell you who was in her group, but they usually came to the bar in pairs.'

'This girl brought her a drink, I think. She's blonde, glamorous; they walked away together.'

He shook his head. 'I don't know who it is; honestly, that described about a dozen girls I served that night. I pour the drinks and take their money. Sorry.'

'Thanks,' Sophie said and gave the nod to Gerard that she was done. She could see the barman was in a gay relationship, which went some way to explaining why he wasn't interested in the gorgeous women he served.

He let the barman go, and the three sat momentarily to discuss the interviews.

'Well, thank you, young lady,' Gerard said. 'We appreciate your time. Do you think this woman with Hope is a clue?'

'No. Maybe, but it is something and not one of the girlfriends she arrived with for the celebration. Could she have left with some other party not her own?'

'Everything's a possibility at the moment,' Rachel assured Sophie.

'I think I should see the football player,' Sophie said.

'Are you a fan?' Gerard teased her.

'I could be,' she said with a grin. 'But he might have seen something? She might have said something to him.'

'We can set it up, but he's on our cold list,' Rachel said.

'And you know what,' Gerard added, 'he's actually a nice kid. He's well mannered, not a smart arse like many of these A-listers are, and he called her the next day... not many follow up when they use that line on a girl.'

Rachel nodded. 'He seemed to genuinely like her. It was telling that he was more worried about Hope than word getting out that he had slept around.'

'Hmm, all might not be well on the home front,' Sophie mused. 'Okay, forget that then, I don't need to talk with him.'

'What if you saw Hope's room?' Rachel asked.

Sophie shook her head. 'It doesn't work that way for me. I need to see people and ask questions. I don't get the vibe from unanimated objects. But I could meet her family... I don't think it would help as they weren't the last to see her, but if you're desperate.'

'God knows we're desperate,' Gerard said, and Rachel agreed to set up the meeting.

As it was only nearing eleven a.m. and her readings didn't start until the afternoon, Sophie took the opportunity to drop by the *Optical Illusion* store. She had questions about Elsopeth's death that only Alfred Lens could answer, and there was no guarantee that she might find an answer if she scurried through all the books on the premises. Sophie wasn't having her best week. For the first time since taking over Aunt Daphne's gig, she couldn't help with the case of the missing girl; additionally,

Murdoch had not contacted her since he was conscious. What was he up to?

Don't think about it.

She checked her phone, no messages. And was Nikolas still angry with her for last night's episode? She sighed. *Whatever, the day can only get better.*

Lukas greeted her warmly, which Sophie needed, as the bell on the door above her announced her arrival.

'You left before I could introduce you to Venetia, again,' he grinned.

'Sorry, I was cheesed off with Nikolas. I think the feeling was mutual,' Sophie joked.

'Ah, Nik, he's always so intense.'

Sophie's expression and laugh relayed her surprise. 'Unlike you.' She studied the handsome man working behind the counter with his light brown hair fashionably mussed, pale blue eyes, dressed in his suit with no tie. 'I remember you breaking all the glass in the front rooms at home and most of the crystal on these shelves.'

'Oh yeah, that,' he said nonchalantly before giving her a grin.

'Yeah, that,' she teased. 'Lucky you have Orli to fix your breaks, or you might need a second job for my glass bill. Am I interrupting?' she wandered closer to see what he was working on.

'No, I'm just servicing a modern watch. Boring. But I like to get the boring stuff out of the way in the morning, and then in the afternoon, I can indulge myself and work on the classic timepieces. So have you heard from... you know who?'

'Not since he tapped my mind the other night. I don't know what's going on, and I've decided not to think about it.'

'How's that going?'

'Pathetically,' Sophie admitted and changed the subject from the Raven. 'Would Venetia be happy to meet me?'

'She suggested it. You could be the best of friends in this generation,' Lukas said and gave a small laugh as if the notion was utterly ridiculous.

'Yeah, that would be weird – her ex is still interested in me, my former protector dating her, and Venetia and me B-F-F's.'

Lukas looked confused, and Sophie filled out the initials.

'Best friends forever.'

He chuckled, and their conversation was interrupted when Alfred and Orli entered the store.

'Uncle said you were here,' Orli hugged Sophie. Sophie always hugged her with a degree of delicacy... Orli, with her shimmering silver hair and the palest of blue eyes, looked fragile, but everyone who knew her powers knew that was far from the truth.

'I've come to speak to the guru and get some answers,' she said with an affectionate look at Alfred.

'Uh oh, I hope I know them,' he said in jest.

'I'll put the kettle on,' Orli said, disappearing out the back to find comfort in a teacup.

Lukas resumed his work, ready to listen in to the conversation, but not before he sent a thought to his grandfather, 'She has not heard from Murdoch.'

His grandfather replied effortlessly without speaking, his voice loud and clear in Lukas's mind. 'No, I believe Murdoch has made a decision. I'll tell you later.'

Sophie took the offered chair in front of Alfred's counter. 'I have finished reading Elsopeth's diary from the late 1740s and Margaret Dillon's diary from the 1940s as well.'

'Goodness, you must have been awake all night reading,' Alfred said.

'It's my fault,' she reinstated as she did every time, angry at herself for not studying under her great aunt.

'You are too hard on yourself, Sophie dear,' Alfred assured her. 'Knowing our past can be useful, but you are forging a new path in a new generation. Not everything is relevant; in fact, a great deal isn't.'

She smiled and relaxed a little. 'Thank you for saying that, Alfred, and yes, I know you are right. But I feel forewarned is forearmed, or is it the other way around?'

'Four arms are definitely better than one,' Lukas piped in, making them laugh.

'You're a big help,' Sophie teased. She sobered and said to Alfred, 'I was shocked.'

'Of course,' he replied.

'What are we talking about?' Lukas frowned and thanked Orli as she brought out the tea and biscuits.

'I overheard,' Orli said in a hushed voice. 'You discovered Elsopeth was murdered?'

'So, it was murder,' Sophie said. 'The diary finished with the news clipping that said the investigation would continue.'

'It was murder,' Alfred confirmed.

'Wow, I didn't know this,' Lukas said. 'Why hasn't someone told me this story before?'

'You can read the stories anytime you like, lad,' Alfred said as he had said many times before to Lukas.

'Besides, it's delicate,' Orli said with a glance to Alfred that held great weight.

'I saw that look,' Sophie said, 'now I'm not sure I want to know, but I have to know, you know what I mean?'

'I want to know,' Lukas said, putting his work down to give his grandfather his full attention.

'It was a dangerous time for all of us with the killing of a powerful witch's daughter, a Raven and shapeshifter in love with her, and a beautiful young lady gone too soon.'

'Will you tell me the outcome, Alfred, or is there an entry I can read?'

'Tell us, please, Grandpa. I'd like to hear it too,' Lukas said. 'Hopefully, the customers will stay away for a while.'

'I'm bad for business,' Sophie smirked, and Orli laughed.

The,n a thought occurred to Sophie. 'Were you there, Alfred? In some form?'

He nodded. 'I was indeed, Sophie. Not in my current form; I'm not that old,' he said, and she laughed.

'You definitely are not,' she agreed.

'But my ancestor was, or rather me then... I was only recently partnered with the accursed as a protector, and the young lady wanted to go to the trial... she had met Elsopeth at a dance and held her in high regard. Given the power of the Raven, her enemy, I felt it was my duty to accompany her each day of the trial. Mind you, he focused on his own grief and did not even notice or bother us.'

'A tense time,' Orli said with a shudder. 'Don't skimp on detail, please, Uncle. It sounds like it was a fascinating time in history.'

Alfred had the attention of the room now and agreed to tell the story, remembering it as it played out at the time.

'It rained for a month until the villain was sentenced to hang... I suspect that was the power of the two grieving Lords in mourning,' he started. 'It is important to note that in that era, there was no police force. That did not come into effect until the late 1820s, so every village or parish as they were known then, had elected officials to act as sergeants and watchmen. Elsopeth's beaus would not accept she took her own life and being powerful men, they influenced the magistrate to initiate prosecution on behalf of the crown and to have the matter seen to in a court with a judge.'

'At first, the suspicion fell on the rival suitors – it was well known that Elsopeth had won the heart of both Lords – Murdoch and Nikolas. And, despite their power and place, both men had to prove their innocence; it was not presumed in those days. Elsopeth had been the envy of every young woman, not just for her beauty but for the men who wanted her hand in marriage. She was also a figure of much intrigue – the spirit woman believed to be half-woman, half-spirit. Rumours of the Lords having powers that were not human were just rumours, and their curses and abilities to transform were only known in the immediate family. Tales of witchcraft and shapeshifters were not uncommon in that era, but not encouraged.'

'And people were punished for anything that appeared unconventional,' Lukas added.

'They were indeed. But the trial was fascinating, and as I worked as a microscope maker then—'

'You worked with glass then too?' Sophie exclaimed in surprise.

'Oh yes, microscopy fascinated me. Optics are a common thread in my ancestral history, as acting is in yours, Sophie, and clockwork in your history, Lukas, if you both look back far enough.'

'Really?' she said, somewhat delighted. 'Sorry, please go on.'

'Well, because of my work, I could attend the trial and continue my craft at night. The court was told that Elsopeth died well before dawn. The poison she drank was in her hot chocolate prepared by the maid who did so every evening. The poison was believed to have been added after the hot chocolate was made. The maid was inconsolable; she truly loved Elsopeth and had no reason to harm the young lady.

'Interestingly, the maid did not take it to Elsopeth's room that evening as the young lady was home earlier than planned. After being assisted out of her ballgown, Elsopeth insisted she would have the hot beverage in the library while she read her book. The maid said she seemed upset, but the library was always Elsopeth's safe place, and she was more relaxed when the maid brought in the hot chocolate and departed, wishing her a good night.

'Naturally, it raised the question, did one of the Lords come to her home? But if so, poison was not usually a choice of murder weapon for a passionate male lover. Both gentlemen could prove their innocence as either their valets or their drivers were with them during the evening and neither had gone to the young lady's house, believing it too late to call and impolite to do so. The usual practice was to send flowers and enquire about her health the next day.

'But several neighbours returning home from their night at the theatre, along with carriage drivers who serviced the strip that Elsopeth lived on, stepped forward to speak of two ladies they had seen visiting Elsopeth that evening. It soon came to light that two ladies had been slighted by the men they loved since Elsopeth made her debut. One was Venetia, who loved Lord Murdoch Ashcroft with a passion that knew no bounds.'

'Sophie gasped. 'No!''

Lukas looked equally as shocked.

Alfred held up his hand. 'We must remember this was several centuries ago, and the people we are today are not the people we were then... we are descendants with no guilt to bear.'

Sophie nodded and exchanged looks with Lukas, who also accepted his grandfather's words.

Alfred continued. 'The other young lady was Miss Sarah Hatt.'

Lukas gasped. 'Sarah? Really?'

'Who is Miss Hatt?' Sophie asked, looking from Alfred to Lukas and then to Orli.

'She was my fiancée until she met Nikolas and fell in love with him. In this generation,' he hurriedly added.

'Ah,' Sophie gave him a sympathetic look. 'I did know of this story; I'm sorry.'

'Thanks. At least I found out before we married.'

Alfred nodded. 'In the 18th century, Miss Sarah Hatt loved Nikolas then too and was determined to be his lady. She was a young lady of good breeding and had a sizeable dowry. But he only had eyes for Elsopeth.'

'Elsopeth's enemies are lining up,' Sophie said with a sigh.

'That is true, Sophie. The two young ladies visited her, professing to be concerned about her sudden departure from the ball. They believed if she were off the scene, they would be the likely choices for the men they loved. They caught her unaware as she had dismissed her staff for the evening. If she had not, they most likely would have been turned away and advised the mistress was not well and not receiving guests. But they did gain entry, and while there, one of them slipped poison into Elsopeth's hot chocolate.'

'Did they admit to poisoning her?' Sophie asked, shocked at the thought of them doing so.

Alfred shook his head. 'No, and they turned on each other. Both claimed to be unaware of the poisoning but believed it to be the other's doing.'

Sophie scoffed.

'Were they both charged with murder?' Lukas asked, horrified at the thought of his current-day love hanging by her neck until she was dead.

'No. Venetia escaped and was never seen again,' Alfred said. 'Miss Sarah Hatt hanged; it was a most distressing affair. The court was often lenient to women, but with powerful Lords demanding justice, well, the rest is history.'

'Wow,' Sophie said, exhaling. 'I didn't see that coming. What a gruesome way to go.' Her hand went to her throat. 'But poor Elsopeth.'

'Poisoning with arsenic was a terrible way to die,' Alfred said. 'There was very little sympathy in the court, I assure you.'

'Did you go to the hanging?' Lukas asked.

'I cannot abide by hanging, especially the fairer sex, as we called the ladies then,' Alfred said, remembering the event as if it were yesterday. 'And no, I did not attend, but it was a public spectacle.'

'A gruesome tale,' Orli agreed and finished her tea before refilling her own and those around her.

'Thank you, Alfred. Well, I can breathe easy around Murdoch and Nikolas again then. But maybe I shouldn't meet Venetia.' Sophie addressed her comment to Lukas.

'Maybe you are right,' he agreed.

'Perhaps you have reasons to be allies in this generation,' Orli said. 'What did you think of Aircraftwoman Margaret Dillon's diary, Sophie? Her unrequited love with the Raven was very dramatic.'

'I was shocked that he was killed by kin,' Sophie said.

Alfred nodded. 'A nephew he barely knew, I believe, but clearly, for some, the curse and its responsibilities run deep.'

Orli agreed. 'They truly believe in maintaining Harley's revenge on the accursed family and want to maintain the rage.'

'But why didn't he save himself in the car when it burst into flames?' Sophie asked.

'Ah, that,' Alfred said. 'I will tell you because we are peacemakers, but it is best kept between us, and you must pledge to me that you will never use this information in the administration of evil, Lukas, Sophie... Orli knows.'

'Goodness,' Sophie's eyes widened. 'I agree.'

Lukas offered his word.

Alfred started, 'You know our line – the doves – are peace seekers agreeing with Bran's way of living and following in Hadley's footsteps, unlike her warring twin brother, Harley?'

Sophie felt Alfred was reinforcing the connection for Lukas more than herself. Was Lukas to be his successor? She had always assumed it would be Orli with all her knowledge.

Alfred continued, 'Well, because we are peacekeepers, we have not met such violent deaths as the Harley line.'

'So they lived by the sword, died by the sword?' Sophie said.

'Precisely, and in those past centuries, witches, in particular, died bound by rope and were then burnt, drowned or hanged. Dreadful,' Alfred shuddered. 'As a consequence, all the Ravens in history are powerless to fire and rope.'

Sophie frowned. 'Meaning that Murdoch the Raven of the 1940s couldn't use his powers to free himself or transform and fly out of the car because the fire had started?'

'Exactly, he had only human strength. Even the latter generation Ravens are powerless around fire and rope. It doesn't affect the dove line.'

'Wow,' Sophie said in a hushed tone. 'Am I correct in thinking then that if there were rope near Murdoch, he would not have the strength to harm me? Could we be together if every time he visited, we had a fire going in the room or rope present? Sounds weird, but I'm up for it.'

'It's not that simple,' Alfred said. 'You will leave him vulnerable to threat, and in the past, that has been detrimental to the Raven... he always has enemies, the shapeshifters for one.'

'But if Murdoch is powerless at that moment, then we should both be safe with each other if we can stay clear of our enemies.'

'In theory, Sophie dear, and I don't wish to frighten you, but enemies have a way of sniffing our vulnerabilities. Remember when you were in-between protectors and Venetia was able to find you in order to seek the Raven? We don't always know what we might awaken.'

'Margaret Dillon must have thought it was odd that the Raven couldn't save himself.'

'Indeed. But it did work in her favour as they could be together, given Margaret saved the Raven's life and broke the curse. Not for all time, sadly, but for her brief time with him at least.'

'If only you could save the current Raven's life,' Orli said to Sophie.

'Maybe next time he does something stupid, you could call me Alfred, and I'll get there as fast as I can,' Sophie joked, and as they enjoyed the break in tension, Sophie stored the rope and fire information in her mind. If they were cautious, they could use this quirk to be together; given the situation was desperate, she would consider all options.

'I hear you,' Lukas said.

Sophie looked surprised. 'What? Oh, you're talking mind to mind.'

'Grandpa is worried I'll store that information about the fire and rope and use it, or tell Venetia.'

Alfred looked a little contrite.

'We've all done things in moments of passion and aggression that we regret. I'm just suggesting caution. The chances of saving a Raven are few and far between,' Alfred said, 'but be open to it, Sophie.'

'Next time, you may not be the accursed and may be back to being the witch Elsopeth again, and you can be together,' Orli said, patting Sophie's hand sympathetically. Sophie guessed Orli was no stranger to unrequited love, but Sophie did not have the patience to wait a generation for something she wanted now.

Sophie looked wistful. 'Ah, fairy tales in a modern world.'

'If I were Prince Charming, who would you be?' Lukas joked as his family ribbed him.

'Given how far I am behind, I'd say sleeping beauty,' Sophie said and sighed.

CHAPTER 15

L UCY HAD PREPARED FOR this day; she was surprised it had taken Jordan so long to make the connection. She had checked him out thoroughly; how could he not have looked her up online? Sure, all the images of Lukas were gone from her accounts, but the online news story about their engagement and the photos they did together were still there. Lucy still bristled at Lukas's resistance to the photo opportunities she had set up – the shots were gorgeous. With her heart-shaped face, straightened brunette hair and dark brown eyes, it had been fun and romantic. Obviously, it was not so for Lukas, especially how he carried on. Jordan would lap that up, she was sure of it. Mind you, if Jordan had discovered something that angered him – his reason for wanting to see her straight away – it didn't stop him from satisfying his own needs first before he confronted her with his discovery.

They lay, sated after a good session of lovemaking. Jordan wasn't the best lover she had ever had, but he wasn't the worst. He had confidence in the sack, and that made a difference. She lay on his chest, running her fingers over his raven tattoo and listening to his heartbeat. He was hers, like putty in her hand, and as long as she kept up the confident front of a model in demand not only for work but also by men, she could keep him on the hook. Men love to think they have the prize catch.

This time, the situation was the opposite of her relationship with Lukas – her feelings for Jordan were short-term at best, a means to an end, but he was falling in love with her. With Lukas, it was love, at least at first, and then it was heightened by her ex being back on the scene and Lucy having to decide whom she loved more. She chose the wrong man; Anders had done what he always did, reeled her in and spat her out, precisely what she intended to do to Jordan once her work was done.

'So, did you need to see me just for this workout, not that I'm complaining,' she teased, basking in their afterglow.

'No, but it's a bonus. I found out something about you.' His hand stroked her head, his fingers running through her hair.

'That I'm good in bed?' she teased, and he laughed humourlessly.

'That you were engaged to Lukas Lens.'

'Yeah,' she said casually, 'he's one of my exes. Did you think I was a virgin? Sorry to disappoint.'

'I'd be worried if you were still a virgin at twenty-eight looking like you do.' His eyes narrowed. 'You know who I am, don't you?' Jordan's voice was menacing, his demeanour cool.

Lucy propped herself up on her elbows and looked at him. 'The cute guy I met at the gym? What's your problem with Lukas Len?'

'If you went out with Lukas Lens and were engaged to him, you know who he is and what he is capable of doing.'

'Yes, I do. But how do you know?' she asked, playing along and knowing full well the connection between the men. She inwardly scoffed, remembering her former best friend whose star kept getting brighter, *and Sophie thought she was the actress.*

'He is my cousin.'

'Really?' Lucy grinned and sat up. His eyes went straight to her breasts, but he did not drop the interrogation.

'Really. So you know what that means?'

'Tell me you're on the Raven side and not the peacemaker side like Lukas, I couldn't bear it.' She rolled her eyes as if that was so boring.

'You're lucky I am since you've just insulted them.' He smiled and crossed his arms across his chest, showing the width of his muscled arms. She was sure he puffed with power and pride, and she played up to it.

'I should have known. You are all things fire, passion and strength.' She climbed onto him, sitting astride. Then she played her trump card, putting her head on the side. 'Is that why you are going out with me? To find out more about him and that side of the family? Is this your way of telling me now?'

She saw the look of panic cross his eyes, that he might lose her, and she knew she had control again.

'Hell no,' he answered quickly. 'I had no idea you went out with him until I checked you out online. I thought you were playing me.'

She frowned. 'What would I get out of that?'

He shrugged. 'Forget it. I just came across him when I was looking at your model shoots. I like to look.'

'Yeah?' she moved slowly on him. 'I am happy to re-enact any of your favourites.'

Jordan gave her a sly grin. 'You're on. Did you meet her, the accursed your ex was protecting before the shapeshifter took over?'

'Sophie.' She said the name like it was unwelcome on her lips. 'We were close, but I dropped her from my friend list. She's full of herself.'

Jordan huffed. 'That's what I've been telling my uncle, the Raven. She's weakened him.'

That rocked in silence for a moment; Lucy webbed her fingers through his as she moved. The curtain moved lightly as a breeze brushed over their naked bodies; the night was about to fall.

'Why did you break up? You and Lukas?'

Lucy gave a small shrug. 'I called it off, not him, for a few reasons. He couldn't say what he wanted or felt; he didn't like going out much, and sometimes I felt like I was managing him. I can't be with a weak man.' Some of that was true, but the latter was not.

Jordan studied her with a smirk on his lips.

'I have none of those issues, babe. I can tell you right now that you are what I want. You can take me anyway, anytime, and I will have you again right now.' He flipped her on her back, taking charge, making sure she could see he was the man, the strong one, and for now, she let him believe it.

'You would be an amazing Raven,' she said, planting a seed in his mind that had already fertilised the idea.

'You could be my Lady Raven,' he smiled as he looked down at her, examining her body.

'Lady Raven,' she whispered with a smile, trying it on. Lucy had no intention of keeping him around; she had a purpose for him and that would come out soon enough. Then, if her plan worked well, Sophie and Jordan could eliminate each other; she'd kill two birds with one stone, so to speak.

Sophie had heeded Alfred's warning about rope and fire, but she still believed it could be a solution if they were careful. There had to be some way that it could be used to her advantage. There had to be! Standing in her office at dusk – Jack and Miss Sharpe had left for the day – Sophie stared out the window at the gardens and the bench, remembering how Elsopeth and Murdoch had sat there and how Venetia had pushed Elsopeth, making her fearful of accepting Murdoch's affection.

'So, you've decided I'm not out to kill you now?' a deep voice behind her said, and Sophie spun around to find Nikolas standing there, smiling.

'You scared me, you boofhead.'

'Boofhead?' He put his head back and laughed. 'Well, that's lovely, isn't it?'

'How did you know?' she asked, a little embarrassed.

'Lukas mentioned you came over to find out who killed Elsopeth. The two Lords were the frontrunners, so I figured you'd look at me differently for a while.'

'Hmm, well, Lord Saggers, you're in the clear.'

He gave a small formal bow as he would have to a lady in a past era. 'I have been known in the past to rough a few people up but usually in the boxing ring, and I would never harm a lady, especially a lady who held my heart in her hands, as Elsopeth did.'

'Ah, Elsopeth, quite the vixen,' Sophie joked. "Sorry about the other night... the fast departure.'

'No, I'm sorry for saying what I said. Are you free tonight... now?'

'Sure. More practice?' Sophie asked.

'No. I want to take you somewhere, show you something. Don't worry, we can go on my bike.'

'Nik, I'm not quite ready—'

'As friends,' he cut her off and rolled his eyes.

She grinned. 'I'm in!'

'I'll return on the bike to get you in thirty minutes. Change into bike gear.'

'My leathers?' she teased.

He raised an eyebrow. 'You have leathers?'

'Well, a jacket.'

He faded with a smile, and Sophie hurried to change; some fun was just what she needed. He was a handsome man, and there would be very few women who wouldn't lose their heart to Nikolas Saggers – a good career, good-looking and good prospects. But she felt a sense of guilt for considering an easy option when she had not yet closed the door on Murdoch.

Sophie was in her jeans, a white T-shirt, a black leather jacket and black boots, waiting for Nikolas when she heard his bike arriving on the grounds. He pulled up, alighted, and offered her a helmet, strapping it under Sophie's chin.

She grinned at him with excitement. 'Thank you, this is just what I need. Don't go too fast, will you?'

'Wouldn't dream of it, but you better hold on tight just in case,' he said with a sly smile and then chuckled when he saw her smirk.

Nikolas showed Sophie where to put her foot to climb on, sat astride the bike and started the engine as she sat and wrapped her arms around his body. They purred out of the grounds; for a while, she forgot everything and had fun. Pure, unadulterated fun. He took the scenic tour of the city – across the bridge, and Sophie looked up at the sparkling night lights beaming down on them from the pylons. She saw the city and the reflecting lights in the river in a new light. Nikolas passed through the city streets with the shop fronts lit up and made his way around the river to a park where modern lantern-shaped lights softly glowed. Opposite was an older part of the city with its grand buildings along the river. In the park, a large group had filled one of the pergolas and were barbequing, couples strolled along paths, some were walking dogs, and a nearby van sold coffee, cold drinks and hot dogs. Nikolas pulled the bike into a parking spot and cut the engine. He waited for Sophie to alight and swung off, helping her with her helmet.

'That was fantastic, even if I now have helmet hair,' she said, exhilarated, fluffing up her hair. 'I've never come across the bridge on the back of a bike.'

'The city and river are beautiful at night.' He nodded to the van. 'A football friend runs it and does a decent hot dog.'

'Dinner then?' she asked, and he grinned and led the way.

'Well, you've moved up in the world,' Nikolas's friend, Alex, said after being introduced to Sophie.

Nikolas smirked at him. 'We're just friends. Actually, I work for Sophie.'

'You do!' she realised, surprised and turned to Alex, 'he's good with figures,' she teased.

'So I've witnessed,' Alex joked. 'You're not looking to start up the footy team again?' he asked Nikolas as he made the two requested hot dogs with mustard and sauce. 'We could be a veteran team.'

'No, the body is a bit past that,' Nikolas informed him, paying and passing Sophie a hotdog and a can of drink. Sophie guessed Nikolas's body could run forever with his regular workouts in wolf form, but she played along.

'You've got to know when to hang up your boots,' she agreed.

'Yeah, maybe we should start a lawn bowls group then,' Alex said in jest and thanked them as another couple came to order.

Nikolas led Sophie over to a bench overlooking the river. 'He makes good money with that nightly van; he has three others around the city. They draw a crowd, especially after midnight when the starving clubbers come out in droves. I do his books.'

She took a bite, nodded with appreciation and said, 'He's not a vampire, is he? Works at night, sleeps during the day.'

Nikolas laughed. 'No, but he'll love that you thought he might be, I'll tell him.'

Sophie sobered. 'Are there vampires?'

'None I've met.'

She exhaled with relief and shrugged. 'Our world is weird, who's to say?'

'Yeah, true.' He gazed across at the old buildings. 'Does this ring any bells for you?'

Sophie blotted her lips with her serviette. 'This now? Why? Have we done this before?'

'No. But it was in that building across from us, the little one in the middle, where I first met you, again, in the 19th century.' He indicated the two-storeyed rendered brick building in the classical style with a copper-sheathed dome, dwarfed by two larger classic buildings on either side.

She turned to him, a look of surprise on her face. 'Really? Do you remember that? Why can't I remember it?'

'Because I was raised to remember, as was the Raven and Orli, and even Lukas, who showed no interest; hence, his memories are limited. Your aunt tried, but I believe your parents were against it.'

'Ah, lucky you,' Sophie said. 'Probably if I'd shown any interest in the clairvoyant side of the business, Daphne could have half-prepared me.'

'The memories will come to you now that you are open to them.'

She finished her hot dog a few mouthfuls behind him and wiped her hands, proclaiming it an excellent dinner. Opening her can of drink, she asked, 'Tell me about our meeting, everything you remember.'

He smiled and sat back with his can of drink and sighed.

'Don't start it with "It was a dark and stormy night" please,' she threatened, and Nikolas chuckled.

'No, from memory, it was a hot and humid summer's day, and I had my coat off and my shirt unbuttoned at the neck, which was most unacceptable in the 1880s, but I was a junior sitting in my place of business and wasn't expecting a visit from a lady.'

'Was your business with me then?'

'No, your father. My firm did his bookkeeping. I was apprenticed or articled, as they say. It was a fun place to work as there were half a dozen of us young blokes. On that day of your visit, my uncle, who owned the business, was detained, and the secretary showed you both through. I can remember scrambling to do my shirt up and put my jacket on, and your father stood in front of you, blocking your view like I was naked. Funny when you think about it now.'

Sophie grinned. 'You rebel. Did I see anything?'

'Well, if you did, it didn't seem to have an adverse effect on you. You didn't have a fit of the vapours and call for smelling salts.'

Sophie huffed. 'Did ladies really do that, or is it just exaggerated in books and films?'

'Trust me, they did it and with great effect. Swooning was big too. I caught many ladies who swooned towards me at balls. I gave them the benefit of the doubt that the room was overcrowded and hot, and their unmentionables were laced too tight, but I suspect a few were performance art.'

Sophie laughed and looked at him with fascination. 'Well, you were obviously the catch of the season. I wish I could remember.'

'Perhaps you will remember this. My uncle arrived back, and your father suggested I might accompany you for a walk along the river while he concluded private business with my uncle.'

'Ooh, were you nervous?' she teased.

'Excited more like it. I was the envy of every young man there; Elsopeth was quite the looker. She, you, took my arm and off we went. I even brought you an ice cream.'

Sophie's eyes widened, and she exclaimed, 'It was at a booth near the steamer that had just come in.'

'Exactly so. Refreshment sales were a big business along there with the incoming steamers and the infantry in town. You chose strawberry ice cream in a little tub. Every time you licked the spoon, I thought I'd die.' He laughed at the memory.

'Why on earth would you remember that kind of detail?' Sophie asked, fascinated.

'Because you were wearing a pink dress as well. I'll never forget that vision of you beside me with your pink ice cream in your pink dress and straw hat with a matching ribbon. A vision of loveliness and way out of my league.'

'Oh wow,' she said and smiled, sipping her drink. 'I can see flashes like I do when I'm wearing the glasses. You were quite dashing if my memory serves me correctly.'

'It does,' he agreed and laughed when she nudged him.

Then, the thought occurred to her, 'What was my uncle's private business?'

'Ah, that. He had no children of his own and left you a sizeable fortune. You were not only beautiful but financially independent. A good catch indeed.'

'Spoken like a true accountant,' Sophie said. 'But we didn't end up together.'

'No. But it was a good day.'

They looked across the river. 'It's a beautiful little building; I'm glad it is still standing,' she said.

'Me too. It's still an accounting firm. No connection to my family, and there's a legal firm on another level.'

'Time goes on.'

'Indeed it does,' Nikolas agreed. 'Hopefully, someone in the next generation will remember us.'

CHAPTER 16

S OPHIE BRUSHED OUT HER flattened helmet hair as she prepared for bed. Another night and not a word or a mind tap from Murdoch. What was going on in his head? Was his family telling him not to contact her? Was he being pressured to keep her at a distance? Regardless, Sophie was over it. If that's how he was going to play the game, so be it, she fumed. There were plenty of fish in the sea, but she'd just like confirmation that this fish was off her hook, so to speak. Sophie wondered if he would now be a Raven in the true sense of the word – her enemy.

She climbed into bed and tried not to think. Too tired to read but buoyed from her night with Nikolas, she lay willing herself to sleep, feeling the comforting presence of Bette Davis at the end of her bed and hearing her soft snuffling. It had been a fun night and a while since she could recall having a night out with a friend. Even though she wasn't looking for love with her protector, Sophie had to admit it was a romantic night, and if she had been open to Nikolas as a lover, she'd probably be swooning. She smiled at her choice of word – swooning – so Elsopeth.

She closed her eyes and exhaled. And waited. A while longer... a half hour, forty-five minutes.

Don't look at the clock. Stop thinking.

Branches scratched at her window, and she thought of Heathcliff opening the window and calling for the deceased Catherine to come in, haunt him, and drive him mad. Another sound, the Raven tap, tap, tapping?

Stop thinking.

What are you doing, Murdoch? Do you miss me as I miss you? Thank you, Nikolas, for giving me a night off from the drama. Where are you, Hope Yardley? Your family is in agony. Aagh!

She surrendered, knowing sleep would not win with the thoughts swirling around in her head. Rising, Sophie left Bette Davis curled up at the end of the bed and went down to the library in her pyjama shorts and matching T-shirt. She always felt a bit pretentious calling it the library – it was Aunt Daphne's favourite room with journals and books on mahogany shelves that reached to the ceiling and beautiful old dimpled leather chairs looking towards the garden or the fireplace that was never lit because the weather did not dictate it. At night, it felt a little eerie – the books were all that remained of the lives that had gone before.

Thanks to Bette Davis, Sophie had previously discovered three precious books – one of them being a journal written by Elsopeth – all hidden with false covers. Maybe Aunt Daphne was worried they would be confiscated and put in the Lens's library, so she hid them. Sadly, with her great aunt gone, Sophie would never know. Tonight, she was on a mission to learn more about her powers.

Pulling the small step ladder into place, she climbed up to where she had left the three volumes safely out of reach on the top shelf. There was *A Victorian Lady's Guide to Being the Best Wife* by Elspeth Marr which was actually the earliest *Personal diary of Miss Elsopeth Rayne* in existence. Sophie had read that diary and all its romantic antics. Next to it was the Charles Dickens classic *Nicholas Nickleby*, which was not the expected Dickens novel but a handwritten volume about the Saggers family... Nikolas, and some of the shapeshifter's story. Beside it, in a book marked, *The Poetry of Edgar Allan Poe* was a volume of handwritten notes exclusively about the Raven with contributions by the cursed descendants. Observations, attacks and cautions.

Tonight, she grabbed Nikolas's ancestors' story and, stepping down, sat near the window under a lamp, leaving the curtains closed so she could not be seen if a "presence" was in the garden like last time. She sped read, searching for her name – or rather Elsopeth's – amongst the words and occasionally smiled at the antics of the ancestral Saggers shapeshifters. Apparently, the animal instinct made them good lovers, but they might have been boasting too. When time permitted, she would read it in more detail, as she had promised with all the volumes stored at the *Optical Illusion* store.

Her ancestor's name came up often but usually in matters of love, not in instances where Elsopeth put her magical powers to any use.

'Elsopeth took my breath away tonight with her beauty...'

'She danced with me, and I could see our future as I held her in my arms...'

'I love walking beside her as her fingers nestle in my fur. I can feel her heartbeat and sense she feels safe and loved...'

And then, at last, something...

'Elsopeth has been up to her usual mischief, summoning the dead for answers.'

'I can summon the dead?' Sophie said, hurrying on but finding no other references to that skill. 'I can summon the dead,' she said again as if convincing herself that was a good idea. Sophie closed the book and put it on the coffee table before her. Rising, she took a deep breath.

'Righto then, let's give this a go. I'll soon know if you're dead, Hope.'

She shivered a little, uneasy at the thought of inviting trouble and entering the deceased's other world. Sophie was sorely tempted to go and wake Mel and ask her to be present, but a glance at the clock told her it was nearing two o'clock and that probably wasn't a great idea.

She inhaled and said solemnly, 'Hope Yardley, come to me.' Sophie grimaced at how stupid that sounded but didn't know how to summon the dead. Nothing happened. Perhaps she's not dead; Sophie brightened and then dismissed that thought. The odds were that poor Hope was gone, took the wrong ride, or went home with the wrong man. She closed her eyes, concentrated on recollecting the image of the young woman's face and with it clear in her mind, said, 'Hope Yardley, I summon you to join me in the now.'

Sophie opened her eyes, looked around the room and yelped in fright, stumbling back against the chair. A beautiful young woman – Hope – was in the corner of the library behind the desk.

Hope jumped with fear at Sophie's yelp and covered her heart with her hand. 'You called me!' she exclaimed.

'I know, sorry, I did,' Sophie said, straightening and slowing her breathing. 'Sorry, Hope, it's just that I've never done this before, and here you are.'

Hope nodded. 'Who are you?'

'Sophie. I'm working for the police, for your family, trying to find you.' Sophie studied the young woman. She was lovely and fresh looking, unaffected... it was hard to explain, but Hope appeared unsure of her beauty, not posing, pouting, or confident.

'I miss them.'

'They are distraught with worry. You're dead then?' Sophie said again with a grimace, given how stupid her question sounded.

'Yes.'

'I'm sorry to hear that.' Sophie sighed.

'Me too.'

'Can you tell me where you are? Who did this? I'm sorry, would you like to take a seat... or a drink? No, of course you don't want a drink,' Sophie shook her head. 'Sorry, I've only just found out I can do this... I think I said that before.'

Hope smiled and then gave a small laugh, and Sophie couldn't help but return her smile.

'I'm okay, standing, thanks. You know my last drink was a glass of champagne. A toast to my life,' she said, her voice dropping.

'I am truly devastated that I couldn't do anything to prevent your death. I get called on after the event to help provide justice. I can do that for you.'

'Yes, please,' Hope rallied. 'That I would like. A woman killed me.'

'What? Why?'

Hope shrugged. 'I don't know. She brought me champagne because she said she was celebrating something and wanted me to have one too. We drank that, and then I was in the ladies toilet and she came in and started talking to me again. She was really nice, and beautiful. She said she liked my hair and touched the back of it and then rammed my face onto the basin, and that's all I remember.'

Sophie gasped and looked stricken. 'How brutal. She killed you?'

'Yes.'

'But why?' she whispered, knowing Hope did not know.

'I don't know. She was like this beautiful assassin. I didn't even know her. It's not like she was my enemy. I didn't want to die yet.'

'Of course not. Hope, where are you?'

'In white light waiting to move on.'

'No, that's good, but I mean, where is your body, you know, your earthly body?' Sophie said.

'Oh, still there. In the back of my car, on a side street near the hotel. I don't know how I got there, but can you go get me?'

'Absolutely.'

'I think I have to go,' she said.

'Do you?' Sophie asked, confused as Hope faded. 'I'll get justice for you, I promise...' her voice faded, realising she was alone. 'What's with the leaving thing?' Sophie muttered, 'Aren't I supposed to send her back, or is that just one of those supernatural myths?'

She looked at the clock. A clue at last, the detectives would be so relieved. But there was no point ringing Detective Oakley at this hour. The body and car were probably going nowhere in the remaining hours before dawn. At daybreak, she would go into the office, ring Gerard from there, and talk with Miss Sharpe about her new superpower.

Sophie climbed the ladder and returned the book. 'I can summon dead people,' she said again as if saying it made it real. 'Could I summon Aunt Daphne to teach me everything

I should know?' The thought cheered her up no end and she vowed to check that too with Miss Sharpe in the morning... well, in a few hours.

CHAPTER 17

MURDOCH WALKED DOWN THE hallway of the police station, oddly pleased to be back in his everyday life, to say hello to his colleagues and feel some control again, to feel useful. The last two nights had been agony, like a druggie on withdrawal. He almost weakened half a dozen times and sent a message to Sophie or appeared in her room. But each time, he coached himself to go one more day, hour, and minute without doing so. It exhausted him, and he wasn't sure he was getting stronger for the absence, no matter how much support the family gave him or how many therapy chats Allanon insisted on subtly having with him. *Enough already*. He was back at his own place now, drinking in the solitude.

Back on the job this morning, Murdoch was even looking forward to seeing his partner – that was a surprise. He greeted the desk sergeant and, arriving at his shared office, walked in to find his chair occupied; Rachel Fletcher, the new girl, looked at home behind his desk, and Gerard sat sprawled at his untidy desk where no part of the timber surface was visible.

'Well, if it isn't the intrepid adventurer back from jumping off cliffs,' Gerard said, rising to greet him and shaking Murdoch's hand while giving him a good slap on the back.

Murdoch winced. 'Yeah, thanks, great to be back.'

Rachel laughed. 'Sounds it.' She offered her hand, and they formally met. 'I'll clear your desk.'

'No, stay there. I'll make myself at home here,' he said, shucking off his jacket and putting it over the chair in front of their small meeting table where he could see the whiteboard and their notes. 'I'll be taking over his desk in a matter of weeks.' He eyed Gerard's desk in a better position near the window. Murdoch lowered himself into the chair a little more gingerly than usual.

'Bit sore?' Gerard asked. 'That'll happen if you jump off a cliff.'

Murdoch ignored him and turned to Rachel. 'So, coping with him?' he nodded in Gerard's direction.

'Teaching an old dog new tricks,' she said with a grin, and Gerard shook his head.

'No respect these days for experience,' he muttered, but his lips twitched in a smile. He returned his focus to Murdoch. 'What the hell were you thinking? Were you having a mid-life crisis?'

'I was responding to a challenge,' Murdoch answered somewhat truthfully... a challenge he had set himself to get her out of his system. 'I assure you, I won't be doing any adventure sports again. I wasn't getting away from you despite what everyone says,' he joked.

Gerard smirked. 'You only had to wait a few weeks. Clearly, you're not cut out for extreme action; you're over thirty now, right? Leave that to the kids.'

'Okay, Grandpa, thanks for the advice. When are you leaving and getting the desk disinfected so I can move in?'

'I thought you two liked each other and got on famously, or that's what I was told,' Rachel said, frowning and looking from one to the other. 'It's more like Grump and Grumpier.'

'We do like each other,' Gerard said.

'This is us getting on,' Murdoch added.

'You wait until you spend the next decade working beside him,' Gerard said with a nod to Murdoch, 'this will be you in ten years.'

'Oh goody,' she said with a smile. 'Anyway, I'm glad you're here, Ashcroft.'

'Ashcroft? We're doing last names?' he asked, surprised.

'Unless you prefer Murdoch or Muddy?'

Murdoch grimaced. Only one person called him Muddy, and he didn't like it anymore when she did it. His mind went straight to Sophie, whom he tried to avoid thinking about.

'Ashcroft's, fine, Fletcher,' he retorted. 'What have you got on the missing girl? I saw the paper this morning. Distraught family, no word from the victim yet?'

'We've got zip,' Gerard said. 'No one saw her leave the hotel, no cameras captured her leaving, no cabs picked her up, and the security guys don't remember her coming or going.'

'She definitely went back there after a quick romp with a footy player, but after that, poof!' Rachel said, throwing her hands in the air like Hope Yardley's disappearance was akin to a rabbit being pulled out of a hat.

Murdoch frowned. He looked to Gerard. 'Did you try...' he hesitated before saying her name, and Gerard understood.

'Yep. Sophie hasn't picked up anything.'

'Unusual,' Murdoch said, surprised.

'Yep. We're taking her to meet Hope's family this morning. Not expecting anything there, but we're turning over every stone.' Gerard sighed.

'Want to come?' Rachel asked.

'No,' Murdoch answered too quickly not to draw suspicious looks from his colleagues. He cleared his throat. 'I'll take another line of questioning.'

'Great,' Gerard said. 'We couldn't get a list of attendees that night because it's a hotel, and they all just wander in and out when they like, but Fletcher stuck up a thing online asking anyone at the hotel to contact us if they saw her. Got about twenty to follow up.'

Murdoch nodded and looked in Rachel's direction. 'I'll take the list.'

She fished the paperwork out of the folder in front of her, rose and handed it to him.

Gerard's phone beeped with a message, and his eyes widened when he saw the name on the screen. He quickly read it.

'It's Sophie, and she's got something. Wants to come in or for us to go to her,' Gerard said.

'Thank God,' Rachel breathed out.

'Go to her,' Murdoch said. 'Let me know before I start on this list. I'll get up to speed on the rest of the file while you're gone.' He eyed Rachel's file on her desk and the notes on the whiteboard.

'You sure you don't want to come?' Gerard frowned. 'You two were as thick as thieves once.'

Murdoch shook his head and said nothing more.

'Right then.' Gerard messaged back that they were on their way and, rising, grabbed his keys and jacket, muttering that he hoped she'd solve the case as the pair departed.

Murdoch exhaled and closed his eyes momentarily. He wanted to go to her so badly he could taste it.

Sophie intended to get up earlier, but given sleep eluded her until sometime after four a.m., she then fell into a deep sleep and bolted awake, wide-eyed, at around seven-thirty. Hurriedly showering and dressing, Sophie startled Miss Sharpe with her arrival just on eight o'clock – Sophie usually arrived around nine despite not having to drive or contend with traffic, but she indulged her night owl habits. Jack arrived moments later – he liked to start early and leave early to get home to train for his chess tournaments.

'What on earth has happened?' Miss Sharpe asked, surprised to see her, and Sophie gave a small laugh.

'I'm only a little earlier.'

'An hour at least,' Jack said, backing up Miss Sharpe. 'Something has gone down.' He sat and watched her, expecting an exciting tale about another presence in the garden.

'Yes! Something big happened last night; I messaged the detectives, and they are on their way. Sorry, Jack...'

'It's all good. Miss Sharpe told me to leave your morning free to work with the detectives,' Jack said.

Sophie looked surprised. 'Oh, right, thank you, Miss Sharpe. Somehow, you always know what I need.'

'I wouldn't be much of an assistant if I didn't, dear. Do tell, what has got you starting work at this hour?'

'Well, last night I summoned the dead!' She stood in front of them, waiting for their shock.

'Excellent, that can be handy if managed well,' Miss Sharpe said briskly. 'Shall I make tea?'

'I expected you would summon them soon enough,' Jack added.

Sophie looked from one to the other as if they were crazy and put her hands on her hips. 'This is big, isn't it? I didn't know I could do that, and I found a note in the Saggers' family volume about Elsopeth doing it, so I called on the missing girl, and she appeared and told me where her body was right now.'

'Oh, so she is dead,' Jack said deflated, 'I had hoped that she might still be alive.'

'As had I,' Miss Sharpe said with a sigh. 'Well, that is a nasty business.'

Sophie gave up. It appeared her team had spent their life living and working around witches, and nothing surprised them as it shocked her. Then, a thought occurred to her.

'You both knew I could do that, didn't you?' she asked, eyes narrowing with suspicion.

'I'm pretty sure you can do many things,' Jack said, 'but I don't know what those things are until you need to do them. You know, witch stuff.' He waved a hand as if that covered the topic.

'Precisely, you are very skilled and a powerful witch, Sophie,' Miss Sharpe said. 'The detectives are arriving now.'

'Well, thanks for believing in me, both of you,' she said, still wearing a bemused look. 'Miss Sharpe, can I summon Aunt Daphne to guide me?' Sophie hoped her question would not offend Miss Sharpe, who was very close to Sophie's aunt.

'She is expecting that, dear,' Miss Sharpe said. 'Well, tea for just you and I then, Jack, as Sophie will be leaving with the detectives.'

'I will? Oh, right, I will. It's been a very confusing twenty-four hours,' she said, and with a look of bewilderment about what just happened, Sophie grabbed her handbag and glasses and rushed outside to meet the detectives before they alighted. They had a car and body to find.

CHAPTER 18

S OPHIE RAN DOWN THE stairs and waved the detectives to a stop before they could park. She opened the back door, 'I'm coming with you; I can get a cab back.'

'We're going somewhere?' Gerard asked.

'Back to the hotel where Hope went missing; I'll explain on the way,' she said, closing the door and putting her seatbelt on.

'Good morning,' Rachel said with a grin, turning to the back seat to smile at Sophie, who laughed.

'Oh yeah, sorry, good morning to you both. Last night, something phenomenal happened.'

'You found Hope and her murderer?' Rachel asked, her expression desperate.

'Half of that. I think I've found Hope's body. I summoned her. That's another story, and please don't tell anyone—' Sophie hurriedly added, and Gerard finished her sentence.

'—and she wouldn't have come if she wasn't dead.'

'Exactly. I'm sorry to say that Hope appeared.'

'We've lost her,' Rachel said, her face falling.

'I suspect we never had a chance, did we, Sophie?' Gerard asked as he stopped at a red light and glanced her way.

'No, you are right. She couldn't tell me much, but some woman befriended her.' Sophie shared what she had learnt from Hope, finishing with, 'The woman followed her into the bathroom and smashed Hope's head on the basin.'

'Good grief!' Rachel exclaimed.

'I know, so brutal,' Sophie agreed. 'Hope doesn't know her or why she did it. She doesn't know how the woman got her back to her car, or even if she stumbled there herself, but she is dead, in there, waiting to be found.'

'We've had no luck finding her car,' Gerard said with suspicion. 'It's not in the hotel car park. Are you sure about this one?'

'Ye of little faith,' she tapped him on the shoulder, and he smirked at Sophie in the rear-view mirror. 'Hope said the car is parked in a dead-end laneway in one of the streets near the hotel.'

'I'm onto it,' Rachel said, grabbing her phone and looking for a map of the area.

'Did she say anything else?' Gerard asked.

'No, but she's upset to be dead.'

'I can imagine. We're looking for a red Mazda hatch,' Gerard said. 'Fletcher, we're almost there, what have you got?'

'Several laneways and... yep, only one is a dead-end, this has to be it,' she confirmed. 'Go past the street the hotel is in, two streets up is the laneway – Larkin Lane.'

Gerard accelerated and drove with a determined look in his eye. No sooner had they reached the corner than all three saw that Sophie's claims were the truth. A small red car sat at the end of the lane. Gerard slowed down; there was no rush to face the gruesome scene.

'What are the chances it'll be unlocked?' Rachel said in a low voice.

'I can probably break in,' Sophie said, and they both glanced at her.

'Supposedly, I can do things I don't know about,' she said and gave a small shrug. Gerard parked a little further away from the car to allow emergency vehicles in when they arrived, which was inevitable now.

The three alighted, and Sophie stood back. Gerard and Rachel put on thin gloves and circled the car. Gerard tried the doors and hatch; all were locked, but then Rachel pounced down near the tyres and lifted a set of keys.

'Ah ha!' she proclaimed, holding them up. 'The killer must have thrown them there when he or she departed.' Rachel pressed the small pad and unlocked the car.

Gerard sighed and moved to the back of the hatchback. 'You don't need to see this if you don't want to,' he said to his partner and Sophie.

'Nope, part of the job,' Rachel said and stood beside him in a show of moral support. Sophie remained further away but close enough to see if there was a body in the back.

Gerard lifted the hatchback doo,r and there she lay. The smell rushed out, assaulting them, but they had found Hope. Now they just had to find her killer.

Murdoch's phone rang, and seeing his partner calling, he answered, 'Solved it?'

'No, but we've got a head start. We've found Hope's body in the boot of her car. You'd better get down here.'

Murdoch hesitated, and Gerard added, 'Sophie's returned to work.'

'Right.' He took the address. 'On my way.'

Murdoch sat back in the chair. Sophie's done it again, he thought. She was as good as her aunt, maybe better. He swallowed the emotion her name brought him and wondered if she was waiting for him – distressed, angry – or perhaps she didn't care if she never heard from him again. All of those reactions he would understand. He was beginning to think it would be better to torment her in his role as a Raven than be separated from her – get a love-hate sort of thing going on. At least then he'd see her.

But for now, he knew his biggest threat was his nephew. Jordan was bristling for a fight and keen for power, and tonight, he'd come face to face with him again at a family birthday dinner for Allanon's son. He wanted to avoid it, but citing work as a legitimate excuse on his first day back was pushing it. He loved the clan, but in the last few weeks, he had seen more of them than he had in a year, and he could do without their looks of concern, Jordan's aggression, and Allanon's constant study.

Murdoch's phone rang as if he conjured him; Allanon's name came up.

He sighed and answered, 'Brother.'

'Hi, just checking to see if you're coming tonight.'

Murdoch hesitated.

'I want you to come.'

'Thanks, but the party will go on.'

'Hardly the point,' Allanon said. 'What's going on with you? What are you feeling, Murdoch?'

It wasn't often his brother used his name with such seriousness, but he had not convinced Allanon he wasn't going to fall from the sky again any time soon.

Murdoch sighed. 'Does being that forward work with your patients?' he asked, rising to pace. He heard his brother chuckle.

'Yeah, they're paying to talk, so most want to get straight to it, except those on court orders.'

'Consider me a court order client,' Murdoch retorted drily and was relieved that Allanon laughed again and didn't take offence.

'Seriously though, wouldn't you feel better just having a quick chat about how you're feeling, you know, see if talking about it might help?'

'Nope. Haven't you got to go? I'm sure I do.'

'Nice try. I'll make you a deal,' Allanon said, and Murdoch groaned.

'Anon, I appreciate all you've done for me, but I don't feel better for opening up. Gerard and I have worked together for years and seen some heavy stuff, but we have never cracked or needed to hold hands. I'm not the type who goes for counselling.' There was silence on the line. 'Okay, what's the deal?' Murdoch gave in.

'Good. Throw me a bone,' Allanon said; the relief in his voice was as if he had a breakthrough with a tough client. 'Give me one feeling, and let me see if I can help you. If I can't say anything that makes you feel understood or supported, or if sharing doesn't work for you, we won't talk of emotions again.'

'Ever?'

'Well, I'll do my best, but it is an occupational hazard,' Allanon joked. 'What's going on in your head? What are you feeling? Where are you at?'

Murdoch's thoughts raced as he considered what to tell his brother and how to voice his anger, desperation, heartache and frustration. He felt there was something ungainly and weak about revealing too much.

'Adrift.'

'What was that?' Allanon asked. 'Adrift?'

'Yep, adrift.'

Allanon hesitated, and Murdoch waited, expecting his brother to have a go at him for offering so little, but he didn't. Instead, he empathised.

'I understand.'

'You do?' Murdoch asked, surprised and lowered himself into the chair behind Gerard's desk, trying it out for size.

'I do. Adrift... you had been working your way to making a life with Sophie. She is your lighthouse, the course you are on for this generation, and now, she could be gone from your future.'

Murdoch swallowed. He couldn't respond, and Allanon continued.

'You miss her laugh, smile, scent, and how she manages you. Gerard's retirement is expected – it has been a long time coming – but Sophie's been on a course towards you, and you were so close to having her.'

Murdoch hung up. He couldn't listen to another word as his brother tapped into his soul and exposed him so perfectly. Everyone within their circle knew of the dangerous consequences of their pairing, what his overwhelming desire to see her could unleash on his family, Sophie and the Lens family.

But Murdoch could not be with her without wanting to kiss or kill her, and he wasn't sure which instinct would be stronger.

Back in the office, Sophie was relieved she could help the detectives and saddened by Hope's death – the waste of all that potential.

'I'm glad I'm a grifter and don't see dead people,' Jack said with a shake of his head after Sophie recounted the story.

'It would be a terrible shock,' Miss Sharpe agreed as the three shared a cup of tea and some of Miss Sharpe's chocolate slice.

'Gerard and Rachel were so calm about finding the body,' Sophie said with a shudder. 'What kind of female would kill for a thrill?'

'Well...' Jack started, 'a few, I imagine.'

'Yeah, I suspect you are right, but maybe it wasn't a thrill kill. Maybe it was emotional – revenge, jealousy, love,' Sophie conceded with a shrug.

'Yeah, I can understand killing for love.'

Sophie raised an eyebrow in his direction, and Miss Sharpe turned to study him.

'I haven't done it,' he assured them.

'Well, it wasn't on your CV,' Miss Sharpe joined in with good humour.

'Phew, on behalf of Miss Sharpe and I, that's a relief,' Sophie joked. 'But something doesn't sit right in Hope's case. If it was a thrill kill, why remove the body? Kill done, killer gone. But this person wanted to hide the evidence of what they did. It couldn't have been easy to get Hope's body out of there unseen and move her car where it wouldn't be easily found. Would someone wanting a thrill kill go to that much trouble?'

'Was stuff stolen?' Jack asked.

'No, detective,' Sophie answered in jest. 'Hope's handbag was in the car, and Gerard said it contained cards, a phone and cash. Why then?'

Miss Sharpe changed the subject. 'Daphne will be excited to see you, Dear, now that you know you can summon her.'

'I can't wait to see my great aunt's face. It'll give her a chance to say, "I told you so", and she will,' Sophie said with a laugh, and Miss Sharpe smiled, agreeing.

'It's amazing what you are discovering,' Jack said enthusiastically, reaching for another slice. 'Why don't you try summoning your aunty now to say hello!'

Sophie looked surprised. 'I could! Would that worry anyone?'

'Not me,' Jack said. 'I'd love to meet her, given she's such a legend, especially around here.'

'Lovely idea,' Miss Sharpe agreed. 'I'm sure Daphne would love a cup of tea and to join us.'

Sophie's mouth fell open and she was about to ask if Aunt Daphne could drink tea but thought better of it. That discussion might go on longer than their tea break if they began on the digestive habits of the deceased. Feeling very self-conscious as the process was new to her, Sophie closed her eyes, as she did when summoning Hope, pictured her aunt and invited her to join them.

'Well, hello at last,' a deep female voice said, making Sophie jump. Sophie's eyes sprung open, and she smiled with delight. Her great aunt looked quite solid, sitting opposite her at the table, next to Miss Sharpe, who was pouring the grand dame a cup of tea.

'Aunt Daphne!'

'Hello, my dear niece, and yes, I told you so,' she winked. 'Hello, dear Valerie, and this must be Jack.'

'Hello, Mrs Shelby,' he said, rising and giving her a small bow.

'So charming, thank you, and please call me Daphne. I knew your mother very well. A little slip of a thing, you obviously take after your father – a gentle giant.'

'That I do,' Jack said happily and resumed his seat.

'Well, I can't stay long,' Aunt Daphne said, addressing Sophie, 'you are not strong enough for that yet, but it will happen in good time.'

Sophie went to speak, 'I'm sorry I ignored—'

'Not to worry, dear,' Daphne cut her off.

'—and thank you for your beautiful house.'

'You are welcome and don't fret. We'll catch up on all that has gone on before,' Aunt Daphne assured her with a wave of her hand. 'But first, a few warnings.'

Sophie bit her lip, wondering if she was in trouble; her aunt was a ghost but still had the power to instil respectful fear in her.

'You did an outstanding job requesting that troublesome presence show itself the other evening before vanquishing it, well done. But, if possible, always give them that opportunity to fight fairly, as your strength is phenomenal... there will be no coming back for them.'

'Did I kill whatever it was?' Sophie asked, alarmed but a little relieved as well.

'No. They were witches and smart enough to depart when they saw your hand actions starting. Others may not be so fortunate.'

'We think it was the Ashcroft twins. Do you know them, Daphne?' Jack asked.

'I believe it was, and yes, I know of the boys, or rather they are young men now. I can tell you the Raven did not send them, but they come from his bloodline. I don't think they realised your strength, Sophie.'

'They were always such nice boys,' Miss Sharpe said with a slight shake of her head, 'well, the youngest twin was a sweet boy.'

'Exactly so, Valerie,' Aunt Daphne agreed. 'The eldest, Jordan, is an angry young man, and you need to be wary of him, Sophie.'

'Jordan,' Sophie said his name to remember it. She would research the twins further later. 'Good thing I didn't eliminate them then,' Sophie said under her breath.

'They'd only have themselves to blame,' Jack added.

'I agree,' Aunt Daphne concurred. 'You need to be careful around Orli too.'

'Orli!' Sophie exclaimed. 'But I love Orli, and she is so kind and peaceful.'

'Exactly,' Aunt Daphne said. 'She is a protector. She has protection spells around the house, which is another reason the twins most likely could not have harmed you unless they could breach them. But by her nature, Orli has to protect. So do not harm anyone – even an enemy – in front of her, as she must intervene.'

'Good grief, I had no idea,' Sophie said.

'Well, that is it for the warnings for now,' Aunt Daphne said, sipping her tea. Sophie noticed that the tea in the cup seemed to be reduced. 'Now, I don't need to warn you about the Raven – he's a very mixed-up young man at the moment, quite torn.'

Sophie wanted to know more but didn't want to discuss it in front of everyone.

'Is he alright?' she asked.

'I wouldn't say so,' Aunt Daphne said with a look to Miss Sharpe, who agreed. 'But he is doing the right thing for your safety by trying to stay away.'

Ah, so that's why I haven't heard from him.

Sophie gave her aunty a nod but wanted to blurt out that she didn't want to be safe. She didn't want him to be sensible and stay away!

'Any quick questions, Sophie dear or anyone?'

'Yes, please,' Sophie jumped in. 'I need to understand my powers. I can only find one Elsopeth diary from the 18th century.'

'Ah, yes. The 19th-century Elsopeth diary is in a shoebox in the attic,' she said. 'I liked to keep them separate in case of a fire so I don't lose everything at once.'

Sophie suspected if there were a fire, the old timber mansion would burn to the ground no matter what rooms held what and where.

Daphne continued. 'The early 20th-century Elsopeth was an actress and could not be bothered keeping a diary. She toured the country treading the boards. You might find some of her reviews if you look up old newspapers. She went by the name of Elsie Shelby and died quite young – in her late twenties, I believe.'

'Wow. My acting days feel like a hundred years ago. I'll explore the attic, thanks, Aunt.'

'Apparently, I'm slipping away,' Aunt Daphne said hurriedly, finishing the cup of tea that Miss Sharpe had placed in front of her. 'It's lovely to see you all. Give my best to dear Alfred. I'll see you at Bridge soon, Valerie.'

With a wave, she faded. They were all momentarily quiet and then resumed eating and talking.

'Well done, Sophie,' Miss Sharpe said, and Sophie grinned.

'Thank you, Miss Sharpe. I feel very uncomfortable doing it, but I'm sure it will become second nature in time.'

'Is Daphne playing Bridge with you, Miss Sharpe?' Jack asked.

'Oh no, but she drops in now and then. I'm playing at her old club, and she likes to say hello during tournaments or social occasions.'

Sophie glanced around; no one thought that was odd. Again, Sophie realised she had much to catch up on to feel truly at home in the witching world. For now, she was impatient to search Hope's social media photos to identify that woman with Hope. If she could talk with someone who might know the mystery woman, the vision would come up in her glasses, but who would that be? It would have to wait until after her three client readings. Then she realised she had not thought about Murdoch for an entire thirty minutes.

CHAPTER 19

Lukas Lens nodded. The room was quiet except for the murmur of voices as Orli fitted a mature customer with glasses at the counter of the *Optical Illusion* store. Lukas was servicing an art deco clock and mind-speaking with his grandfather; Alfred's words were coming through loud and clear. Lukas, however, wasn't proficient at reading what his grandfather was thinking and needed to concentrate.

'Do not think the worse, lad,' Alfred said, soothing him, 'I am sure there is an innocent explanation. Venetia is very taken with you.'

Lukas was not as sure. His mistrust of women ran deep – a former fiancée who called it off when she met Nikolas, Lucy whose deceit he could smell on her, and now Venetia was exiting her car from across the street, and he could tell from her scent even before she entered the shop that she had been in the company of Jordan Ashcroft – Murdoch's nephew. It was a gift he wished he did not possess.

'He may have requested to see her,' Alfred continued. 'I suspect they go way back, given Venetia's past relationship with Jordan's uncle, Murdoch.'

Lukas nodded again, keeping his head low, working on the timepiece before him and trying not to get worked up. He couldn't risk his eyes flaring yellow with a customer in the shop or glass shattering, but he struggled with his anger. He could feel Orli's worried glances his way.

'Say nothing about it to her, Grandpa, please,' Lukas said in his mind, 'I want her to raise the subject and tell me she has been with him. I want to know I can trust her.'

'As you wish,' Alfred answered back.

The customer paid Orli and with an assurance that she was delighted with her new glasses, bid them goodbye, the bell tinkling after her as Orli held the door open for her, keeping it open for Venetia.

'Hello!' Orli said, welcoming the sophisticated witch and moving aside so Venetia could enter.

As always, Venetia's beauty caught the eye of passers-by on the footpath, and she sidled into the store, greeting the family, lingering longer on Lukas. He felt the tug and shift as his heartbeat skipped and fell into rhythm with hers.

'A pleasure to see you, young lady,' Alfred greeted her kindly. 'Are you taking Lukas out for afternoon tea?'

Lukas knew his grandfather was keen to get him out of the store.

'Oh no, Mr Lens,' she said, slipping onto a stool in front of Lukas's counter as invited. 'I have come with news, but I won't hold you up for too long from your work.'

'We always welcome visitors, hold us up as long as you like,' Orli said graciously.

Lukas was aware he still hadn't spoken, but he feared the anger that might rush from his mouth and the rush of energy from his eyes shattering all before him. But then, his anger diffused; Venetia was honest and upfront.

'I have just met with Jordan Ashcroft,' she said. 'He sent me a phone message; I don't know how he got my number... probably raided his uncle's phone.' She shrugged. 'Anyway, he asked me to meet with him, and you won't believe what he wanted.'

'I told you all would be well, lad.' Lukas received the message and relaxed, giving his grandfather a small smile. Venetia would not be telling him this if she met with Jordan with romantic intent.

'Were you in danger?' he thought to ask.

'Ah, he speaks,' she teased. 'You are jealous?'

'Yes. I am jealous of every man who gets to spend a moment in your company,' he said, and she softened, her eyes radiating her love for him.

'You are my man, I have no interest in Jordan Ashcroft,' she scoffed and reached across the counter for Lukas's hand. He accepted her hand, rubbing his thumb gently over her smooth skin. 'If Jordan's power was as big as his ego, he might have something to crow about.'

Orli suppressed a smile at her comment, as did Alfred, but Lukas chuckled, happy to hear the man whom he thought might be competition, diminished.

'He wanted me to consider going back to his uncle.'

'Good grief,' Alfred said, 'and Jordan thought he could organise that?'

Venetia laughed. 'Yes, I believe he meant to persuade me. His dislike of Sophie is quite intense, given he admits to barely knowing her. He pronounced her cursed and unsuitable for his uncle in this generation. Of course, he didn't put it quite as nicely as that,' she added.

'I can imagine,' Orli said, her sympathy for Sophie evident.

'I told him I had lost my heart to another and had no interest in resuming with his uncle, even if he were to find himself single.'

Lukas kissed her hand, and she smiled at his old-fashioned gesture.

'But this is the interesting part...' Venetia looked around to ensure she had their attention.

'Do tell,' Orli said, holding her breath.

'You will never believe who Jordan's new girlfriend is, a woman he claimed to have met at the gym, but we all know better...'

'Who?' Lukas asked, genuinely interested.

'Lucy. Jordan Ashcroft is dating Lucy, who is seven or eight years his senior. It is in keeping with her usual groupie habits. I could not believe it.'

Lukas's eyes narrowed, and he looked at his grandfather. Immediately, Venetia stiffened.

'Do you still harbour hopes of reuniting with her?' Venetia asked, her voice demanding.

'Absolutely not,' Lukas returned his attention to Venetia. 'No interest whatsoever, I called it off. Can't you hear my heartbeat for you?'

She exhaled and smiled, touching her own heart. 'Yes.'

'But this is dangerous,' Lukas added.

'I fear you are right,' Alfred said.

'What do you mean?' Venetia asked, not yet catching on.

'There's only one reason Lucy would have sought our Jordan to partner with,' Orli said. 'Murdoch is at his most vulnerable, and Jordan hates that Murdoch loves the accursed. Lucy will subtly persuade Jordan that he could be the next Raven and do the job better and put the accursed in their place.'

'Oh my,' Venetia said, 'of course. But if I got back with his uncle, then Sophie could go back to being just the accursed and not the woman weakening the Raven.'

'This could lead to a power showdown between Jordan and Murdoch,' Alfred said.

'But do we know who is to be the next Raven?' Lukas asked. 'It may not be Jordan.'

Alfred shook his head. 'Only Murdoch knows that; if it is Jordan, I suspect the road ahead will be very violent.'

The first two of Sophie's readings went as she expected. She had completed so many readings now that her style was relaxed and easy, her nerves non-existent. Jack's workload had lightened a little, but anytime Sophie was featured in the news – should she help the police solve a case or be profiled – the demands for her time increased again. They both enjoyed the "down" times more.

'Your last client for the day is Kimberley Porter, aged twenty-five. She was adopted and is trying to find her mum,' Jack said as he gave Sophie the standard summary he provided before every reading.

'Poor Kimberley.' Sophie sighed. 'She's not interested in finding her dad, too?'

'She didn't mention him, so maybe not today,' Jack said with a shrug. He looked to the garden path where a slim woman with dyed red hair, wearing a blue dress and white runners, was walking towards them. 'This will be her, right on time.'

'Thanks, Jack,' Sophie said and cleaned her glasses. Jack usually met the clients, took the payment if they hadn't prepaid online already, which Kimberley had, and introduced them to Sophie. After introductions, Sophie put on her glasses.

'Thank you for seeing me. I've been waiting for three months, but it is worth it, and I'm grateful for any help you can give me,' Kimberley said, her blue eyes already teary.

'This is very raw for you,' Sophie said, not needing the glasses to tell her that.

'My adopted mother passed away a few years ago from cancer. She was a wonderful mother, and I wanted to allow some time, just out of respect for her, before looking for my birth mother. My sister doesn't want to know, but I do.'

'Is she your blood sister?' Sophie asked, and Kimberley shook her head in the negative. 'No, she was adopted too, but we grew up as sisters. She doesn't think any good will come from seeking the parents who didn't want us.'

'May I ask if your adopted or birth dad is still alive?'

'My adopted dad is, and he understands my search. I want to find Mum first in case my real dad abandoned her, and that's the reason she had to give me up. I don't know if I'll seek him then.' She took a deep breath and got a grip on her emotions. 'It's just that I'm hoping there's a reason she gave me up.'

'Of course, I understand,' Sophie said. 'You haven't found anything?'

'I was told my birth files were not computerised and were lost in the flooding of the government building in which they were stored. I can't even tell you my mother's surname.' Her voice rose with emotion, and she cleared her throat and calmed herself again. 'I'm not usually this emotional, sorry. I've been researching for months; it just feels so... last chance today.'

'But it is not, of course,' Sophie said. 'Just the beginning.'

Kimberley nodded. 'Thank you, you are right. I will find her.'

It was times like these when Sophie was pleased the room felt calm and welcoming, and she felt Kimberley relaxing as she began to notice her surroundings and heed Sophie's words.

'I hope I can help you. I normally see the past, present and future. I'll obviously focus on your past to see if I can help you identify your mum, and then we can look to the future to see where she might be now.'

Kimberley nodded enthusiastically. 'Thank you.'

Sophie smiled. 'In your own time, at a calm pace, tell me anything you know or can remember about your birth mother, anything you might have been told, or failing that, your earliest childhood memories.'

Kimberley nodded and began. The images appeared above Kimberley's head, and Sophie squinted at them.

'Stop!' she ordered. Kimberley reeled back. 'Sorry, it's just that now and then I see an image I might need, and if you talk on, I could lose it.'

'Oh,' Kimberley breathed a sigh of relief.

'Can you tell me a little more about your first house memory?'

'Sure.' Kimberley began again, and Sophie saw her. A young woman with a babe in her arms and another child in the cradle, two the same age or near enough. She saw a grave, a funeral procession, the two children, and a man who could be their father signing paperwork. There was another woman at the funeral who looked like the deceased, so like her.

'Back, back, the paperwork,' Sophie muttered. 'Sorry, not you, Kimberley. Carry on, I'm talking to myself.'

Kimberley nodded and, looking slightly confused, picked up her train of thought and continued. 'I was told my mother loved all things yellow...'

Sophie saw the adoption papers, the headstone, and yellow roses on the casket. Then came the name. She stopped Kimberley.

'You saw something? You can help?'

Sophie nodded. 'Let me warn you first, as I warn every one of my clients – this is the truth I know. You don't have to choose to believe it, but I know it to be so. It may be painful, so please think carefully about whether you want to know. You can go away and think about it, and we'll get you back in whenever you are ready, with no waiting. There's no pressure.'

Kimberley leant forward. 'Thank you, Sophie. I want to know, I assure you.'

Sophie nodded. 'Your family name is Walters; your mother was Bernadette Walters.'

Kimberley inhaled sharply, repeated the name and then rushed to tap it into her phone. She looked back at Sophie expectantly.

'I'm very sorry to tell you this, Kimberley,' Sophie lowered her voice. 'Your mum has passed away.'

The young woman's emotions spilled over, and Sophie pushed the box of tissues on her desk towards her.

'I'm fine, really,' she said, sniffling.

'If it is any consolation,' Sophie continued, 'your mum died when you were very young, I suggest you were only a few years old from the image I saw... so you didn't just miss meeting her, that would be terrible.'

'Terrible,' Kimberley agreed. 'Do you know what she died of?'

Sophie shook her head. 'I think it was an illness, perhaps. I didn't see an accident. Shall I go on?'

'Yes, please,' Kimberley said with much insistence, dabbing at her face with the tissue.

'I saw a man whom I believe was your father signing paperwork. He looked grief-stricken. I'm surmising that perhaps he didn't cope with the loss of your mum and could not raise you... and your sister alone.'

Her head reeled up, and Kimberley's mouth dropped open. 'Sister?'

Sophie nodded. 'There were two babies. I don't know if you were twins or had a year or so apart, but you were both very young. And... I believe your mum might have been a twin, too. So you might have an aunty out there who looks just like your mum if she is still with us today. I saw her at the funeral.'

Kimberley gasped and clapped her hands together in delight. 'I knew my mum wouldn't have abandoned me.' She shook her head. 'I might have a sister and aunty. I wonder why my aunty couldn't take us,' she pondered.

'I think your mum and her sister were very young,' Sophie said with a small shrug.

'It's good news; it really is,' Kimberley said, rising and embracing Sophie. A happy client was a good result all around, and now Sophie could spend the last office hour searching through Hope Yardley's photos online and trying to identify that mystery woman.

CHAPTER 20

MURDOCH DEPARTED HOPE YARDLEY'S death
scene and, taking Detective Rachel Fletcher's word
for it, didn't buy a present for his nephew whose birthday
dinner he was en route to now. He didn't relish seeing
Allanon after cutting him off on the phone but figured he'd
be forgiven if he showed up.

'Cash is king with kids,' Rachel had said, so he picked up
a birthday card with a cute dog on it, scribbled a message
and stuck cash in it. He grabbed a bunch of flowers while
there for Bree, the hostess and Allanon's wife. It would
surprise Allanon that he came, let alone bearing gifts.

He drove the route on autopilot, thinking of the case,
not thinking of Sophie as best he could, and occasionally
grimacing at the thought of the shapeshifter hanging
around her.

Nicholas Saggers. The shapeshifter, always on the scene.

You have never won her heart in our history, go love someone else. You will have her this century over my dead body.

He realised that was probably a reality. Damn, he hated this pain. Life was much simpler when his life was just work and friends. The occasional drink with the boys, casual relationships when needed, nothing that caused the all-consuming and non-stop ache he felt now.

Justin's car was present when Murdoch pulled into his brother's driveway. Jordan, the hothead twin brother, had not yet arrived from work or the gym. Of course, Murdoch knew who the next Raven would be, but there was danger in releasing that information too early; there was also the problem of not releasing it at all, and the person was then thrust into the role unprepared. A bit like Sophie – even though he's not thinking of her. She did have plenty of warnings from her aunt that she was to follow in her footsteps as a clairvoyant... Daphne might not have mentioned the witch part.

Murdoch was comfortable with his chosen successor, but all could change should he have a child. He couldn't see that happening any time soon, but the thought of doing so with Sophie was too much for him to dwell on. Never in history had Elsopeth lived long enough to procreate, and he was quietly terrified of calling forward fate.

Entering the house, Murdoch was immediately ensconced into the family with hugs and kisses from the ladies present, appreciation for the flowers, and back slaps from Allanon and Justin. Sometimes, he wondered why they bothered with him when he felt as if he brought so little to the family.

'Happy birthday, kid,' Murdoch said, kissing Noah on the top of his head and presenting the card.

'Thanks, Uncle Murdoch,' he said, still of an age to be comfortable in being kissed and hugged by family. He tore open the envelope, and Murdoch saw Rachel was right.

'Cute dog!' he said, admiring the card and opening it; his eyes bulged at the cash enclosed. 'Brilliant, thanks Uncle Murdoch, look Mum! I can get the game now.' He hugged Murdoch and ran off.

'Fifty dollars is way too much for a nine-year-old, Murdoch,' Bree scolded him for his generosity.

'Is it?' he asked, surprised and shrugged.

'Do you remember what you got from Dad for your ninth birthday?' Allanon asked.

'A kick in the pants,' Murdoch guessed.

'Yeah, that's about it.' Allanon laughed. 'Thank God for Mum. Here's Jordan now with the girl he wants us to meet.' Murdoch turned to see his nephew's car coming up the winding driveway. 'Come on, we'll go out the back. Justin's out there, and we'll have a few moments of sanity before the party begins.'

'Are you calling us insane? Is that a clinical diagnosis?' Bree asked, her eyebrows raised, giving her husband a suspicious look.

'It certainly is,' he said, kissing her on the cheek.

'Get out of here you two.' She laughed, enjoying a glass of wine with Justin's girlfriend.

The men wandered to the firepit at the back of the block, where it was dark, quiet and cool. They could see Justin sitting there alone. He was always in Jordan's shadow, the quieter of the twins, and his uncles rarely had the chance to enjoy his company alone. He smiled as they approached.

'Are you taking after your Uncle Murdoch and avoiding the crowds?' Allanon asked, sitting down beside him.

Justin grinned. 'You know what they say, still waters run deep.'

'That's us,' Murdoch agreed. 'Deep.'

The men laughed and spoke of each other's day, and then Jordan could be seen heading towards them, a lady by his side. Murdoch squinted, looked again and bristled.

'What is it?' Allanon asked, picking up on his tension.

'What's the new girlfriend's name?' he asked.

'Lucy,' Justin answered. 'She's a looker, a model, apparently.'

A breath hissed through Murdoch's teeth, and they stood as the couple arrived. Lucy looked glamorous, as expected from a model out to make a good impression with her new boyfriend's family. She was different somehow, Murdoch thought, sexier than she was with Lukas. Maybe she adapted depending on the man she needed to ensnare, he thought uncharitably. Did she decide she needed to be more sensual to get Jordan – a younger man – across the line? Her dress was fitted and low cut, the skirt reasonably high, her dark hair was down and voluminous, and she acted coy and flirty around her new love.

Jordan stopped in front of them. 'Uncle Murdoch, Uncle Allanon, Justin, this is Lucy; Lucy, this is the family,' he said with a smile at his relatives. Allanon and Justin greeted her enthusiastically, and Lucy shook hands with the men, refraining from doing so with Murdoch.

Lucy laughed. 'That's so sweet that you still call them uncle.'

Allanon smiled. 'We raised the twins from young boys. Should they forget, calling us uncle reminds them that we are family and old enough to be respected,' he teased his nephews.

Lucy turned to Murdoch. 'Hello again,' she said, smiling at him.

'You know each other?' Jordan asked, taken aback. 'Oh, of course, Lucy was Sophie's friend.'

Murdoch was surprised Jordan knew and that it didn't bother him.

'It's been a while,' Lucy smiled up at him. 'Still doing the police thing?'

Murdoch studied her. 'You can't be expecting civil conversation after the way you threw your best friend under the bus.'

Lucy's eyes widened in surprise. 'Why would you care if she is supposed to be your enemy?'

Jordan scoffed beside her. 'Exactly. What's the saying, Uncle Allanon, about enemy and friends?'

Allanon looked uncomfortable, not wanting to side against his brother or nephew. He put his hands in his pockets and rocked on his heels. 'Ah, it's something like "The enemy of my enemy is my friend",' he answered.

'Perfect,' Jordan crowed. 'You and Lucy should be best friends, Uncle Murdoch.'

'I'm partial to loyalty,' Murdoch muttered.

'Look what she did to me!' Lucy exclaimed, forgetting her coy act in the moment.

'What did she do?' Murdoch asked with genuine curiosity. 'Steal your limelight for a minute in the press, in a field that's not even your line of work?'

'She was seeing Lukas all the time, putting pressure on our relationship, and she knew our engagement press story was coming out, but she usurped it with her crime story.'

Murdoch laughed, amazed at how Lucy's perspective was so distorted. 'I suppose she could have held off solving a murder until your engagement photos appeared so you would get more likes,' he scoffed. 'As for your ex-fiancé, it was his responsibility to protect her. You wouldn't have met him without Sophie. I believe she introduced you both, didn't she?'

Lucy didn't answer, and her displeasure showed on her face. She turned to Jordan. 'Babe, I think I'll join the ladies.'

'Good to meet you, Lucy,' Allanon said, trying to save the situation for Jordan's sake. Justin nodded, not as convinced. His loyalty to his brother ran deep, and Murdoch sensed his wariness about his twin's new girlfriend. She departed with a backward glance at Murdoch.

Jordan smirked at Murdoch as if baiting him. The two men remained standing.

'You can't be serious,' Murdoch said in a low voice.

Jordan shrugged. 'She's sexy and sweet, good in bed and keen. What's not to love?'

'What's going on?' Allanon asked them, confused and looking between his brother and nephew.

'Why do you think she's going out with you, Jordan?' Murdoch asked.

Jordan huffed. 'Because she's got good taste.'

'You don't think she has an agenda here?' he continued.

'Like what?' Jordan was sneering now as he stood straighter to meet his uncle eye to eye and attempted to loom over him.

'Settle down, you two,' Allanon said, reading their body language. 'Jordan, sit down.'

Instead, the young man crossed his arms across his chest and widened his stance.

Murdoch could see Bree coming towards them, probably to get Allanon to start the barbeque and begin dinner.

'We'll discuss this later,' Murdoch said.

'No. I want to know what agenda you think she would have?' Jordan asked.

'Where did you meet?' Murdoch asked.

'The gym.'

'A place where lots of couples meet,' Justin added, entering the discussion.

'Your girlfriend, who was supposed to be Sophie's best friend, went to the media and told them Sophie has no skills, and she lost Lukas because she slept around with her ex-boyfriend – I bet she didn't tell you that. Then, of all people, she meets you at the gym and let me guess... she's been telling you what a great Raven you would make, how powerful you would be, and how you wouldn't put up with any crap from Sophie or me.'

It was lightning fast, and Murdoch's defences were down; Jordan struck him in the face with a tight fist, sending him backward, spiralling to the ground. Bree screamed and ran to Murdoch, who was up before she could reach him.

'Jordan, what the hell!' she yelled as Allanon pushed Jordan back, and Justin watched, shocked.

Murdoch dusted himself down and looked at his nephew. Blood ran from his nose, and he swiped the flow with his hand. The group stilled.

'He didn't mean to—' Allanon interjected.

'Apologise, Jordan,' Bree insisted, glaring at her nephew.

Murdoch's eyes flared black. Not even his family knew what he was capable of doing or the strength it took to restrain himself from instinctively lashing out. His body shook slightly with the restraint of controlling himself.

Generational fear and respect for the Raven ran deep, and his stillness created more fear and caution within them. Jordan had just stirred a beast, and the young man shuffled; his bravado slipped. The air around them felt thick. The silence that descended was deafening. Not even the night noises of nature or the distant sound of a car could be heard.

A glance at the surrounding trees made Murdoch's eyes darken to the full spectrum of black, and Allanon followed his gaze and gasped. The branches were lined with black birds – Ravens.

'Christ,' Allanon muttered. 'Go,' he whispered to his wife, hurriedly pushing her away, and Murdoch could sense her fear as she did as asked, departing quickly without looking back – heading inside to the children.

Justin moved in front of his brother in an extraordinary display of braveness. 'Uncle, I apologise on behalf of Jordan. Violence is never the answer, and your questions certainly did not provoke that response,' he said most eloquently. 'But Jordan really likes Lucy, and none of us wants to see him hurt or betrayed.'

All eyes were upon Murdoch. Justin remained in front of his twin, oddly sacrificing himself for his stronger, reactive brother.

Murdoch nodded his thanks to Justin. He swallowed and reined in his pain and anger; the power required to do so drained him when his body was still recovering. His eyes lightened in colour, and he looked at the trees and slightly inclined his head. The birds rose from the branches, flying into the night. He heard Allanon exhale with relief.

'I will let you have that blow this time, Jordan, since I misread the depth of your feelings for her and for your brother's sake. But know this. Next time, regardless of family, love and loyalty, you will not be as fortunate, nor can I guarantee my restraint.'

Jordan swallowed and nodded.

'She has chosen you for a reason,' Murdoch added. 'I am not saying you are not worthy of love, but I know her. *She* is not worthy of you.'

Murdoch saw Jordan's defences fall; his body deflated at his uncle's compliment. Murdoch nodded to his brother and Justin, and walked away. He heard Jordan exhale, and his brother allowed him to leave, knowing it was safer for all of them. Lucy would keep for now, but Murdoch had no doubt of the alliance forming.

Sophie pulled herself up the ladder to the attic and flicked on a light switch within reach. One bulb hanging from the ceiling came on, lighting the room sufficiently and surprising her that it still worked. It was an angular space, as most attics were, with large timber beams high above them showing the bones of the roof.

'Safe to enter,' she joked, making way for Mel to come off the ladder and sneezing several times as the dust was disturbed by their entrance. 'I think I've wasted your time,' Sophie said, glancing around.

The attic was oddly empty. Given Aunt Daphne's house was full of curiosities, Sophie expected the opposite – a cluttered collection.

'Wow,' Mel said, looking around once she had stepped off the ladder. 'I thought we would be wading through clutter and relics.'

'Me too, it's a bit disappointing. But then again, if it was full of old, dusty garbage, that would have been worse.'

'True,' Mel said, 'we'll find what you were looking for sooner.' Several large timber trunks were pushed to the corner of the room, along with a painting easel... as if it were a long-forgotten hobby.

Something furry scurried by them. Both ladies yelped and jumped out of its path. Nikolas appeared.

'What?' he looked around, ducking in the lower part of the room. He was still dressed in his work suit and looked less than impressed at his dusty surroundings.

'Mouse, I think,' Sophie said and shuddered.

Nikolas rolled his eyes and straightened. Mel laughed.

'You are such a great protector,' Sophie teased him. 'Thanks for coming to my rescue yet again. But we should get a system going. What if I'm watching a horror movie and scream... I'd hate to waste your time.'

'What if you are in the throes of passion,' Mel said wide-eyed. 'If you're a screamer, Nikolas might appear.'

He gave them both a wry look. 'I don't need to see that. A system then. Yell my name.'

Sophie nodded and then bit her lip. 'As long as I remember to do that under duress. What if I'm being kidnapped and I scream, but before I can yell your name, a hand goes across my mouth, and I can't get the word out!'

'Then you are on your own,' Nikolas said and grinned as she narrowed her eyes at him. 'Where are we?'

'In Aunt Daphne's attic. She told me today that one of Elsopeth's diaries is here.'

'You saw her today? Deceased Daphne?'

'She dropped in for tea when I summoned her,' Sophie gloated.

'Well, aren't you getting better at this witch stuff,' Nikolas teased her.

'Sure am, so be warned! Speaking of which, will you transform for us, become your wolf dog?'

'No, and you won't wear me down.'

She pouted and Mel laughed.

'Okay, maybe one day I will,' he conceded, and Sophie smiled. 'I'm out of here since you don't need me.' He looked around. 'I thought Daphne would be a huge hoarder, given how much stuff she had downstairs in the house.'

'So did we. Maybe she had everything she owned on display,' Sophie said and shrugged. 'Sorry, I hope I didn't interrupt something important by screaming.'

'I was just leaving work.'

'Will you come back later and become a wolf?'

Mel laughed again at her persistence.

He rolled his eyes. 'You are adamant to see the wolf, aren't you?'

'I can't wait,' she admitted. 'I want to run my hand through your fur,' she teased.

He groaned. 'I'm never telling you anything again that you can use against me.'

'I'm serious,' she said sincerely.

'It would be the coolest thing to have a boyfriend who could turn into a wolf,' Mel said and sighed. 'You'd always feel safe.'

'Go on, wolf for us,' Sophie begged.

Nikolas smiled and shook his head. 'One day, when you least expect it, I'll appear as the wolf. Listen out for a growl.'

'Really?' Sophie said, excited. 'When, though? One day soon?'

'Maybe.' He disappeared.

'Yeah, I won't hold my breath,' she said to the space where he once stood. 'I'll take this trunk. Want to take that one?'

'Yes!' Mel raced to it.

They both opened the lids and gasped, looking at each other.

'Mine's empty,' Sophie said, her voice falling flat.

'Mine too.'

'I think this attic was once full, and someone's cleared out Aunt Daphne's stuff. But why?' Sophie sank and sat cross-legged next to the trunk.

'Witch goods' sales?' Mel suggested. 'I bet everything in here was sold.'

Sophie laughed and then sobered. 'Really? Is there such a thing?'

'You bet. Daphne's stuff would go for a high price given she was really respected for her skills.'

'But she wasn't a witch, just a cursed clairvoyant.'

'She had power and the sight, that's enough for some collectors,' Mel said most knowledgeably on the subject.

Sophie shook her head. 'The world is just too weird.' And then a thought occurred to her; she knelt up, put her hand tentatively inside the trunk to see if it had a false bottom and gasped.

'Mel! The trunk is full, look!' They could now see the contents – layers of women's clothing carefully laid out with fabric and tissue paper around them.

'Oh my, that's brilliant!' Mel gasped. 'Daphne must have got Orli to make them look empty to protect the goods.'

Sophie shook her head. 'Aunt Daphne keeps surprising.'

'There must be something good in here then,' Mel said, looking at the trunk nearest her. 'Shall I?'

'Yes, please,' Sophie said and watched.

'It doesn't work for me,' Mel said, sinking her hand into the trunk and finding it empty. Sophie stood and hurried to Mel's chest, wading her hand in and the spell of cover lifted. It was full of trinkets and several books.

'Amazing,' Mel proclaimed.

'Oh good, diaries, hopefully!' Sophie brightened. She returned to her trunk and removed the first few layers of clothing. They were tagged.

'Look at this, Mel, it's like a collection of cursed outfits. Maybe each of the accursed ancestors donated an item.' She held up a striking patterned dress. 'I remember Aunt Daphne wearing this outfit when she was in her forties, she loved it.' Below was a military uniform with a tag reading "Aircraftwoman Margaret Dillon 1942". Sophie dug deeper and found a very flattened ballgown with the label "Miss Hannah Shelby 1879".

'You will have to add an outfit,' Mel suggested, 'something that says "you".'

Sophie chuckled. 'Jeans and white runners. Or my boots. Rather unglamorous compared to these. I should get some mannequins and put them on display in that long hallway.

The accursed through time,' Sophie said, brightening at the thought. 'What have you got?'

'Some nice art deco stuff. I'm sure Lukas would love that old clock and watch.'

Sophie studied them and agreed. 'Let's keep them out for him.'

'And, five volumes – diaries,' Mel counted them and handed them over. She looked into the bottom of the chest and lifted out a large cloth dress bag. 'Ooh, I think this is another dress.'

Mel placed the bag down and started to open the layers. 'It's wrapped in cotton muslin,' she said, looking up at Sophie. 'My great grandma used it to preserve fabrics, so this dress has to be old.'

Sophie moved closer to help unpack the carefully preserved dress that appeared to be quite elaborate when revealed – an exquisite gown in pale pink and white satin with cream lacing that had yellowed only a little over time. Miniature pink roses were embroidered around the neckline, and a wide pink satin ribbon featured below the bustline.

'Wow, it's so feminine. Whoever owned this must have come from money,' Mel said. 'It's beautiful.'

'It's held up rather well,' Sophie said, lifting the top half gently out of the bag. 'Look!'

A label inside read "E. Rayne".

'This dress didn't belong to one of the cursed; it belonged to Elsopeth Rayne and was probably stored with her diary,' Sophie said, touching the fabric gently. 'How amazing to think one of my ancestors wore this.'

'Maybe Elsopeth wore it when Nikolas or Murdoch were romancing her, and she swooned and fanned herself,' Mel said, making the actions.

Sophie laughed. 'Or she didn't put up with either of them and used that fan to beat them away! The diary will tell.' She reached for the five volumes and glanced into each one. They were all written by Elsopeth – the 19th-century Elsopeth. 'Excellent.'

'More research on just what kind of witch you are!' Mel exclaimed.

'Or hope to be,' Sophie added and returned the dress to the bag, covering it with the fabric. She vowed to try the dress on later that night when alone... the temptation was too great not to do so.

CHAPTER 21

J ORDAN WAS QUIET AS he drove Lucy home after the family evening celebrations. He regretted falling out with his uncle. As a kid, he had always loved and looked up to Murdoch; he wanted to be just like him. It wouldn't have been so bad if he hadn't struck him, but his fists were always faster than his mouth, and the birthday atmosphere was strained after that. Jordan was conscious of Lucy's hand rubbing up and down his leg as he drove, but Murdoch's words kept running through his mind.

She has an agenda. Meeting you was too coincidental. She is not worthy of you.

Then his anger flared at Murdoch for protecting the cursed witch, and he allowed Lucy to regain a hold of his affections.

'I really like your family,' she said, 'thanks for introducing me. You will have to meet mine next.'

He glanced at her and smiled. 'Yeah, that'd be good. My kin liked you too, except for Murdoch.'

Lucy gave a little shrug. 'Every family has one,' she said and made him laugh. 'Justin told me you visited Sophie to stir her up, and she retaliated. He seemed to regret it.'

'He's like Uncle Allanon, too compassionate for his own good; I've got to watch out for him,' Jordan said. 'That was pretty brave what he did tonight, though, stepping in front of me like that.'

'I saw you from the kitchen window. I thought you'd push him away and stand up to Murdoch more,' Lucy said, 'or did you not want to embarrass Justin?'

Jordan gave a brief nod. 'Justin's the peacekeeper... if he steps in, I've learnt to let him, mainly because he's not a fighter, and I don't want to put him in harm's way. Besides, he's good for me and reminds me to shut up occasionally.'

Lucy squeezed his arm and smiled. 'Weird how you can be so physically alike as twins and so different.'

'Yeah. It's good, too. We don't attract the same girls, so more for me,' he said in jest.

She smiled. 'That's for sure. I like my men strong and bold, who stand up for things and go for it when they think something is wrong, like you did about Sophie.'

Her words started to ring hollow, and everything she said made Jordan wonder if she did have an agenda. She had just brought the subject back to Sophie again.

Jordan's eyes narrowed, thinking about the accursed. 'Yeah, Uncle Murdoch wouldn't have had his accident if the witch hadn't pushed him to the edge. I just wanted to let her know she is being watched.'

Lucy turned side on to face him. 'Let's do it again, now. The two of us.'

He glanced her way and back at the road. 'Yeah?'

'Yeah! Why should Justin have all the fun? Take me along this time, please,' she begged. 'Why not?'

'Because the family has warned me not to do it, and because I can make a fast getaway, you can't.'

'Then we'll stir her to come out into the garden and I can make a subtle escape while you freak her out a little more. You can come to me wherever I'm waiting. It'll be fun!'

'You're a wicked girl, Lucy, my babe,' he said, warming to the idea, a smile spreading across his face.

She leaned over, giving Jordan a good view of her cleavage should he take his eyes off the road. 'Let's do it, Raven-to-be,' she teased, and he laughed with pleasure.

'Why not,' he said, turning his car towards Sophie's mansion. 'Spook and run.'

'Spook and run,' she agreed, smiling like the cat that had got the cream.

After Mel had turned in for the night and Bette Davis had settled herself in her usual comfortable position on the end of the bed, Sophie studied Elsopeth's gown draped over a chair in the corner of the room. It was stunning. Mel was right; the detail spoke of money, the fabric was thick, satin, and high quality, and she could imagine a woman of wealth and class wearing the gown. Sophie gently touched and lifted the fabric of the skirt; it was heavy, but it didn't have the full skirt that Elsopeth, who tripped into the Raven's arms in 1744, would have worn. It was straight and layered; Sophie imagined it would highlight the figure and make a lovely silhouette in a ballroom or formal garden.

From the date in one of the journals from the trunk, Sophie guessed the dress was worn around 1825, and hopefully, Elsopeth would write about wearing it. Pink and white colouring, the breasts were meant to feature and heave no doubt, Sophie thought, amused, and below the bustline was a pink satin ribbon that tied around the back drawing the bodice in closer against the body. The detail on the neckline, small sleeves, and hemline was beautiful – lace with small roses stitched above it. So feminine and sweet. Was the 1825 Elsopeth a sweet girl?

Sophie stripped, headed to the shower and afterwards, scurried through her underwear draw to find a bra that would push her cleavage higher to match the dress and small satin pants that matched in colour – not that Elsopeth would have worn anything as racy as that under her clothing back then. Still, Sophie wanted to feel beautiful, even if she was alone and her love life was a mess.

Non-existent more like it, she scoffed. 'I've got a guy who can't come near me for fear he'll extinguish me, another who is romancing me subtly but pretending he's not, yep, clearly I'm a catch,' she told Bette Davis. Next, Sophie retrieved a pair of white ballet slippers she had worn in some production a few years back and slipped them on.

Sophie lay the dress on the bed without disturbing Bette Davis and undid the small clasp at the back of the neck. She left as many of the clips done up as possible, knowing she couldn't reach them otherwise and lifting the skirts, she lowered the dress over her head. It felt heavy, cool and silky on her skin. Turning, she faced the mirror and couldn't help but admire her reflection and the feminine dress. She did up the clasps at the back and tied the ribbon below her bustline. Sophie fluffed out her blonde hair and let it loose, unlike the Elsopeth who first wore this dress whose hairstyle would have been coiffured and held in place with pins to show off an elegant neckline. But it was late in the evening, and it was a small concession she could justify should she have company by saying she was preparing for bed.

Sophie smiled and turned side on and back, feeling the small swish of the skirt.

'So feminine,' she said, giving a low bow to an imaginary dance partner before swirling around the room. She stopped to accept a make-believe glass of champagne, sip it daintily, and observe the pleasantries of the dance with other guests and her imaginary dance partner. A banging noise interrupted her fantasy.

What was that?

A noise downstairs, like a window was being rattled, tested for entry, and again. She strained, listening. Bette Davis lifted her head; she had registered the noise. At that moment, Sophie wished she had a large dog instead of a cat, and thought momentarily of Nikolas. She looked down at the dress; there was no time to change, and besides, Mel was in the house – she felt responsible for her.

'I'm protected,' she said quietly, 'Orli's protection charms are in place, don't worry, Bette Davis.' She felt a little easier remembering that, and moving to the bedroom door, Sophie glanced both ways down the hallway, declared it all clear, and ventured to the grand staircase – her nickname for it.

There were no shadows or figures in the windows as Sophie gingerly descended the stairs, lifting her skirt to avoid going head over heels.

'Oh my God,' Mel said, tip-toeing down the hallway in a shiny pair of yellow pyjama pants and a matching oversized top.

'Did you hear it too?' Sophie whispered.

Mel gasped, gaping at Sophie.

'Oh, the dress,' Sophie looked down at her gown, 'I couldn't resist.'

'You freaked me out. I thought I'd stepped back in time and was in some weird sort of portal,' Mel said, her hand on her heart. 'And I did hear it and felt it too.' She held up her hands.

A loud bang on the front door made them both jump, and Mel yelped in fright.

'Who's there?' Sophie called, moving to the door. She glanced out the window nearby but could see nothing or no one near the door, on the steps or in the garden nearby.

'There's a force out there again,' Mel said, moving her fingers. 'I'm tingling, but it's not as strong as last time.'

Again, there was banging on the door, something hit the window making Sophie scream. The thumping and rattling increased as a wind out of nowhere felt like it shook the house to its foundations.

'Do you think one of Murdoch's nephews is here to scare me again?' Sophie yelled to Mel over the roar of the wind. 'Maybe he's had a big night on the drink and wants to stir up more trouble.'

'It feels like the same as before,' Mel said, 'only not quite as strong.' She wrapped her arms around her, and Sophie saw Mel's eyes were huge with fear.

Sophie reached for the door handle.

'No!' Mel yelled. 'We're safe in here. If Orli has spells in place, we should stay in.'

'Mel, this is not fair on you or me,' Sophie said, jumping again at a hit on the glass panel nearest her. 'Please go to your room and lock the door. I'll give you the all-clear when you can come out.'

'No, I can't leave–'

'You need to. I am not putting up with this,' Sophie flinched again as she heard glass shatter and several garden lights went out, their bulbs and glass shells fracturing. 'Quick, Mel, go.'

Mel turned and ran down the hallway to her room, and with her gone from sight, Sophie yelled out, 'Nikolas, help!'

Without waiting, she opened the door and stepped outside. The wind whipped Sophie's hair around her; it was darker now, and the closest garden lights were shattered. She heard a gasp, a female voice, and a male laugh.

'Show yourself,' Sophie demanded, and not seeing the force that was present, she was shoved, falling back into the doorway. Sophie scurried to her feet and rushed down the front stairs, her hands raised to retaliate. The flying dust and leaves made it hard to keep her eyes open, and the wind whipped her hair around her. It was then that Sophie heard a low feral growl. The atmosphere shifted; there was movement and a rush, and then everything stilled, not a sound or a voice. She was alone – temporarily blinded by dust and the force of the wind.

Sophie blinked rapidly to clear her vision and stepped into the garden, realising that she was walking in the footsteps of her ancestor, wearing the dress she once wore, maybe even in the company of a man she once met here. Treading along the path in her delicate ballet slippers, she avoided the broken glass and raised her skirt slightly as she ventured deeper into the garden and crossed the small bridge over the ornamental creek. Then, she heard a low growl again, closer this time and whipping around, an enormous white wolf appeared through the tree line.

Sophie gasped. 'Nikolas?'

It nodded, perhaps so she would not fear it, and came towards her. The wolf was beautiful, and she could see its dark eyes, Nikolas's eyes. Hesitantly, Sophie reached out her hand and touched it, the wolf muzzled her hand with affection and Sophie smiled.

'My, you are beautiful. Thank you for coming.'

The pair walked back to the house together.

The last time Murdoch had flown, it hadn't ended well. Fuelled by exhaustion and despair, he flew until he fell from the sky. He wasn't keen to retake flight anytime soon, but he knew Jordan was up to something; he could sense it, or maybe it was the cop in him that recognised Lucy would lead Jordan astray and get him in trouble. If she was true to form and with his nephew primed for a purpose, the sooner she could accomplish her mission – destroy Sophie – the better. Murdoch needed to warn Sophie, and yeah, he wanted to see her and this was a valid excuse.

As he drove away from his brother's house, he thought of how to warn her – tap her a message, contact the Lens family, or send a message via Allanon. None appealed to him because his heart was pumping, and his need to see her was constantly intruding every moment of the day and night. The mention of her name or the reminders of her existence made it worse. Murdoch had to pass her mansion on his way home; he decided to drive by and see if her lights were on.

And then what? Wait until her lights go off and go in? Try and reach her in a dream?

Risk it and call her down to the garden?

Murdoch hated it when he was logical, but his feelings for Sophie quickly rendered him irrational. He drove past her home and returned, parking outside the perimeter and cutting the ignition. He watched as lights in various rooms on different levels went on and off until several hours later, it was just her bedroom light left on upstairs.

Murdoch felt better for being there; knowing she was nearby greatly eased his suffering. He wondered if she could sense him; her protector most likely could.

Just then, Murdoch sat upright. He recognised the car; Jordan parked away from him, not seeing his uncle or expecting to see him in the dark car nearby. He and Lucy got out of the car, laughing and holding hands. Murdoch's anger rose. He checked his car's interior light was off and quietly exited. Murdoch knew the grounds so well that he easily shadowed them to the entrance of Sophie's home.

They were going to taunt her. Lucy was egging Jordan on, laughing and flirting, getting him to use his limited witch powers to create a false storm and aggressive front. Murdoch's blood boiled; he had warned Jordan. Their assault began... amateur stuff, thumping, howling, Lucy whooping, hissing and clinging on to Jordan. Expecting Sophie or her protector to storm out of the house, Murdoch vowed not to interfere until he needed to; he would deal with Jordan later. He saw his nephew send Lucy back to the car, and she ran laughing back through the trees, not seeing or sensing him nearby. She had no powers to speak of, only intuition, which he noticed did not serve her well, given an aggressive, powerful male could have reached out and grabbed her as she ran past and finished her life effortlessly.

And then, he sensed the protector arriving. The shapeshifter in his wolf form was trailing through the garden towards Jordan; the door flung open. Elsopeth came out onto the balcony in all her beauty... her hair wild about her, wearing a pale pink gown, looking more beautiful than he remembered. She raised her hands, and all stilled. Murdoch saw Jordan using his skills to vanish, and from where he stood, he could see Jordan reappear near the car where Lucy waited. His nephew jumped into the vehicle, grinning like some kid who had just played his first prank, and the pair sped away.

Murdoch turned back to the house, Elsopeth was in the garden now, her hand on the wolf's head, like Murdoch had seen before. The growl he heard was from his own chest, not that of the wolf, and they disappeared inside, Elsopeth closing the door behind her.

CHAPTER 22

NIKOLAS EMERGED FROM THE bathroom in a T-shirt that only just fitted him and a pair of running shorts that belonged to Mel, and while they were long enough, they left a lot to be desired.

Sophie laughed at seeing him.

'Maybe you should leave a few things here in case you wolf-out and can't go home naked,' she teased.

'Wolf-out? Is that like max-out?'

'The same. You are a beautiful wolf.'

'It's been said,' he teased, accepting the coffee she had made for them both while he was changing. They sat on the seat in the bay window of her bedroom, looking out at the garden and peering into the shadowy patches where the lights had been shattered, leaving a spill of darkness. Sophie looked the part wearing her ancestor's dress and sitting in the frame of the old-fashioned window seat.

'You look most becoming,' Nikolas said, and Sophie grinned.

'Most becoming? How easily you fall back into "old" speak,' she teased him, 'but thank you, kind Sir.'

He chuckled. 'Dare I ask why? A costume party or a siren call?'

Sophie noticed his demeanour was playful, but his eyes and tight smile betrayed an element of possessiveness. She kept her response light, not wishing to hurt or offend him.

'I was playing dress up. After you left the attic, Mel and I found this and some of the clothes the accursed wore in one of the trunks. It's rather beautiful.' She ran her hand over her satin skirt.

'It is that.'

'Thank you for coming over. Mel thinks it was the same force as last time, but not as strong.'

'Probably just one of the two nephew idiots then,' Nikolas said drily. 'I wonder if the Raven knows.'

'I could message him, but he might not care. He might think that's the least I deserve,' Sophie said, giving a small shrug.

Nikolas looked out into the dark garden. 'He's out there.'

Sophie snapped to look at him and then out the window. 'Who? The Raven?'

Nikolas nodded. 'He's in the garden. I don't think he comes every night. I would have sensed it, but he's here tonight.'

'Was he here when the attack happened? That would mean he was okay with it then.' Sophie's eyes narrowed with anger.

Nikolas did not deny it. 'He was here, he is your enemy,' he said bluntly.

'Maybe Mel should move out for her own safety.'

'Maybe you both should. The offer still stands for you and Mel to crash at my place.'

'Thanks,' Sophie said but shook her head in the negative. 'I'm not running from my home because of him or his dopey nephews or whoever the force is that's giving me a hard time. I'm supposed to be a strong witch... bring it on.'

Nikolas sighed. 'Yeah, I was worried you'd say that. I should stay.'

'I'll be fine, thanks. You will be the first I call if I need to. She studied him and smiled. 'Come as a wolf anytime.'

'You liked the hairy beast, huh?' he teased.

'What's not to like?' Sophie said with a smile that spoke of sincerity before turning her gaze again to the garden. She could easily allow the handsome, enigmatic Nikolas Saggers to romance her, but her heart had not closed to Murdoch yet, and she needed that closure. She could not do what Elsopeth did and be torn between them both, and she sensed Nikolas knew that which is why he was slowly winning his way into her affection but not taking it that step further, not risking rejection.

'It's the dress. I bet that's what's drawn the Raven here tonight. I wonder if he can sense Elsopeth from it,' Sophie said, returning her attention to the room and looking at the pink gown she wore and pooled around her.

'It is beautiful; you look beautiful in it,' Nikolas said candidly and comfortably.

'Really? Thank you. I bet you're quite adept at complimenting the ladies in ballgowns.'

He laughed. 'Plenty of practice, but only when deserving. I remember Elsopeth wearing it.'

'Do you?' Sophie's eyes lit up. 'Tell me about it, please.'

He leant back on the bay window frame. 'Okay. It was a dark and stormy night...'

Sophie frowned at him, and he laughed.

'Oh, you want the real version?'

'Yes, including the compliments,' she said, taking another sip of her coffee and preparing for a recollection that she hoped would give her the male romantic perspective. 'Remember, I've found the 1825 diaries of Elsopeth, so I will be cross-checking your account.'

'Ah,' he said, grimacing, 'then I can't make up a story for the blanks in my memory.'

She gave him a smirk, and Nikolas looked her in the eyes and said, 'Trust me, the last time I saw Elsopeth in that dress, I will never forget. It nearly killed me.' He brightened. 'Do you have my ancestor's volume here?'

'Right here,' Sophie said having read from it only last evening. She fetched it, and he seemed to know exactly where the entry was recorded.

'Allow me to read it straight from my ancestor's lips.'

Sophie happily agreed and sat back to enjoy his reading.

Extract from the journals of The Duke of Montmount, Nikolas Charles Saggers

March 19, 1825

A desperate situation

My estates were in order, and the accounts were up to date – I have a new and very good bookkeeper assistant for that – Mr William Burton. Nevertheless, the estates still require my vigilance. Thus, today we rode to the farthest village to inspect the tenants' properties; I make this journey every six months or so depending on the season and demands on my schedule. My young assistant, William, was with me. He was the son of a friend, and I agreed as a favour to offer him a position in my employ. William was proving to be a keen and clever young man.

As well as my work with the tenants, we intended to stay the week at my country estate as the ride was taxing, and it allowed me extra time for any unfinished business and to be seen, which is the expectation in the village of a duke. Of course, we had not managed to avoid the expected invitations from those in our social set including an offer to dinner at the Howlett's residence this evening with a group of the village's influential figures and dinner the following evening at the priest's humbler abode. No doubt some of the ladies were also hurriedly arranging a ball so all the single daughters of consequence could be paraded. Word spread fast when the house staff heard of my imminent visit.

William was excited. It was above his station, and he would enjoy the spoils of a life he hoped for in the future. The first night we stopped at an inn not far from the village so the next day's journey would be short and I could arrive early, work for the day, and then it was only a short trip to my estate. William had done an admirable job organising our time – we met tenants at the arranged hour and had tradesmen at our call. The tenants had cleaned and prepared their properties as expected – they were hard-working and respectable people. I agreed to new roofing for several cottages, new fencing where required, and I ensured those families who had just celebrated births were given a gift of money and linen to assist. My visit was welcome when there were rewards to be had.

We arrived at my country estate late in the day, and the servants had everything prepared. I was pleased that William was humble and polite and did not let his elevated position make him arrogant. I was often asked if he were my younger brother; we were both tall, with dark hair and dark eyes, but that's where the comparison ended. William was not of magical persuasion and must never see me when I run at night.

He was shown to his rooms, and I retired to bathe and change; an hour later, we departed for dinner at the Howlett residence bordering my estate – I took William as he was invited and why should I suffer alone. Their home was imposing, the grounds even more so and as we exited from the carriage, I could hear laughter and lively chatter from within. It sounded like it was not going to be an intimate dinner.

William laughed at my reticence, but it was still a novelty for him. I braced myself, adopted my smile and accepted the bows required to a duke, meeting Mr Howlett senior, his wife, two married sons, their wives, another single son, the great aunt, and several guests staying with them for a brief while. William was in the company of the Howletts' unmarried son of similar age.

Just when I thought I had been introduced to all present, two young misses entered the room laughing and then restrained themselves on seeing the company gathered.

'Forgive us, Father, we were late returning from town,' a beautiful young woman said and curtsied. She moved slightly, allowing me to see the girl who had come in behind her.

'My daughter, Caroline,' Mr Howlett said, offering Caroline an indulgent smile, 'and her friend, Miss Elsopeth Rayne.'

'Your Grace,' Elsopeth said, surprised at seeing me and dropping into the customary curtsy.

I bowed, momentarily lost for words. 'Miss Caroline, Miss Elsopeth,' was the best I could do. The last time I had seen Elsopeth, she had danced with me at a ball and refused a second dance claiming her card was full. The Raven had appeared to claim her but I was out riding the next day and came upon her again. Or rather, she passed me on her mount, inviting a chase, so of course I had to accept. We had a lovely morning sharing our mutual passion for riding and trekking through the woods. Many young ladies would not want to get their boots dirty.

And here she is, in all her beauty, in a pale pink dress, stealing my heart. I could see no one else in the room. Fortunately, I was able to steal some time with her before being seated at the dining table.

'This is a surprise.'

'Caroline is a friend I met through our great aunts who play bridge together. I am often

invited to the estate and I much prefer the
country to the city.'

'As do I. Have you been riding?'

She gave me a smile that said she well
remembered our last encounter.

'Often, and here. I shall be riding in the morning
in the woods. There are many wonderful trails.'

'I know.'

'Of course,' she flushed, 'this is where you have
your country estate.'

'Adjoining this one,' I informed her. 'May I join
you?'

'Yes, please,' she said most enthusiastically, and the morning could not come soon enough. I then had to endure sitting opposite the senior Howletts; Elsopeth was seated opposite the Howletts' single son of marriageable age. I was not happy and entirely distracted watching them talk and laugh. I had the pleasure of speaking with her again briefly and sitting through a musical recital she was invited to give with Caroline. Then, the great-aunt sat and played the piano and encouraged us to dance. I wasted no time asking Elsopeth for a dance and she graced me with a turn of the floor.

As we whirled around the dance floor, Elsopeth looking so feminine and spirited in her beautiful pale dress, I knew this would be the woman I would spend my life with, until Miss Caroline Howlett suggested with a laugh that Elsopeth did not monopolise my time. My anger rose in a flash but turned to ice as Caroline teased Elsopeth, saying, 'after all, you are betrothed to Lord Ashcroft, are you not?'

The Raven. The thought was a stab to my heart.

Sophie gasped at Nikolas's passionate reading of the story. 'Again? Is it always you two in pursuit of the same lady?'

'Yes, and it has only ever been one lady,' Nikolas clarified. 'I have never won.'

'Never? Perhaps that is not your destiny then,' Sophie said, studying him. 'Maybe there is someone else for you.'

He cleared his throat and rose.

'Maybe. Thank you for the coffee. You know how to reach me,' he said with a small smile, and with Sophie's thanks ringing in his ears, Nikolas vanished in his customary fashion.

She sighed, knowing she had hurt him with her casualness, but it was the best she could do for now. A glance to the clock told her it was just after midnight; Sophie rose, and with another inspection of herself in the mirror, she ran a brush through her hair, which had become quite tangled from the wind earlier, and set out to face Murdoch head-on. She would go to the garden and see if he was still present, even if she had to play the role of Elsopeth to protect them both.

Sophie debated whether to put her hair up as Elsopeth would have worn it but decided against it. She was sure the Murdoch of the past had run his hands through Elsopeth's long hair many a time, releasing the pins and savouring seeing her behind closed doors. A thought occurred to her, and she opened her closet and scurried through a box of Aunt Daphne's remembrances, finding the Old English Lavender perfume her aunt favoured. No doubt it was a fragrance that women of Elsopeth's era would have dabbed on themselves along with talcum powder. She found both and applied them liberally.

'I can play this role,' she said to herself in the mirror. 'I am an actress at heart.'

Lowering her chin and eyes, she prepared to play the demure lady of the house and departed her room, taking the stairs to the front door, where she drew a deep breath. She would have to remain in character, speak with the gentility of the past, or say very little at all to be safe and allow him to lead. It was a price she was more than willing to pay. Sophie opened the front door.

CHAPTER 23

MURDOCH DECIDED TO DRAW Sophie – Elsopeth – to the window, as he regularly did a century ago. Sensing the protector was gone, he stood below the wing of the mansion that housed her room, waiting as he once did for her to appear in all her fineness, her eyes as willing to see him, her hand quick to take his own. He considered whether he should have changed into formal wear rather than his work suit and was relieved that at least he had gone straight to his brother's from work and not changed into jeans... would Elsopeth have rejected him in confusion? But this wasn't a dream. Nevertheless, it was Elsopeth... he knew that dress; he had proposed to her when she wore it and being sentimental, he assumed Elsopeth had preserved the dress in memory of that night.

Before Murdoch could decide on the safest course of action to protect them both from the rage that fought with his passion, the front door opened, and he turned towards it.

Elsopeth appeared, slightly lifting her skirt to take the few steps down into the garden. His heart stilled, she had that power over him from the first day he set eyes on her, that was the last day he would call Venetia his love.

Elsopeth looked around as if seeking him and continued down into the garden, through the maze of trees, along the path and over the small bridge. He followed her, and sensing him, she whirled around, her breath hitching.

'Murdoch!' Her hand went to her heart. Then she whispered, 'Lord Ashcroft' and curtsied.

He fought the instinct to rush to her and forced himself to remain rooted on the spot, only her name escaping his lips.

'Elsopeth.'

They stood transfixed by the relief of seeing each other, suspending all the emotions that were to follow.

'It might be dangerous to come to me,' he said. From where he stood, he could smell her familiar lavender scent and the freshness of her skin. He closed his eyes momentarily to regain himself. When he opened them, she was still there in all her beauty; it was not a dream, but it was her and he didn't care to question how or why, he just desired her ravenously.

'I don't care if I am in danger, and I do not believe that. It is worse for me not to be by your side,' Elsopeth said, and then she lifted her dress slightly and started towards him. Murdoch needed no further encouragement and rushed to her, holding her so tightly that both felt relief ebbing through them.

'I have missed you,' he whispered into her hair.

'I have been waiting for you, day in, day out.'

'I know... but the other half... it's a serious matter – your life. I've been waiting so long, I wouldn't risk that.'

'But I am Elsopeth now; we are in no danger,' she said, and he sensed the fear within her regardless of her words of bravery. Murdoch was conscious that their intimacy in this generation had been in sleep, through dreams, in stolen time, but the Elsopeth of his past was no stranger to his lovemaking, and he wanted to keep it that way so he could have her here and now. Her actions told him she felt the same way; her hands travelled up his back, touching his neck and down his arms, the need burning through his suit jacket.

'I have to have you,' he hissed, his body in turmoil. 'How you tempt me, Elsopeth.'

'Then take me,' Elsopeth insisted. 'Here, now, Murdoch.'

Murdoch needed no encouragement; it was as if she offered a drowning man a cool glass of water and refusal was not possible. Removing his coat, he lay it on the grass mound bordering the small pond lit by the lamps that remained unbroken. He lowered Elsopeth to it and was surprised how keenly she embraced his lovemaking, with a hunger that he thought only he possessed.

It was as if the floodgates within him opened to emotion; she filled him, and the need to be inside her was so overwhelming. When they connected, they both inhaled with the relief it provided. Murdoch slowed himself; he needed this to last in case he couldn't see her again in her guise as Elsopeth.

'I love you,' she whispered as he moved in and out of her, slowly, needy, building the passion for both. He looked at her, the flush of love on her face, but Murdoch was surprised to see tears in her eyes; Elsopeth had never been one to show raw emotion.

He responded, touching her cheek. 'I love you, always have, always will.'

Murdoch strived to be gentle, keeping his movements slow, which was nothing short of agony given his state of arousal. But the pain was exquisite, and the release was shattering and glorious – that was the word Elsopeth whispered as she came down from her place of exultation. They lay together in the cool, dark night, dressing enough to be modest and laying in each other's arms.

'When can you next see me?' Elsopeth asked, touching his rough cheek where the day's stubble had begun to appear.

'When you can next appear as yourself or call me in a dream,' he confirmed. 'Not before, for fear I will... you know.' He didn't want to mention the need to find a solution or refer to the now in case the moment snapped and his violence came to the fore.

She sat up slightly, and being the gentleman, Murdoch rose to assist her to her feet.

'I best let you return to your bed.' He brushed himself off as Elsopeth straightened her dress, and then she took a deep breath and became most serious.

'Murdoch...'

'Yes?' he responded, leaning down to retrieve his jacket off the lawn and dusting it off.

'How will you know it is me? How do I let you know I need to see you?'

'I will be watching you, as I am meant to,' he said, his voice a little threatening and he started to back away.

She gave a brisk nod and, lifting her skirts, headed quickly to the house. He watched until she entered, stopping momentarily to look back at him before closing the door.

He exhaled with the turmoil building within him. It would have to do for now. A momentary reprieve where he could convince himself – his inner rage – that he was romancing Elsopeth. If she slipped or appeared as Sophie, he would be responsible for the consequences, and he didn't wish to live with that, ever.

Sophie felt wonderfully light the following day, as if a load had been lifted from her shoulders and the world looked wonderful again.

Mel glanced at her now and then over the top of her teacup and smiled. 'It was truly that good?'

Sophie grinned. 'It truly was, and I will keep up the Elsopeth front for as long as I have to.'

'You will need more dresses then,' Mel stated matter-of-factly.

Sophie's eyes widened. 'Yes! I never thought of that. I don't have time to look through Elsopeth's diaries to find her favourite dresses or colours, but I suspect they were all similar in that era.'

'Maybe Nikolas can tell you,' Mel teased, finishing a bite of toast.

'Hmm, that's risky. I don't want him getting amorous... I just want him protecting me at this stage.'

'I wish Jack was a shapeshift and a grifter.'

'He might be,' Sophie said.

'No, I've read up on grifters... they are unique unto themselves. But don't get me wrong,' she said with a coy look, 'he will be more than enough for me.'

Sophie chuckled. 'I've no doubt he will be. Well, I'll have to visit some of my theatre friends and check out the costume cupboards... I'm bound to find a few suitable dresses.'

They wished each other a good day, and after Mel departed, Sophie poured herself another cup of tea and grabbed her phone. Last night, she had intended to check out more of Hope Yardley's social feed and that of the football player the police had cleared, but she had been distracted. The thought of Murdoch and their garden romp brought a smile to her face again. It felt so right, oddly, given that their time together in this generation had been minimal – more in the pursuit of crime-solving than romance- but that pursuit had produced hours and hours in each other's company. Perhaps the concept of a soul mate was real.

'Time for a little research,' Sophie said, focussing her attention on Hope's social pages again and thumbing through the images. She could not see the woman who brought Hope the drink at the bar. Sophie moved on to search for the football player Matt Sutton. He was a big deal – young, handsome, newly-appointed captain of the Vikings and the world at his feet.

'Bet you've got an influencer girlfriend hanging off your arm, Matt,' Sophie said, studying him. He didn't have his own social media footprint, which impressed her, given he could be making a killing from sponsor endorsements as a lot of the big names did. Maybe he was nice and down to earth like Gerard and Rachel had claimed. Instead, she found the Vikings' social media pages and discovered the recent Best and Fairest award night photos. Scrolling through all the shots of the players in black tie with their gorgeous girls on their arms, she found Matt and gasped.

It was her! The woman from the hotel who brought Hope a drink was on Matt's arm. A million thoughts rushed through Sophie's mind.

So, this was Matt's fiancée?

Why was she in the bar?

Was she a friend of Hope's? No... she must have caught them together, and what... followed Hope back to the bar?

Or was she at the bar and saw them leave?

Sophie hurriedly looked for the caption and the woman's name – Imogen Harper – and a quick search revealed a lot about the girlfriend or rather fiancée of Matt Sutton.

'Woah,' she exclaimed, seeing Imogen's massive number of followers with her beauty and lifestyle presence. 'I imagine Matt is crucial to your profile, Imogen.'

Shot after shot of beautiful Imogen in revealing gym wear and swimwear, pouting, out and about, clinging onto Matt's arm, and on it went. Sophie went to ring Detective Oakley and hesitated. She wanted to see Matt first, to see if, somehow, he was involved or knew something about it. Would he speak with her? Worth a try, she mused and rang the Vikings' club.

'They're here now, training,' the guy who answered the phone told her. 'I can pull him off the field if it's urgent.'

'No, that won't be necessary,' Sophie assured him, 'how long will they be training for this morning?'

'Another hour at least.'

'Thank you, I'm on my way.'

Sophie left a note for Jack, saying that she was working on the case of the missing girl and would arrive before eleven a.m. She grabbed her keys and headed to the Vikings' home ground; not that she had any idea where that was, but her masculine-voiced, well-spoken car navigator knew the way. If only her navigator was dateable and had no hang-ups, Sophie amused herself as she bubbled with excitement about her discovery.

'Thank goodness,' she muttered on her arrival to find a smattering of die-hard fans watching training from the stands, and grateful she wouldn't be the only one. She sat nearby them where she could exit quickly and wait for Matt outside.

Like a footy groupie, she grimaced at the thought. He was easy to pick from the crowd – the boy-next-door good looks, natural flair, with an easy grin. Sophie slipped on her glasses. As he neared while doing training sprints, she could see his recent past, but without direct questions, there was nothing that would assist her line of questioning; she would need to speak with him.

It was another twenty minutes until they were released from training and another fifteen until he appeared showered and heading to his car.

'Matt,' she called, and he looked around warily. Probably accustomed to keen female fans, she thought with a sigh. At least he didn't dive into his car and lock the doors. She made her way to him, leaving her glasses on, which was often tricky given the images swirling above the top frame, but the lenses that Orli had framed for her were just clear glass.

'Hi,' she said, approaching. 'I'm Sophie Carell, I'm working with Detectives Oakley and Fletcher, trying to find Hope.'

'Oh, right.' He licked his lower lip and looked around quickly, ensuring no one was nearby to hear the discussion.

'Can I ask you just two quick questions?' She found numbers worked well, and people rarely objected if they knew escape was imminent.

He nodded. 'Okay, but I told the detectives everything I know.'

'I know, and you are not a suspect, but we're getting desperate to find Hope.'

'Yeah, of course.' He dropped his sports bag on the ground and leaned on his car, looking a little more relaxed now that Sophie had told him he was in the clear. He really was a beautiful specimen of manhood and not polished like she imagined his fiancée would be.

'She was sweet,' he said without prompting. 'I heard they found her body.'

Sophie read the sadness in his voice; she wondered if that was the kind of girl Matt wanted, not the woman who had made a career from being his partner.

'Yes, we had hoped that Hope was still alive.'

He nodded, and Sophie got down to business.

'You met Hope at a bar, I believe. Is that true, and was that the first time you met her?'

'Yep. It was just a drink after the game for one of the guy's birthdays. We aren't allowed to have big drinking sessions during the season. Hope was there, and we got talking.'

Sophie saw from her visions that his story was true. She saw them meeting, introducing themselves and felt the interest between them.

'My second and last question,' she said, 'Was your fiancée, Imogen, with you at any time that evening at the hotel?'

'No, we both had things on that night. I didn't see her until we were in bed.'

And that was a lie.

CHAPTER 24

DETECTIVE GERARD OAKLEY ANSWERED the phone on the second ring.

'Hello, young lady, clairvoyant extraordinaire, solved my case for me?' he teased.

'Yes.'

There was a stunned silence on the line as Sophie waited for him to say something while she watched Matt depart with a wave. She had asked her two questions and kept to her word. Now Sophie had enough for the detectives to step in and do their bit.

'You're serious?' he asked.

'Absolutely, I'd never lie to you about that, especially with so much at stake.' Sophie leaned against her car and looked to the stadium as other players departed after training. 'I'm at the Vikings' home ground, but leaving now. Can you meet me somewhere, or I can come into the office?'

'It's safe to come in; Murdoch's not here,' Gerard said. 'Fletcher and I are both in.'

'On my way.' She hung up, and as she turned to enter her car, she saw him – Murdoch – leaving the stadium. He had been at training, too, asking questions and no doubt double-checking on his partners' first interview takes and talking with Matt Sutton's drinking friends that night. As always, she was struck by his presence: strong, dark, gorgeous. She glanced around for his car and found it between two similar dark vehicles.

He sensed her immediately; their eyes locked. He was the Raven; she was his prey, and her breath hitched at the cold look he gave her. Where was the desperate need and affection from last night? The heat and passion? It was because she was Sophie, dressed as Sophie, and his enemy instinct was inherent.

With the press of a button, she unlocked her car and opened the driver's door without taking her eyes off Murdoch.

She saw him mouth the word "Go", and with that, she slipped into the front seat, locking the door for what good that might do. She started the car and turned to leave. If she was returning to his office, she hoped Gerard intended to call Murdoch and tell him to stay away for a while. It was crazy how nervous she felt, but she feared that side of him as much as she loved the other side.

Could she match him for power? Maybe.

A glance in the rear-view mirror told her Murdoch had not moved, and he stood watching her car until she could no longer see him, and only then did she feel the foreboding chill that surrounded her melt away.

Gerard stood before his whiteboard, looking at the photos pinned by magnets and Rachel's notes.

'You know,' he said to his young partner, 'it shits me when we can't solve a case, but a clairvoyant can. Not that I'm not bloody grateful for the help, but what are we missing?'

Rachel came and stood beside him. She glanced at the photos and shook her head. 'I'll be dammed if I know. I feel like I've lived and breathed this case for a week... it's invaded my sleep... I have no life.'

He huffed in amusement, knowing all too well how a case could consume you. They heard footsteps hurriedly approaching, and both looked to the doorway as Sophie appeared.

'Hi! I haven't got long,' she made her excuses when in essence, she was trying to get away before Murdoch returned.

'He's not here. He rang a minute ago and is off to see Hope's parents,' Gerard assured her, and Sophie visibly relaxed.

'So you won't work with me and Ashcroft when Oakley leaves on his permanent fishing trip?' Rachel asked and smirked at her senior partner.

'Be careful young lady, or I might decide to stay another year,' he threatened her.

Sophie smiled and gave a small shrug. 'We'll work something out. I've got a lead for you on Hope's case... a strong lead.'

Gerard offered her a chair at their small meeting table, and she accepted the coffee Rachel pushed towards her.

'I remembered how you liked it and ordered it when I heard you were coming.'

'Thank you,' Sophie said gratefully, accepting the cafe-made cappuccino and feeling the need for caffeine after what the glasses revealed. Taking a long sip, she noted the strained look on Gerard's worn face and the hopeful expression on Rachel's younger face, and then she gave it to them.

'Matt Sutton's fiancée killed Hope in the bathroom of the hotel. I don't know how yet, as I've only seen it through Matt's eyes, and the body was in a cubicle when he arrived.'

Gerard's eyes narrowed in anger. 'He played us well.'

Sophie nodded. 'I went to training this morning after I found a photo of him and his fiancée on the Vikings' social media pages, and I immediately recognised her as the woman at the bar who bought Hope a drink. I saw her through the barman's gaze,' Sophie hurriedly explained.

'Amazing,' Rachel said in awe.

'Matt helped Imogen get Hope's body to the car, and he followed her in his car while she dumped the car in the dead-end street before they both sped off.'

'I can't believe it,' Gerard said, shocked, and hurriedly added, 'but I do if you've seen it.' He ran a hand over his jaw.

'I wanted him to be innocent; he seemed so genuine,' Rachel said, her voice a mixture of remorse and frustration. 'We've wasted all that time...'

'He still might be innocent,' Sophie said, 'we don't know the full story.'

'How can he be if you saw him assisting in the disposal of a body?' Gerard asked. 'A young woman he had just had sex with is dead, and he helped get rid of her.'

'From the quick images I saw, I believe that he might have been threatened and coerced. Matt looked genuinely shocked and even terrified. The visions were short and sharp, but I heard a snatch where his fiancée said if he didn't help, she would tell everyone he did it. She threatened to ruin his career and his life.'

'She's succeeded at that already,' Rachel said.

'We need to get the fiancée in here now. Imogen?' Gerard asked.

'Imogen Harper,' Sophie informed him.

Rachel's eyes widened. 'I know her. She's an influencer with a huge following. She's very glam.'

'She is,' Sophie agreed. 'Having spoken with Matt, I have to agree with your assessment. He's like a country boy and she seems so worldly.'

'I'd say she's the boss,' Gerard agreed. 'We'll need you to sit in on the interview, can you?'

'Of course,' she nodded. 'I'll leave you to it. Let me know when and where, and I'll be there.'

Gerard rose and smiled. 'Just in the nick of time, too, Sophie. I'd hate to retire with another cold case.'

She shook her head. 'I am too good to you,' she teased.

'That you are,' Gerard Oakley, cynic and former non-believer, agreed.

CHAPTER 25

IMOGEN HARPER – MANICURED to within an inch of her life and dressed head to toe in white – tried to look composed and relaxed as she sat in the interview room, her fiance beside her. She had caught the eye of every male as she made her way down the hallway of the police station. Sophie was far enough behind to see how men reacted to Imogen's body on display in fitted workout gear, the striking blonde hair, and her pout and breasts pushed up to best advantage. It was not hard to imagine how Imogen would have won the heart of a nice country lad on his rise in the football world. She definitely did the hard yards, as Matt had done on the field.

Sophie imagined she would be putting on the same front if she were in Imogen's shoes; it was only a matter of time until the woman called for legal support. Gerard intended to interview the glamorous couple separately as well, but for now, he had told Sophie he wanted to see how they reacted to each other, and he'd be doing a bit of bluffing as he went along.

With all parties seated at the table, all eyes were on Detective Gerard Oakley, the senior detective in the room. Sophie noticed Rachel observed him as if studying the master or an old-time professor who knew his topic. In the next room, watching through the glazed window, was Murdoch; Sophie could feel his eyes upon her even if she couldn't see him. If she reached out and touched the glass, would it be hot?

'You're the clairvoyant,' Imogen said more as a statement than a question, and Sophie nodded, slipping on her glasses. Imogen laughed, looking to her fiancée for a similar reaction, but he remained stony-faced; too much at stake.

'You know anything she says won't stand up in the courtroom,' Imogen said, smirking.

Gerard raced an eyebrow in her direction. 'Thanks for advising us of the law, Ms Harper. Whatever would we have done without you?'

Rachel restrained a laugh and added, 'Sophie advises us, and we gather evidence. Proof which we have found.'

Matt shuffled uncomfortably, moving his long legs in front of him and visibly moving away from Imogen. Too late now, Sophie thought.

'Why did you buy Hope Yardley, who was a stranger to you, a drink?' Sophie asked.

Imogen looked surprised. 'I don't legally need to answer questions from a clairvoyant.'

'This will take some time if you wish to play that game, Ms Harper, and I'm sure your fans will miss your content more than ours will.'

Sophie hid her smile as the older cop showed he wasn't a dinosaur after all.

Rachel hid her grin, asking the same question, 'Why did you buy Hope Yardley a drink? You didn't know her, did you, Ms Harper?'

Imogen shrugged with indifference. 'Firstly, I can't even remember going to that hotel if I did. My girlfriends and I did a lot of bar hopping that night and I bought lots of people a drink. I wouldn't know Hope from Harry.'

'Well, we beg to differ, Ms Harper,' Gerard said, 'because we have CCTV footage and a witness who recalls you being there and buying yourself and Hope a drink. You spent some time talking to her... there was no Harry in sight.'

Imogen scowled, which was not her usual pose and not pretty.

'The witness said they recognised you because they followed you online,' Rachel said.

'We didn't know you were loverboy's fiancée or you would have been in here much soon,' Gerard said with a nod to Matt.

Sophie could almost hear Imogen's mind working overtime, trying to fabricate her next lie, but the images above her head did not change – her target that night had been Hope Yardley.

'Why were you there?' Gerard asked. 'Your fiancé told us it was a boys' night out celebrating a birthday and that you both had different events.'

'We did, he's right. I wasn't there. Which hotel was it again?' Imogen played the role of a confused party girl but Sophie corrected her.

'You arrived just in time to see Matt leaving with Hope,' Sophie said, reading the images, 'and you followed them back to your home.'

Matt snapped to look at Imogen.

'Why did you come at all? We both had functions on. Why didn't you just meet me at home as we agreed?' he said in a low and angry voice.

She narrowed her eyes. 'You don't get to speak to me with attitude, and I did meet you at home.'

'But not before you went to the bar,' Sophie said. 'You drove, so I'm guessing you can't claim to be drunk and have forgotten everything.'

'I would never drink and drive.' Imogen had her brand to protect, which was always foremost in her mind. She cleared her throat. 'I was on my way home and thought I'd drop in and see if Matt was ready to go home too and we could share a ride.'

'So now you are saying you were there and remember the hotel. And then?' Rachel asked.

'Matt wasn't there, so I went home,' she said casually.

Matt went to speak, and she placed her hand on his leg. He closed his mouth. Sophie wondered how many times over the years she had shut him down; apparently, she had perfected the art.

'I am seeing that you went home, discovered Matt and Hope in bed and waited outside in your car. You followed the taxi with Hope in it back to the hotel, where you confronted Hope in the bathroom.'

'Ridiculous,' Imogen said and scoffed, pushing a strand of her long blonde hair behind her ear.

Sophie stiffened and turned to the coated glass window between the two rooms; although she could not see him, the Raven's stare was so intense she felt her skin crawl. It eased for a moment as he must have looked away. She wished Murdoch would go away and let Gerard and Rachel finish the case. He had missed the start of it anyway with his hospital stint; it's not like he was deep into it.

'Please continue, Sophie,' Gerard said, bringing her attention to the group around the table.

Sophie knew Gerard hoped one of them would crack before he would have to parade out any evidence they had, which was a bit slim on the ground. Sophie continued to read from the images that flew around Imogen's head as the influencer panicked and thought of lies and alibis.

'You threatened Hope, told her to steer clear of Matt, and when she refused and told you he had got her number, you shoved her.' Sophie grimaced at the images she saw, and Matt sat back, looking skyward.

Sophie continued, 'Hope was frightened. She asked who you were and tried to leave, but you grabbed her and hit her head against the basin until she fell to the ground.'

Everyone in the room, including Matt, grimaced at the image of that young girl in the last moments of her life; Imogen did not bat an eye.

'You dragged her into the cubicle and, using your fingernail, spun the dial on the outside of the door to "Occupied". Then you called Matt.'

Imogen was about to deny it again when Gerard said, 'We have fibres and hairs from Hope's body and her car that will no doubt match you both.'

Matt leant forward, put his face in his hands and groaned.

'It's not what you think,' he said, which was as good as an admission for Sophie and then, the performance began. Imogen straightened, moved her chair away from Matt's and said, 'I demand to see a lawyer. I am the victim here. Matt raped that girl, and when she threatened to tell and ruin his career, he called me in desperation to help him.'

He spun around to face her. 'What? That didn't happen,' he exploded and rose, pacing, his hands behind his head.

'Sit down,' Gerard ordered as Rachel rose to restrain him.

Matt dropped back into his chair, his face masked in panic. 'She called me,' he told the detectives, 'that's the honest truth. You can see that, can't you?' he asked Sophie. He turned to Gerard and Rachel. 'You'll see the time she called on my phone. She rang and said if I didn't help, she would make up that story that she just told you, and my life would be ruined. I'd go away for rape and murder. You've got to believe me.'

'I suggest you both get legal representation and we'll continue this separately, no one is leaving the station,' Gerard said and rose. He opened the door and organised for two constables to separate the pair into different interview rooms and manage the phone calls to legal teams. They waited until Imogen and Matt had been removed, and then the three discussed what had just happened. Sophie slipped off her glasses.

'So Matt's version is the truth?' Gerard asked, and Sophie nodded.

'She had him completely believing he was going down for rape and murder. I saw a snatch of her wanting to bury Hope, but he wouldn't have it. I guess that's good or else her family might not have found her.'

'Thank you,' Gerard said. 'We'll get their statements, and Fletcher, let's get those hairs and fibres and test them against the pair.'

'Sure, Oakley, but how do we prove who's telling the truth?'

'The phone call will be in Matt's log. If his return to the hotel is not on camera, someone might remember when he arrived back there,' Gerard said.

'He's hard to miss,' Sophie agreed, given the football player's profile.

Gerard agreed. 'I don't think proving he was an accessory will be difficult. What happens to him after that is out of hands, but I do feel sorry for the poor kid,' Gerard said.

'Me too,' Sophie said and sighed. 'Imogen's an ambitious woman.'

'She's a piece of work,' Rachel agreed. 'We might also get lucky and find footage on a camera somewhere of Imogen following Hope's taxi back to the hotel.'

'Hell hath no fury like a woman scorned,' Gerard said with a smirk at the two girls as the three of them rose.

'I'll get back to work.' She accepted their thanks, pleased to get out of the room and away from the intensity of the Raven nearby.

Then, she made a mistake.

Sophie had been avoiding looking towards the glass, but as the last one out of the room, she glanced towards it, knowing he was on the other side.

The sound was like a gunshot as the glass shattered between the rooms with an almighty bang. In front of her, Gerard,

Rachel, and a passing officer dropped to the ground. Sophie disappeared.

'Get down and stay down,' Gerard roared.

'Where did that come from?' Fletcher hissed, staying low, assessing the risk.

'Gunshot. Was it a gunshot?' the officer beside her asked, not moving as other officers hurried towards the scene, flattening themselves against the wall as they cased the area.

Sophie was still there and saw them looking around for the source of the noise and for her.

Murdoch exited the small room, and the three on the ground braced, expecting a gunman. 'No one panic; the glass just shattered,' he announced.

'What the hell?' Gerard gingerly rose. 'Where's Sophie?'

'She must have hot-footed it out of here,' Rachel said, rising to her feet and glancing around as more office staff arrived to find out what was happening. The constable beside her jumped up and continued on his way.

'Stand down, there's nothing to see here,' Gerard said, dismissing the officers and curious onlookers. He turned to Murdoch. 'How the hell did that happen?'

'No idea, but I'm glad it didn't happen during the interview,' Murdoch said.

Sophie watched them all from her invisible state, and she saw Murdoch slowly looking around, aware that she was still there and out of sight. She departed before her body physically reappeared, pleased with her handy skill under pressure. The thought of what might have happened if she could not disappear under pressure and they were facing each other did not bear thinking about. Sophie hoped that day would never come.

CHAPTER 26

I F LUCY WAS SEETHING at the publicity Sophie received since her former best friend was dubbed the "hottest clairvoyant in town" by one journalist, today's front page of the newspaper and online media sites did not help her mood. Splashed all over it, was a story that would make for compulsive viewing as the court case unfolded and Imogen Harper put on her best performance to prove her innocence. The beauty influencer and the football captain, and there at the centre of it was Sophie Carell, again.

'I bet your Uncle is all over her now,' Lucy said as they did their morning workout.

'Who?' Jordan asked.

She rolled her eyes. 'Sophie has solved another big case. Here it is now.' She nodded to the gym TV screen and the news playing in the background; they both watched.

Jordan scoffed as he ran on the treadmill beside her. 'It was a pretty good effort, though; you've got to be impressed,' he conceded. 'I feel sorry for the poor bastard manipulated by his chick.'

Lucy's blood boiled. She slowed down and stepped off the runner; another woman stepped up, taking her place. The gym was full at this early hour, and getting access to the equipment was a game of speed.

'Hey, are you finishing up?' he called after her.

'Yep, I've got a shoot this morning,' she called over her shoulder. A little bit of cold treatment and jealousy was just what Jordan needed to bring him back in line. She headed to the showers, aware of how good she looked in her gym gear and ensuring Jordan got a good look at her flirting with one of the instructors on the way there.

For the anger coming off her, it was surprising the shower water did not steam as it hit her skin.

He can't possibly be wowed by her too. What the hell! It's time. She has to fall from grace, and so does her idiot lover, and if Jordan can't step up, then I'm wasting my time here.

When she emerged from the ladies' changing room, Jordan was all over her like he was waiting for his possession.

'Tonight?' he asked.

'Depends on how long my shoot runs – today's photographer is brilliant and a perfectionist. Sometimes we all go out afterwards.' She overplayed it slightly, but whatever it took.

She gave him a quick kiss and left him watching her. He'd be ripe tonight to do her bidding, especially after she posted a few shots from the shoot. She smiled at the thought that her time would come and Sophie and Jordan would not be part of it.

The blue silk gown was magnificent and it might have been worn a little earlier than the last Elsopeth's era, but close enough. Sophie added a pale lime gown to her small pile of dresses at the insistence of her costume dressmaking friend. She promised to guard them with her life.

'Don't worry. We're not doing any more Shakespeare this year, so there's no rush to get them back,' her friend assured her.

Returning to the car and laying four gowns on the back seat, Sophie was relieved and pleased with her morning efforts. At the police station, her transparent form had lasted long enough to get her to the car park before she started to return in body, even if she did startle an elderly lady coming into the station who hadn't seen her there a moment ago – a small price to pay.

Sophie knew from the images she had seen of Imogen Harper's future that the influencer would spend a long time in jail with no hairdresser, manicurist or social media following.

Matt's career would take a huge dive, but not for long – he was painted as the victim who saw no way out and was manipulated. After a few years, his career would be resurrected, and he would captain a team again. Sophie had also seen in his future that he ended up with a nice girl who looked remarkably like Hope Yardley; his remorse was genuine.

Back in her car, Sophie wanted to quickly visit the Lens' men and then return to the office for her afternoon readings that Jack would have ready, along with a few media interviews she had promised to do.

The sight of the *Optical Illusion* store always made Sophie happy, a little piece of paradise in the village with three of her favourite people in the world inside. Mid-morning was a beautiful time to visit with the glass catching the soft light before the sun rose directly overhead. Nabbing a park across the road, she exited, crossed the street and entered the small store, the bell announcing her arrival.

Sophie froze. *Venetia!*

The glamourous beauty stood opposite Lukas as he fitted a watch to her wrist. But there was no stepping away now. She was here, and it was time for them to meet.

CHAPTER 27

'AH, SOPHIE, I WAS expecting you, welcome,' Alfred Lens said, moving from behind the counter to fully open the door for her as Sophie gingerly stepped inside.

'You were?' Lukas asked, 'I mean, hi, Sophie.'

You could have warned us, Grandpa! He sent the message to Alfred.

Better to not overthink it, lad, the response came back.

Orli appeared from the back room, 'Sophie, how lovely to see you,' she said, looking nervously from Sophie to Venetia and back. 'Tea?' she offered as if it could abate the wars of the world.

Both ladies were dressed for success – Sophie had been at the station this morning, and Venetia had business on her mind.

'At last, we meet,' Venetia said with a smile, a hint of European accent in the melodic lilt of her voice.

'In case introductions are needed,' Alfred said, 'Miss Sophie Carell, may I present Miss Venetia Cawthorn.'

Experience first-hand had taught Alfred the proper etiquette of introductions over the centuries. As Sophie and Venetia were the same sex and of similar age, the order in which he introduced the ladies was not of consequence. But, both ladies smiled at his charming old-fashioned style.

'A pleasure,' Venetia said with a small bow of her head.

'Hello, at last. It feels like we have always known each other,' Sophie said, studying her, 'but I am not experienced enough yet to recall our introductions.'

'And that is probably a good thing,' Venetia laughed.

Sophie accepted the seat in front of Alfred's counter and gratefully declined Orli's offer of tea.

'Venetia is designing jewellery for bespoke clients,' Lukas said, looking at his girlfriend with pride. 'This one is a modern watch with an antique face.'

Venetia moved her wrist so Sophie could see the face of the silver watch she wore.

'I brought it in so Lukas could sync it with his heart as I intend to wear it to promote my line,' she explained.

'It's beautiful. How talented you are,' Sophie said with sincerity.

'Speaking of talent, we saw the headlines, congratulations,' Orli said, moving completely into the room now.

'Ah, thank you. A horrible case, but at least the murderer will be punished, even though my visions show she does not believe for a moment she will be,' Sophie said with a shake of her head. 'She is so manipulative, and it was a vicious, cold-hearted attack.'

'Women, we are frightening creatures,' Venetia said, and Sophie gave her a smile of agreement.

'You can say that again,' Lukas agreed and laughed at the looks they shot him.

'I hope you were warned about Lucy,' Venetia said with a glance to Alfred and Lukas, 'that she has partnered with the Raven's nephew and her agenda appears most obvious to everyone except Jordan.'

'Thank you, yes, the nephew twins have paid me a visit late at night, the eldest twice,' Sophie said, narrowing her eyes in annoyance at the memory.

Lukas's eyes flared yellow. 'You didn't tell us that.'

'Nikolas came,' Sophie told him, and his eyes reverted to their palest of blue as he calmed himself.

Alfred spoke up. 'Venetia had an unsavoury experience with Jordan, too.'

'Yes,' she agreed and told of Jordan trying to convince her to woo his uncle again to distract him from Sophie. 'He is determined that the Raven will treat you as the enemy in this lifetime,' Venetia said, 'but be assured, I will not. So should you need me...'

'Thank you,' Sophie said, her eyes widening in surprise. 'That is a great comfort. How powerful is Jordan?'

Venetia looked to Alfred for his thoughts.

'I would agree with your initial assessment, Venetia dear,' Alfred said, 'his ego is bigger than his talent. But, he is ambitious, Sophie, and raw ambition can be a powerful motivator.'

Sophie nodded. 'That's what the recent murder was all about – Imogen Harper and her ambitions. Can I speak of the Raven, or would you prefer I do so in your absence?' she asked Venetia, who waved her hand casually.

'I have found my love for this generation. Nothing you say will distress me.'

The look Lukas and Venetia exchanged convinced everyone present of that.

'Lucky you,' Sophie said. 'I seem to either drive men away, or they are trying to eliminate me,' she said in jest, making them all smile. 'I saw the Raven last night – not in a dream – but in person; I was dressed as Elsopeth by coincide... I found a dress in a trunk in Aunt Daphne's attic.'

'And he came, believing you to be Elsopeth?' Lukas asked, surprised.

'Yes, and we managed to be together without combusting,' Sophie said in jest. 'Again, this morning I saw him, but this time I was back to being me, in this time and place.' She told of seeing him this morning at the football stadium and the shattering glass at the station.

'Where was Nikolas?' Alfred asked, concerned.

'I didn't call for him, but he did momentarily appear at the station; I sent him away, assuring him of my safety given the Raven was behind glass, so to speak.'

'So are you going to spend the rest of this century dressing as Elsopeth to be with him?' Orli asked, 'There has to be a better way.'

'I am yet to find it,' Sophie said. 'I picked up some old-fashioned gowns from the theatre costume department this morning.' She laughed at their reactions and shrugged. 'Whatever it takes for now.'

Venetia made a knowing sound. 'Ah, I remember the dress you wore the first time the Raven saw you in a ballroom, and mind you, he strode straight over and demanded the waltzes in your dance card. I was most angry with both of you.'

'How amazing that you were there and remember,' Sophie said.

'When was this, Venetia?' Alfred asked, always keen to talk of history.

'It was the 18th century when the gowns were big in skirt and tight in bodice. When we had laces down the back and those terribly tight corsets,' Venetia said.

'And the gentlemen had to tackle those ridiculous cravats that got more elaborate in style and jackets that you couldn't move in, but we were expected to bow and rescue dropped handkerchiefs and ladies' fans all evening,' Alfred recalled and laughed.

'I can only imagine the number of scented handkerchiefs dropped at your feet, Alfred,' Sophie teased him.

'Enough to keep me fit,' he joked and laughed when he saw his grandson's look of disbelief. 'I saw that look, lad.'

'It sounds charming,' Orli said with a soft sigh.

'Your dress was gold, Sophie, or rather Elsopeth's dress was gold... shiny gold satin, and it was beautiful.'

'We have it here,' Orli said, all eyes turning to her. She explained, 'Our historical artifacts collection is on the attic floor above Uncle Alfred's residence.'

'Oh wow,' Sophie said, looking at Alfred. 'I didn't know you had a museum here of sorts.'

'More of a collection of misfitting relics, but we do our best to preserve the bits and pieces. You say Daphne had a dress in a trunk. Was it actually one of Elsopeth's dresses?'

'Yes, apparently. Aunt Daphne dropped in, or rather I summoned her, and she sends her best to you, Alfred,' Sophie said with a smile, and Alfred applauded her effort.

'Bravo, young lady!'

Sophie bowed in her seat. 'I'm a slow learner but getting there. Aunt Daphne also had the uniform of Aircraftwoman Margaret Dillon from World War II; she was the accursed who fell in love with the Raven who was murdered by his family, allegedly,' Sophie explained and Lukas grinned at her legal disclaimer.

'Allegedly? You've been hanging around the cops for too long.'

'Why didn't Daphne give us the items for the artifacts collection, I wonder?' Orli said.

'I can't say, but she has hoarded a few things, including Elsopeth's diaries,' Sophie said with a shrug. 'I believe she was scared of fire and everything being destroyed if it were all in one place.'

'Understandable,' Lukas said.

'Except I have protection charms on all the items,' Orli assured them.

'Sophie dear, like the diaries, you are welcome to access the collections at any time. Rummage up there in the attic to your heart's content; they are all preserved carefully, and there are some obscure things.'

'Like what?' Lukas asked, as he was as out of the loop as Sophie when it came to his family's treasures.

'Well, items relevant to their era,' Alfred explained. 'Locks of hair were often preserved and given as gifts in past eras. We have Saghani's lock of hair.'

'No!' Sophie said, amazed. 'Oh wow, the witch who started it all.'

'I think your ancestor, Samuel, started it,' Lukas said, giving her a wry look.

'Let's not get caught up on technicalities,' she teased and returned her attention to Alfred.

'Indeed,' Alfred said and chuckled. 'We have death portraits as they were quite common in those days.'

Venetia shuddered. 'Awful things. I am so glad that morbid habit is done and dusted.'

'Do you have death portraits of all of us or rather our ancestors?' Sophie asked and continued without waiting for an answer, 'Would Elsopeth and Venetia, and even you, Alfred, have a death portrait stored?'

'Yes, several,' he said matter-of-factly, laughing at Sophie's grimace. 'There's also the occasional outfit... like Elsopeth's beautiful gold dress, the Raven's uniform during the Napoleonic Wars and so on. And some lovely lockets with portraits of ancestors hand drawn in them – that was quite the thing then, too.'

'True,' Venetia said, holding up a locket from around her own neck and flicking it open to reveal two antique portraits.

'My beloved parents... these are not as old as they look, but I had them designed in the fashion of yesteryear.'

'Beautiful,' Orli observed. 'What do you think, Uncle, would Elsopeth's gold dress hold up to being worn?'

'Oh, I believe so. It might smell of mothballs and need a good airing, but if required, a little magic can bring it back to life,' he said with a wink in Sophie's direction and a smile at her excited grin. 'I am picking up Miss Sharpe from the office this evening at six p.m. for a night at the theatre; I shall retrieve it and bring it with me then.'

'Oh, that would be amazing, thank you, Alfred. I hope it fits!'

'What happens if you see Sophie in costume with the Raven when you are returning Miss Sharpe after the theatre?' Orli asked, thinking ahead.

'Ah, good thought. I could offer to drive Miss Sharpe to her residence, but she doesn't like me driving too far in the evening. She worries I'm too old for it,' he said, smiling. 'Imagine that?'

The young people laughed affectionately with him.

'We will keep a very low profile and remain on the office side of the building, Sophie,' Alfred assured her, 'but good thinking, Orli.'

'Thank you, I'm sure it will be fine. Should you see me, just be sure to call me Elsopeth; I promise not to do anything amorous in the garden that might shock you both!' Then Sophie grinned. 'I remember reading about that ball you spoke of Venetia in Elsopeth's diary. Didn't you come and slap me in my garden that night?' she teased.

'Oh, that sounds very much like me,' Venetia agreed without a hint of embarrassment. 'I promise not to do it next time you wear the dress.'

Sophie laughed. 'I'm almost disappointed.'

Alfred smiled, enjoying the harmonious discussion between the witches in his beloved store and home, and communicated a mind message to his grandson. *'See, lad, all will be well between the ladies in this lifetime.'*

CHAPTER 28

J USTIN LOOKED AT HIS twin brother sitting opposite at their place of work and tried to understand Jordan's anger, given they both had the same parents, the same upbringing, and equal space in the womb although he suspected Jordan took up more. Neither was favoured over the other and their love of each other was binding. Was rage inherited? Was one of their parents quick to anger? He thought to check that with his psychologist uncle, Allanon.

The boys had started a security company called Apollo Security – in Greek mythology, the raven was the messenger of the god Apollo, and Jordan had once been into online mythology games. Jordan looked after the manpower and training that suited his gym-sculpted body, taking the gigs he wanted for himself first; Justin looked after the contracts and marketing, and several office ladies took care of the paperwork and payments. Jordan's ambitions evolved solely around Apollo Security, while for Justin, it was a means to an end – he was in his third year of studying law.

Justin chose his words carefully. 'Uncle Murdoch knows you and Lucy went to Sophie's place again last night, so don't think you've gotten away with it. He is bound to seek you out to talk about it.'

Jordan rolled his eyes.

'Did you expect anything less?'

'I am not a kid and not putting up with any more lectures,' Jordan stated bravely when not in his uncle's presence.

'Why provoke him?' Justin asked with exasperation.

'If Uncle hasn't got the guts to put the accursed in her place, I will do it for him.'

'He loves her. What would you do if you discovered that Lucy was the accursed?'

'I'd have her under my thumb right from the start,' Jordan said with a smile. Justin believed it.

'This is not a new romance,' Justin reminded his twin. 'Uncle has loved her for generations.'

'Yeah, well, bad luck that this generation, his witch is also the accursed, but he can't have it both ways. Man up and call it what it is – they are enemies, and he has a tradition to uphold. He's supposed to be the chosen, a role model.'

Justin huffed. 'The curse is outdated. I'm sure Saghani would never have meant to cause fear and pain in generations of innocent people just to avenge her death.'

'Why would you think that?' Jordan disagreed. 'I bet she'd be thrilled; she set the curse and applied it to all the murderer Samuel Rayne's descendants. It's what Harley wanted, too. That's why the family split, and that dove flock went and did the peace thing,' he scoffed and folded his arms across his chest, making his arms bulge. Justin recognised it as an intimidation gesture, but he had never feared his twin nor had grounds to do so.

Justin rose and filled his water glass at the dispenser in the corner of the office. 'Actually, Harley did soften a little in his beliefs.'

'Yeah? And how would you know that?'

'I read his logs. Did you?'

Jordan shook his head. Reading wasn't his thing, as Justin knew.

'They weren't eloquent, more like a diary of happenings and jottings, but a few were revealing.'

'Like what?'

'Well,' Justin continued, 'he fell in love with one of the accursed he was harassing. I think he initially enjoyed causing her terror, but from his notes, he was attracted to her beauty.

Is that what you mean by "under your thumb"? Is that what you would do to the girl you love?'

'That's exactly what I mean.' Jordan said, smiling in a sinister fashion. 'And there you go, evidence that Harley might have thought she was hot, but he still did his duty.'

'If you want to call it a duty. It reads like he became obsessed with her. He couldn't bear to see any other man with her but didn't want to admit his weakness of loving her.'

'Bullshit,' Jordan said, rising, his temper flaring. 'Harley was the strongest of all in our line. I don't believe he loved her; he was just enjoying the power of tormenting her, more like it.'

Justin shrugged. 'He called her beautiful and feminine, or if memory serves me, he used the word "delicate". Harley wanted her, and I remember clearly that he wrote how he could crush her when she looked at another man. His ramblings were sinister, but there's no doubt she bewitched him. Why would I make it up?'

'To get me to take it easy on Uncle Murdoch and his cursed witch.'

'Read it for yourself then.'

'Just saying I believe you, what happened to her? I bet Harley didn't get with her,' Jordan scoffed.

'She killed herself.'

'Yeah? Wow,' Jordan took that information in. 'Then he didn't go easy on her.'

'Harley must have made her life a misery, and from what he wrote, I suspect she was terrified of him. She was like Lucy, not magical, just a normal human. Harley must have been real proud,' Justin said drily.

'Was he?'

Justin shrugged. 'For what it's worth, I thought it read like he was devastated, but what would I know? All I'm saying is maybe it's time love and forgiveness conquer all.'

'Ah, my little brother, the dreamer,' Jordan said, reminding Justin that he was born second – seventeen minutes later but enough for Jordan to pull rank.

'You might change your mind when you fall in love,' Justin shot back. He didn't take favourably to being called a dreamer when he felt his feet were firmly planted on the ground and not in some generational family feud that had no place in a modern world.

Jordan bristled. 'What makes you think I'm not?'

'Because you have no compassion. And trust me, when you fall in love, you'll move mountains for her.'

'Right. Well, I'm off to move some mountains,' he said, rising and giving his brother a wink.

'What does that mean exactly?' Justin asked suspiciously.

Jordan stopped in the doorway. 'Lucy wants to revisit Sophie tonight and continue our good work. She likes to see me in action, it turns her on, apparently.' Jordan shook his head and grinned at the thought. 'Yeah, she's quite a spitfire, my girl.'

'And what will you do when you visit?' Justin's voice belayed his displeasure. 'Don't let her lead you around by the nose, brother.'

Jordan gave a short laugh. 'Hardly. We intend to do what Uncle Murdoch is not... remind the witch of her place. Lucy wants to rock her confidence, make the cursed go underground and shun the media for her own safety. I want her to know that the family curse is serious, and she may win over Uncle with her charms, but there's more than one descendant in the Raven line.'

Justin saw how his brother's face hardened and asked, 'If Lucy wasn't pushing for this, would you still do it?'

Jordan shrugged. 'Probably. It'd be something to have the witch bending to my whims.'

'She has a name, you know.'

'You're soft, brother, but don't worry, I'll do my best not to hurt Uncle in the process.' Jordan walked out of the office with a grin and stepped back in momentarily. 'You wouldn't dob me into Uncle Murdoch, bro?'

Justin gave a small shake of his head in the negative. 'She will retaliate, you might get hurt.'

'I can move fast,' he grinned, proving that by departing in a hurry, leaving Justin to worry about what was to come... and he had a fair idea; he could sense it. After all, Justin was the Raven who would follow in his Uncle Murdoch's footsteps when the day came if that day came. It was why he was reading the history, preparing for the surge of power that would overtake his body. Justin decided he would be there tonight, too, for no other reason than to stop his brother's destruction. Sophie was a much stronger witch than Jordan could ever hope to be, despite the egging of Lucy telling him otherwise, and Sophie had every right to protect herself.

Justin made a quick call.

'What's wrong?' Allanon answered the phone, and Justin chuckled.

'Nothing, don't panic.' He heard his uncle exhale with relief. 'I don't only call when there's a drama.'

'Yeah, you do; otherwise, you would see me at home tonight and not call at all,' his uncle reminded him.

'Oh right, fair point. Any chance I can drop in and see you?'

'Sure. I have a few hours between appointments if you can come now.'

Justin could hear the concern in his uncle's voice. 'On my way.' he hung up and grabbed his wallet and keys, telling the office ladies he would return in a few hours. His uncle was intuitive; he read people for a living, and this was a situation Justin didn't want on his conscience if he should have done something to stop it. He drove on autopilot, his mind going over scenarios and was surprised when he arrived so quickly. Justin knew the minute he entered Allanon's office that his uncle was expecting trouble. He took the offered seat as his uncle closed the door behind him.

'Is this where your patients sit?' Justin joked.

'Yes, now tell me what brings you here today, young man, you look like a fairly balanced sort of lad,' Allanon joked.

'I am, thank you, doctor, I was well brought up,' he joked, 'but my brother is a nutter.'

'Ah,' Allanon nodded, understanding what the visit was about. They both smiled and sobered quickly, given the jest hit close to home.

'Jordan and Lucy are returning to Sophie's tonight; they want to harass her some more, and Lucy thinks if they scare Sophie enough, she'll drop out of the limelight. Jordan just wants to punish her because he believes she is weakening Uncle Murdoch.'

Allanon groaned. 'I can't say I'm surprised. He's always held Harley up to be some hero and is acting increasingly like a vengeful Raven. We haven't seen that sort of personality for a generation or more.'

'Even Harley softened in the end, well, I think he did when the accursed took her life.'

Allanon nodded. 'That's how I read it, too.'

Justin waited while Allanon thought for a moment.

'I don't think we should tell Murdoch.'

'Nor do I,' Justin agreed. 'I'm going to be there, where I can keep an eye on Jordan and step in if necessary. Is there somewhere I can hide without being seen?'

'That's easy. The gardens are huge, with plenty of mazes and twists and turns. I will come with you.'

'No, but thanks, Uncle,' Justin shook his head. 'It could end up like a circus if I have to step forward and Sophie finds me, Jordan, Lucy and you there as well, maybe even Murdoch if he is going to her at night... I am not sure if that is happening. I'm strong enough in spirit.'

He could feel his uncle studying him until he nodded and agreed. 'I believe you are, and Lucy is powerless, so there won't be too many forces present.' He shook his head. 'What is wrong with that boy?' Allanon muttered more to himself than the twin present.

'Can anger be inherited, you know, a characteristic of our nature passed down from parent to child?'

'Hmm, you'll find different schools of thought on that,' Allanon said, 'but your parents weren't angry folk. Anger has been linked to genes, like the serotonin gene, and mental illness, and some believe it can be attributed to experiences in early development – what we witness, what we learn.'

'A learned behaviour? Well, you and Aunty Bree are the calmest people I've ever met, so we didn't grow up in a hothouse.'

Allanon gave a grateful smile for the kind words. 'Jordan has his own issues of abandonment and responsibility, especially to you. He loves you beyond all measure.'

'And I love him.'

Allanon nodded. 'I think the cursed history gives Jordan a sense of family stability; it makes him feel that he is part of something bigger.' Allanon chose his words carefully.

'I can see that,' Justin agreed. 'I also think Uncle Murdoch is right, and Lucy has her own agenda.'

'On that, we are all agreed,' Allanon said.

Orli arrived at Nikolas's estate ready to free herself from her earthly form. Their routine on the first Wednesday of every month was to meet late afternoon at his residence to enjoy the forest. Today was that day, and Orli loved the freedom of flight. She could fly above him as Nikolas ran in his wolf form through the forest before the sun set – doves were not night creatures, and if she stayed near him, she was safe.

After stretching their bodies to feel their natural animal states, they would transform back to their human forms, neither alarmed by their immodesty when respect was afforded by both parties and privacy granted as much as possible. Sometimes, Nikolas would cook dinner afterwards, or they would go to the *Bell and Gate* English Pub, where Nikolas was a regular, and Orli had become known.

She couldn't remember when it had started, well over a year ago, but she remembered why. She had been to his home when Nikolas was mourning the loss of his mother. Oril had come in her dove form, that of a mourning dove. He recognised it was not a creature native to the area and saw it as a sign of hope. He stopped to observe the pale bird, and then Orli transformed. Nikolas later said seeing the graceful bird gave him great peace. Identifying with the mourning dove, which returned to the same place every year if they had nested there previously, Orli felt that pull – the need to nest with Nikolas. She became a monthly guest; maybe it would end one day when they both found themselves with their partners for this generation, or maybe not.

Orli was no stranger to waiting for the shapeshifter to come around to her. Every generation, he had denied himself of her love, not believing the ethereal beauty would be interested in a hairy, rough beast such as himself. He sought a non-magical person, then found himself captured by Elsopeth, Sophie, or some other attractive woman in his orbit until he saw the bright and shiny thing before him that he never believed he could have. Orli would wait, but not forever. The life span of a mourning dove was under two years, and that was the lifespan of her love. In past generations, if he had not found her by then, Orli would have moved on to love another, but her heart wanted him.

He ran, and she followed, watching as he transformed, his limbs taking shape into the large white wolf, his pack of dogs running beside him, and she stayed above him, graceful, fluid, safe. Maybe tonight, she thought, maybe tonight he would recognise their love. Time ticked by.

CHAPTER 29

I T WAS LIKE A scene from Edgar Allan Poe's poem, *The Raven*, Sophie mused, scattered lines returning to her from her classroom days and her recent re-reading. She looked out from her upstairs bedroom window at the bright, large moon slowly engulfed by dark clouds and had to admit to a sense of foreboding.

Once upon a midnight dreary.

A glance at the clock told her it was nearing ten p.m. Almost midnight, Sophie thought and turned to look at her reflection again in the full-length mirror. The dress was breathtaking. That it fitted surprised her, but the lacing at the back allowed for some sins and loosening, as Elsopeth had been younger when she had worn it and not as womanly as Sophie's figure was now.

Earlier, Mel had gushed at the feel and touch of the rich gold satin fabric in all its fineness and happily laced Sophie from the back, teasing if she needed someone to unlace her, to wake her if required. Sophie took Mel's teasing with good grace, but now alone and waiting, she was not without some inner nerves.

What if the Raven didn't show up tonight? How many nights would she dress, wait, and live, hoping to see him and feel his touch? The anticipation in her chest was shortening her breath, along with the fitted gown. She marvelled at how the ladies of yesteryear coped with such dresses after a night of dancing and exertion. No wonder their breasts were always heaving, and they fainted regularly, she thought. She heard the mournful cry of a bird and paused, wondering if it could be the Raven warning of his imminent arrival at her home to her bed.

So that now, to still the beating of my heart, I stood repeating

Tis some visitor entreating entrance at my chamber door–

But no, again, it was a false alarm. She was very much alone. Another glance to the mirror. Sophie's hair was loose around her shoulders, her small ballet slippers were hidden below the dress folds, and her lavender perfume scent was subtle but hopefully reminiscent of the era. The window rattled, and eagerly, she glanced outside.

Back into the chamber turning, all my soul within me burning,

Soon again I heard a tapping somewhat louder than before.

'Tis the wind and nothing more!"

It was nothing but the wind. Sophie scolded herself. 'Get a grip.' She ran her hand down the dress and then felt a little bump in the fabric, finding a tucked-away pocket in the skirt. She felt inside, hoping to find a small note or a potential suitor's long-forgotten card. Instead, she found a dainty lace handkerchief, and holding it to her nose, she could smell a mixture of mothballs and a touch of lavender, no doubt stained into the fabric forever more. She smiled at the thought of the fabric touching Elsopeth's face and now her own. Re-pocketing it, she sighed and looked outside again, deciding whether to go to the garden and wait.

'Where are you, Murdoch? I am ready for you,' she whispered as the moon became a sliver of light, the rest hidden.

Deep into that darkness peering, long I stood there wondering, fearing,

Doubting, dreaming dreams no mortal ever dared to dream before.

And then Sophie heard a tapping... a small stone against the window. Her heart leapt, and she hurried closer to the window, almost tripping on the length of her dress. She looked down. He was there, the Raven, in formal wear slightly askew and looking handsomely mussed – a dark suit, white shirt open at the neck, and the shiniest black dress shoes. His slow smile was a balm to her longing.

Sophie held up her hand to ask him to wait, and he nodded, his eyes relaying his pleasure at seeing her.

Presently my soul grew stronger; hesitating then no longer.

The risk of spending time with the Raven did not even occur to Sophie, and if Nikolas had appeared as her protector, warning her not to go, she would not have heeded his words. This, now, was more important to her than playing it safe. She carefully descended the grand staircase, opened the door, and gasped at finding him waiting right on the doorstep. Murdoch grinned and gave a small bow, presenting from the hand behind his back a single, long-stemmed yellow rose.

'My favourite, thank you, Your Grace.'

He laughed. 'We are back to being formal, Lady Elsopeth?'

She laughed, enjoying the moment and showing appreciation for the gift by inhaling the scent of the perfect rose.

'Breathtaking, Elsopeth,' he said. 'I remember the first time you wore this gown.'

'You demanded all my waltzes,' Sophie said, happy to play the role. Murdoch chuckled at the memory. 'I would have demanded your hand and heart right then, but I suspected that might not have won you over.'

Sophie did her best to emulate how she thought Elsopeth might react... teasing but naive, flirtatious yet innocent, strong as needed but feminine. She offered her hand to him, and he raised it to his lips to kiss but then just as quickly wrapped his arm around her and pulled her against him, taking her in a more passionate kiss as Sophie gasped and leant into him, allowing him to lead. There was something delicious about allowing him to be the strong one and not always hold her own.

She wanted to invite him upstairs but doubted such a thing would come out of Elsopeth's mouth, and she was right when he pulled back as if regaining control of his emotions. Despite their last unguarded passionate scene in the garden, she acted – demurely looking down, but when she looked up, Sophie was disconcerted by the intensity in his dark eyes, an intensity that spoke of generations of love and waiting, of patience and passion. Her breath grew shallower, and Murdoch cleared his throat. Remembering himself, he crooked his arm and offered it to her. 'Forgive me. Shall we take a turn around the gardens?'

Sophie looked skyward. 'It is so dark; I feel as if it is going to storm any moment.'

'I had arranged a large and beautiful moon to shine down upon us, but this weather appeared from nowhere,' he teased, and Sophie laughed, slipping her hand into the crook of his arm and allowing herself to be led.

Something in his silent presence made her desperate to know him more, to be the only one to whom he revealed himself. Then, she realised she could do this every night for as long as necessary just to have the chance to be with him. And she also grasped how foolish that was and the half-life it would give her – the thought of yet another chance at love slipping by her shadowed her face.

'I am sorry if I took liberties and it has upset you,' Murdoch said, slipping into the past so easily, having lived a full life in the centuries before.

'Oh no,' Sophie assured him, 'you did not upset me, nor could you with that passionate display,' she teased, and he smiled sheepishly, unaccustomed to being teased for being romantic. 'I...' she remembered to use old world speak, 'I unashamedly want more.'

He snapped to look at her and did not need further encouragement, bringing his lips to hers, his hand caressing her face as he held her closer. It was then that they heard a twig snap and a voice nearby hushing another. They were not alone. Murdoch pulled away, moving Sophie to his side for protection.

'Come out, whoever is there,' he demanded, and the air was still. No sound could be heard, nor did anyone step out of the dark gardens around them.

'Perhaps it was just a night animal, a rodent,' Sophie offered, wrinkling her nose at the thought.

'No,' Murdoch said. He knew it was Jordan. Despite the dark, Ravens by nature had acute sight, and while his sense of smell was not noteworthy, he could see the shape of his nephew and the outline of the woman, Lucy.

'What is it?' Sophie asked, mindful not to mention Jordan's name in case that brought them into the now and put her at risk.

He spoke aloud so he could be heard. 'It is a presence I acknowledge and advise to leave.' His eyes were black and threatening, and Sophie took a step back. His hand shot out to hold her. 'You don't need to fear me,' he said.

And then Jordan stepped out of the shadows, Lucy by his side.

Sophie gasped. 'You!' The sight of the woman she once held so dear and who betrayed her still caused a stab of pain.

Lucy smirked and stood close to the younger man, who resembled Murdoch and the Raven clan.

As if afraid, the slip of moon disappeared completely behind a thunderous cloud, leaving them with only the glow of two distant garden lights; the remaining had not been repaired since they were damaged – of all the thoughts racing through her head, Sophie remembered that was Nikolas's job as the business manager and property overseer.

'I warned you, Jordan,' the Raven said, but still, he did not act angrily, and all present waited for a display of his strength.

Maybe it was because of Allanon, what he owed his brother, that made him so restrained with his nephew, Sophie wondered, and she stepped forward to abate the situation.

'No, Murdoch!' Sophie said, 'They will go now, go!' she ordered them.

'I don't take orders from you, witch,' Jordan hissed, and Lucy smiled, enjoying her boyfriend's show of power. He stepped forward to challenge his uncle, and Murdoch's eyes became darker than the night.

'You are on my private property,' Sophie reminded him, believing the property claim as Elsopeth would still hold true.

The Raven said in a low and threatening voice, 'I love you as family, Jordan, but do not make me do something we'll both regret – you more than me. Take the girl, and go while you can.'

'Girl?' Lucy said and grimaced at him. She was not one for being sidelined.

'No, Uncle. You are a disgrace to Harley and the Raven descendants. I am taking your mantle,' Jordan said with a wicked smile and stepped forward.

'Nikolas!' Sophie screamed.

'Don't call him!' Murdoch snapped at her, and hearing her gasp of fear, he held up his hands. 'I will protect you, Elsopeth, you don't—'

'Elsopeth?' Lucy exclaimed.

Their words were cut off as Nikolas appeared with Orli beside him. Sophie stepped back towards them, creating a divide – the Ravens and the Doves – the ancient enemy sides with Sophie now as its cause for this generation's warring.

'What is it? We were together; Orli sensed trouble earlier,' Nikolas explained to Sophie and then looked at the Raven clan and snarled. 'What are you all doing here?'

'Wolf,' Jordan hissed.

With that, Justin stepped out of the darkness of the garden, startling his brother and Lucy. He looked at his uncle and Sophie and held up his hands.

'I knew Jordan was coming here tonight,' he said with a look to his brother. 'I didn't dob you in, but I couldn't let you come and risk your life.'

Jordan laughed. 'Risk my life? You forget how strong I am, bro, as a witch and physically.'

'I know exactly how strong you are, Jordan; I know everything about you. I am half you. And I know this girl has an agenda of evil and that what happens to you doesn't interest her in the long run.'

'Girl again,' Lucy said, annoyed. 'The girl has a name.'

Sophie watched the interplay and saw the look of annoyance Jordan flashed Lucy. She didn't defend her love for him but rather her own standing.

'I apologise for my brother's arrival,' Justin addressed Murdoch and Sophie. 'We will leave now. Jordan, step down, this is not your destiny.'

'You don't apologise for me, bro, and you don't order me around, witch,' he said again, glaring at Sophie until Nikolas moved in front of her. Jordan realised what Justin had said. 'What do you mean this is not my destiny?' His jaw locked as he looked from his brother to his uncle. 'I am the natural inheritor of the role.'

Justin gave a slight shake of his head.

'I am the future Raven,' he said again louder.

'You are not,' Murdoch said.

As if there was not enough tension in the air, an elderly voice could be heard, and Alfred Lens and Miss Sharpe were hurrying up the path, arriving back from the theatre. Sophie heard him ask Miss Sharpe to go inside, wait with Mel and secure the doors. Sophie felt hopeless standing in her ballgown surrounded by pacifiers and agitators, herself the cause of the tension. If she had walked away from Murdoch... but she couldn't, and now she could add guilt to her emotions with Alfred and Orli dragged into the situation of her making.

As Alfred arrived, despite the tension, all heads nodded in his direction, and he acknowledged the compliment with a quick reciprocal nod of greeting. Before he could speak, Lukas and Venetia appeared beside them.

'Oh, great,' Murdoch could be heard to say at the sight of his former love, Venetia.

Sophie rolled her eyes. 'Lukas, please go. You both don't need to place yourself in harm's way.'

'I heard Grandpa's words of alarm to Miss Sharpe.'

'Now you develop the skill,' Alfred said with a sigh. 'All is well, Lukas, Venetia dear.' He turned to the group. 'Shall we call it a night and depart,' he asked of the intruders in Sophie's garden. 'I am sure the Raven and...' he hesitated as he was just about to say Sophie's name but assumed as the Raven was still in Sophie's company, he still believed her to be Elsopeth. He finished, 'I am sure the Raven and the lady of the house have much to discuss.'

'Exactly right. Go, all of you and leave her alone or you will have me to answer to,' Nikolas addressed Murdoch. 'You can't be together in this lifetime. Accept it, or we will have this out here and now for good.'

The Raven scoffed. 'Don't threaten me, Shapeshifter or—'

'No!' Sophie said, moving Nikolas back and away from in front of her. 'This is my home and my choice of who is a guest here. Thank you for coming when I called, Nikolas, thank you to all of you, and my apologies, Alfred, for placing this in your lap,' she said to the support group near her, 'but I want Jordan and Lucy to leave and stay away for good. Everyone else, thank you and please don't be concerned, it is safe to leave us.' She hoped that would dismiss them.

'I am not leaving so that you can seduce my uncle with your spells, witch,' Jordan said with a huff.

'Do not speak to her like that,' Venetia said, defending Sophie as promised. 'Your uncle does not need his weakling nephew witch to protect his honour.'

'You're defending the witch now?' Jordan's teeth bared in anger. 'My uncle is not the man you knew; he no longer knows what is good for him or the family. Call me weak again, and you will experience a display to change your mind.'

Lukas's eyes flared yellow at the insult to his girlfriend as he moved towards Jordan. Sophie ordered him back, and all eyes were on the Raven, expecting an explosion. Alfred looked deceptively calm.

Nikolas moved closer and whispered in Sophie's ear, 'Despite your golden gown, the Raven cannot possibly believe you are Elsopeth with all the current day progenies around him. Sophie, you are not safe.'

She gave a small nod of understanding, and he stepped back. Sophie ran a hand down her dress near the pocket, knowing she had something upon her to ensure her protection and that of the Lens family – the doves. The feel of it in her possession was reassuring.

'The Raven and I can be together, safely,' she told Jordan, 'I have found a way, and it is your uncle's choice, not yours. Go love the deceitful woman you are with and leave us alone.'

Lucy hissed like a cat, and Jordan stepped forward, but not before the Raven and Justin both moved to force him back.

'I have this, Uncle,' Justin assured him and growled at his brother and Lucy to leave.

'You have it?' Lucy huffed, 'Your brother has to protect you!'

Jordan went to protest, no one demoralised his twin, but Justin spoke up first.

'I may not be prone to anger, but I am tired of my brother's misplaced bravado, tired of stepping in when rational deserts him, as it appears to have, again.'

Jordan ignored his twin and asked Sophie, 'How can you be together without weakening and destroying him? Sure, you're a witch, but you're cursed, and you can't beat Saghani's curse or the power of our Raven clan.'

'A curse which you deserve,' Lucy added, standing taller beside him.

Sophie turned to the Raven and spoke to him as if no one else existed. 'I need to tell you something.'

'I am listening,' Murdoch assured her, speaking to her as if she were Elsopeth.

She delivered the words slowly, 'I am Sophie. Not Elsopeth, I am Sophie.'

Murdoch's eyes widened in alarm, waiting for the fire within him to rage and destroy her. His eyes reflected his alarm. The Raven stepped back, breathing through his teeth. 'Go quickly.'

'No.'

'Sophie, go before I lose control.'

'But you won't. We can be together.'

She put her hand into the small pocket of her dress and pulled out a token of sorts. Murdoch frowned, trying to see what her hand was clasped around, and then she uncurled her fingers to show him. It was a coil of rope.

'Oh, Sophie,' Murdoch moaned, 'what have you done?'

CHAPTER 30

F OR A MOMENT, THE air stilled as the realisation of
what this meant to each person present hit home;
Murdoch held Sophie's gaze. To see them, nothing else
existed in the world but the two of them. Sophie bit her lip,
her eyes pleading for forgiveness.

'I was desperate.'

'I understand. It's over now.'

'No, no, Murdoch, don't say that,' she rushed to take his
hands, the rope still within her palm, and he let her. She
brought one of his hands to her lips.

'I was selfish. I wanted you,' she said. 'I'm sorry.'

'Don't be upset. I've never wanted the Raven life; I never
had a choice.'

Jordan laughed, a deep, sinister laugh. 'But you can't
give it up. It has to be taken from you, and the witch has
brought you to your knees, Uncle. Didn't I tell you she
would?'

'Another Sophie betrayal,' Lucy said in a sing-song voice beside her boyfriend. 'All she ever thinks about is herself.'

'No, never a betrayal,' Sophie said, only speaking to the Raven.

They all heard the low growl, and before anyone could react, Nikolas leapt towards Murdoch, his body changing in flight.

'Nik, no!' Sophie screamed in fright as Murdoch's hands were yanked from her grasp, and he hit the ground, the white wolf snarling and attacking the defenceless Raven, ripping at him with his powerful jaw. Justin leapt to his uncle's defence, throwing himself on the wolf's back as pandemonium broke out, the Raven clan defenceless in the rope's presence.

'Look what you have done, witch!' Jordan roared.

'Orli, take it and go,' Alfred said, and with a flick of his wrist, he removed the rope coil from Sophie's enclosed grip and hurled it towards Orli. 'Get it away.'

'Yes, Uncle.' Orli snatched it from the air and disappeared.

The Raven's power was restored with force, each man feeling the rush within them. Jordan bellowed, using all the power in his body to send a bolt of pain to the wolf. His force field misfired, hitting his brother, Justin, who fell from the wolf's back, his eyes fixed in shock at his brother as he collapsed to the ground.

'No!' Jordan rushed to his twin's side.

Murdoch battled the wolf, his anger surging, his eyes black, his power immense. The noise was deafening with the roar of two cursed beings. The wolf flew through the air, propelled by the Raven, landed, and flung himself back at Murdoch, crashing nearby as Murdoch dodged the huge white beast.

Alfred held up his hands, and the whole scene froze. Silence reined.

The strongest witch had acted; no one could move. They stood or lay immobile, alive, panting, frightened, angry, shocked. The wolf returned to his human form; Nikolas lay naked, unharmed, unable to move.

Beside him, Murdoch was bleeding badly, his throat torn from the savage attack when he was powerless, his breathing ragged. Justin lay motionless, his eyes glass; Jordan wailed in terror at his prone brother.

'Help him.'

'Murdoch's still alive,' Lucy said between clenched teeth.

'Shut up!' Jordan snarled at her. 'My brother...'

Orli reappeared and froze as she entered Alfred's sphere, but not before she uttered Nikolas's name, seeing him laying on his side and bleeding.

And then Sophie broke free.

'Do as you must, Sophie,' Alfred said, acknowledging the strongest witch present now. Her strength had overcome his; no one else was capable of moving.

'Forgive me, Alfred. You warned me, please forgive me,' she said and ran to Murdoch and Justin, placing her hands on both men. Murdoch gulped for air, his strength fading.

'Save them, please save them,' Jordan begged.

Sophie closed her eyes. A bright light radiated from her fingers to the flesh of the Raven men and trailed over their skin, threads of heat repairing and restoring. Murdoch slumped, his neck wounds closing, his breathing returning to normal as the blood, bites, and scratches faded from his body. Justin did not move.

'I'm okay. Help Justin, Sophie,' Murdoch muttered, trying to rise but held motionless by Alfred's force.

Sophie placed her hand on Justin's heart. Behind her, she could hear Jordan egging his brother to life, the desperation in his voice.

'Is this the war you wanted, Jordan?' Murdoch asked. 'You have it.'

Lucy went to speak and shut up when she saw the glare Murdoch gave her.

The light was radiating from Justin's body now, and with a shudder, he opened his eyes and gasped, taking in a lungful of air. Sophie sat back on her haunches and breathed a sigh of relief.

'You saved him,' Jordan said.

'Of course,' Sophie said, looking at Jordan with more compassion than he had ever given her.

'Why? We're your enemy.'

'Why are we enemies?' Sophie asked. 'I like your lovely, gentle brother and your uncle, Allanon, and I love your uncle, Murdoch,' she said unabashedly, putting it out there. She saw the smile on Murdoch's lips.

'And my Uncle Alfred has already saved Murdoch once before,' Orli reminded Jordan. 'Why can we not co-exist?'

Alfred spoke up. 'If Sophie agrees, I will release you all now, but can we declare the war for this generation over? Can peace prevail?'

Nikolas snickered. Sophie rose and threw his discarded shirt over his naked state. Her anger at him for his loss of control was evident. Yes, he was a hunter, and a weakened prey was not shown mercy, but he was also human, and she suspected – knew – the rivalry had more to do with his desire to win her than his hunting instinct.

'We can't stop something that runs deep in our DNA,' Nikolas said with a glance at Murdoch. 'Only the curser can remove a curse, and the shapeshifters will always instinctively hunt.'

'But yet we have kept the peace for the past two generations,' Alfred said, 'and I understand that is how everyone wanted it. We are all powerful. If we kill one, another will die in revenge, and on it will go until no one is standing and all hearts are broken.'

'Wise words,' Sophie whispered.

'Respect and caution from both sides,' Murdoch agreed.

'Exactly,' Alfred said.

'I'm sorry, Uncle Murdoch, sorry, Justin,' Jordan mumbled. 'I could have killed you.' He swallowed, staring at his brother.

'But Sophie saved me,' Justin said gratefully.

'You're kidding?' Lucy squealed. 'You wouldn't need saving if she wasn't trying to weaken your uncle with her selfish needs!'

'It's called love, Lucy.' Murdoch said drily. 'I have loved this woman for generations. I will be with her any way I can.'

'And now you can,' Alfred said and smiled.

Nikolas grunted. 'Can we get released?'

'How can we be together?' Sophie asked, ignoring Nikolas. She turned to look at Alfred – she was still the only one in the group who could move, her gold dress glistening in the moonlight that had broken through the clouds.

He smiled. 'Remember Aircraftwoman Margaret Dillon? When she saved the Raven from the burning car, he lost the burning desire to destroy her. You saved the Raven from destruction; let's hope his desire to destroy you is quelled. '

'If it's not, I'm on hand,' Nikolas said, glaring at Murdoch, who gave him a look of dismissal.

'You were lucky I was defenceless, or Sophie would be restoring you if she chose to,' Murdoch told him.

Sophie looked at Murdoch, and the look they shared was full of hope.

'Are we agreed that there shall be peace so Uncle Alfred can release us?' Orli asked.

There were words of agreement and nods of heads amongst the worn-out group, even from Nikolas, and Alfred released the spell with a flick of his hand.

CHAPTER 31

ORLI WAVED A HAND towards the broken glass garden lamps and restored them immediately; she had a lot of practice doing so when Lukas lost his temper in the *Optical Illusion* store over the years.

There was a strange energy as the group moved, stretched their limbs, and checked their injuries. Before departing to dress, Nikolas ordered Sophie to test her theory. He glared at the Raven. 'Test you can be near him without him reacting.'

'Gladly,' the Raven said, smirking at Nikolas as he won the girl again. He moved towards Sophie in her gold gown and offered his hands. She accepted, and he pulled her towards him in a tight embrace. Everyone watched, breaths hitched, but nothing happened – the Raven's anger did not rise, and his eyes did not flare. The pair smiled, freed to love.

'Excellent,' Alfred said, relieved.

Jordan embraced Justin, then pulled away, holding his brother by the shoulders. He exhaled, his words full of pain, 'I thought I'd lost you.'

'Yeah, that'd be a great loss,' Justin teased him.

'You're it, aren't you?' Jordan asked. 'The next Raven?'

Justin hesitated. 'Only if Uncle Murdoch departs this world too soon or has no descendant in this generation.'

'I think you best leave,' Venetia said to Lucy.

'I'll leave with my boyfriend when we are good and ready, thanks,' Lucy said.

Jordan fished in his pocket and gave her a set of car keys. 'Here's your keys. I'm going home with Justin.'

Her face flushed with anger, and she snatched the keys from his palm and stormed off down the path.

'Well, I shall check on Miss Sharpe and Miss Karta and bid you good evening,' Alfred said with a small bow. Again, all parties turned to acknowledge the elderly statesman who prevented a war this evening.

'Beer?' Jordan asked his twin.

'Hell yeah,' Justin said, and the men bid the remaining group good night and left, walking towards the road where Justin had parked earlier.

'Let's go,' Lukas said, taking Venetia's hand. She coiled herself around him lovingly, and the pair vanished.

Orli took Nikolas's arm. 'You are not needed tonight. Let me clean your wounds,' she said of the punches and scrapes he had received when the Raven returned to power. Only Alfred's quick action prevented the Raven from using the force of his fiery powers and destroying Nikolas.

Nikolas gave her a no,d and taking her hand, the pair disappeared. At last, the Raven and the strongest witch were alone in the quiet of the garden.

Sophie whispered, 'I am so sorry for—'

Murdoch cut her off. 'I dreamt of you. Missed you. I couldn't focus for wanting you.'

Her breath hitched. 'Let's never be separated again. Not in this lifetime.'

'Not in this lifetime,' he agreed. Murdoch cleared the emotion from his throat. 'Did I mention I love this dress?'

Sophie smiled, pleased that he should say that to her after all that had happened.

'I believe you did. I could wear it often if you like, and we could role-play. There are some interesting uniforms upstairs, too,' she teased.

'Best show me then,' he said, and extending his hand, she took it, but as Sophie began to lead him inside, she was gently tugged back into his embrace. 'Let me just enjoy this moment alone with you here in the garden, where we have met before so many times,' he whispered into her ear as she pressed up against him.

'We've done it,' she said, 'we can be together.'

'I was never in any doubt that we would find a way to be together in this lifetime.'

She pulled back and smiled, 'really?' Her eyes narrowed. 'You know, when I first met you, you were in love with someone else.'

'You were not ready. My ex-fiancée's cousin,' he recalled. 'I wasn't with her, could never be.'

'But what if you were? What would become of us?'

'We were fated.'

Sophie's eyes widened with surprise. 'Are you saying she would have died if you were together so we could be united by fate?'

'It's not important now, we're together.'

'Nonetheless, tell me,' she said, pressing him.

He grinned at her. 'And that attitude got us in trouble the first time you dismissed me.'

'I didn't dismiss you... I didn't mean to—'

He kissed her to stop the words and, on pulling away, saw the unanswered questions in her eyes.

'No one would have died by our union. I'm saying it worked out the way it did because we were fated, and our journey crossed paths with others on their own shorter or longer journeys. That's the best way I can think to explain it.' He touched her face. 'Don't overthink it Elso... Sophie.'

The intensity in his dark eyes made her pause and appreciate the history between them.

'Oh, I'm still in Elsopeth's dress.'

'Yes, you are. A dangerous move on your part.'

'But aren't you glad for it?' she teased, and he smiled.

'More than I can say.'

'Let's go inside,' Sophie said, keen to be with him body and soul. 'Be with me.'

'For the love of you, I would go anywhere.' And this time, he did follow, and the pair made their way back through the garden into the mansion.

EPILOGUE

Fʀᴏᴍ ᴛʜᴇ Lᴇɴs ꜰᴀᴍɪʟʏ journals – an entry by Alfred Lens, this current day.

Today marks exactly one year since the "Night of Reckoning" as we refer to it – the night that a truce was called for this generation and a promise of prevailing peace agreed to by all parties. A year... how quickly time flies, and I am pleased we finally arrived at the agreement; I was always waiting for fate to call.

Our duties have not changed for the Lens family – we are still the guardians of history and protectors of the accursed. Nikolas was right that stormy evening when he said only the curser could remove a curse, but there are factors at play that Saghani could not have foreseen. Even my sight does not allow me to see that far into the future as my days left in this generation are few.

Speaking of protectors and for journal readers who wish to understand what became of us all when the truce was called, I shall provide a little detail. Nikolas Saggers stood down as Sophie's protector after that night; she could not forgive him for allowing his base instincts to attack the defenceless Murdoch, although they have repaired their friendship since. Nikolas has always been that way; it is why in history, Elsopeth was never with him despite his attempts to claim her as his own. He still manages Sophie's estate and I am pleased to say he has partnered with my niece, Orli. Her gentle soul keeps his restless side at bay, and they run and fly together when the need arises. They are in love, and he will always protect her, I know that to be true.

My grandson, Lukas, cannot resume duties as Sophie's protector as he stood down from the role some time ago and the window of resumption has long since passed. He remains in love with the beautiful Venetia, and their hearts are truly in sync, which is a great comfort to me. It is agreed that with her powers, Sophie does not need a protector in this generation – she is the first of the accursed not to need our resources, but she does like to avail herself of the journals, and I am pleased to say, our company.

Sophie and the Raven have been together since that evening when she placed her hands upon him and his nephew and saved them; if only her ancestral father had done the same for Saghani and not condemned her, our lives and paths would have been so different. The pair live in the mansion Daphne left Sophie, which no doubt would delight Daphne as she always had a soft spot for Murdoch.

Sophie is doing fewer readings these days as her time is taken in motherhood duties – more on that shortly. Her psychic role continues but, in another form, and she still retains the visions when wearing the glasses as Aircraftwoman Margaret Dillon – another Raven rescuer – did before her. Sophie has chosen to work closely with Detective Rachel Fletcher on cold cases, and their results for the past year have been outstanding; they are a fine pair of capable young ladies.

I believe Sophie's assistant, Jack, has enjoyed the research aspect of this new role and is happily distracted with his new amore, Miss Melino Karta, potion maker, who formerly resided with Sophie and now lives in another wing of the mansion with the talented grifter.

The Raven – Murdoch – continues to police but has been given a young protege to develop. I believe that causes him some consternation, and no doubt he misses his former partner, Detective Gerard Oakley, whom I am not sure he has forgiven for mentioning Sophie in his farewell speech, thus losing Murdoch his bet.

The young ones are surprised at the inroads Detective Oakley made in opening his mind and accepting change at the end of his career, but I am not. We seniors have lived through considerable change and are quite adept at adapting.

A child was born, conceived in the garden when Sophie first appeared as Elsopeth to the Raven. Their son, Dane, is not yet one year of age and takes after the Raven clan in features. His parents are not wed – I know that is what modern young people do, but I understand Murdoch is keen to make Sophie his wife. She insists on regaining her figure first and laughs that she sounds like Lucy, her former friend, who is long gone from their lives but occasionally appears in advertising, reminding us of a time best forgotten.

I am sorry to say that Murdoch's nephew who thought he loved Lucy is still quick to temper, but Sophie will be forever in his protection since saving his twin brother, Justin. He will not hear a word against Sophie, thus proving he has some redeeming qualities. Justin will step down from the Raven-succession role when the young Ashcroft comes of age.

And, this is the mystery we are all most interested in seeing unfold. Young Dane's father – Murdoch – is the strongest power of the Raven clan, and his mother – Sophie – is the strongest witch of her time and related to the cursed. What will Dane Ashcroft be? A cursed, a Raven, a witch beyond compare? Will his existence end Saghani's curse if both sides of the warring families exist within him? Time will tell.

The concern is not mine, as I will not be around to see what unfolds. Time has a shadow, and I can feel it encroaching, coming for me, and I will meet it happily. My wife has been gone many years now and waits for me on the other side. My sons Mendel and Chauncey have departed this world, and I am confident I leave our legacy in good hands with my grandson, Lukas, and niece, Orli – respectable young people with good morals.

Orli will step into my shoes, and I have no doubt she will do an admirable job as her strength and skills surpass all others except for Sophie. Lukas is not ready for the task. If I feel remiss at not training him well for the role, I think only of my father's heavy hand and accept my failings as I could not do the same to my grandson. Orli will decide what is best for her descendants and successor when the time comes.

My dearest friend, Miss Sharpe, left this world six months ago after a short illness she bore with no fuss. She took my remaining joy of life with her and left an enormous hole in Sophie's heart.

My work here is done, my life has been a grand adventure, and it has been an honour to serve.

A note from Lukas Lens, grandson of Alfred Lens.

This was the last entry for my grandfather, Alfred Quill Lens, who passed away in his sleep the day after his 80th birthday. Hundreds of mourning doves and ravens lined the telegraph wires of his street like a guard of honour for his soul. He died as he lived, with dignity.

The End.

NEXT IN THIS SERIES

Next in *The Clairvoyant's Glasses* series: The Raven's Son is coming in early 2025.

Special thanks to:

Karri Klawiter, Art by Karri for creating the beautiful covers for this series.

Lisa Randall, Raylen Chen, and Bev Goltz for love, suggestions, and encouragement.

ALSO BY HELEN GOLTZ:

THE LADY MORTICIAN'S VISIONS (historical
mystery/romance/paranormal twist)

The Missing Brides

The Fake Child

The Dastardly Debutante

The Deathly Dolls

The Potent Perfume

The Watery Grave

More to come....

**Miss Hayward & the Detective Series (historical
mystery/romance):**

Murder at the Carnival

The Artist's Missing Muse

Mystery at the Asylum

The Mortician's Clue (introducing Phoebe and staff from
The Economic Undertaker)

Murder in Bridal Lane

The Clairvoyant's Glasses (paranormal/romance)
Volume 1 – A vision unexpected
Volume 2 – Time has a shadow
Volume 3 – Love knows no bounds
Volume 4 – Fate comes to call
Volume 5 – The Raven's Son (coming in 2025)

The Jesse Clarke series (cosy mystery):
Death by Sugar
Death by Disguise
Death by Reunion

The Mitchell Parker series (crime thriller):
Mastermind
Graveyard of the Atlantic
The Fourth Reich

Writing as Jack Adams (mystery suspense):
Poster Girl
Delaney and Murphy childhood friends' series:
Asylum
Stalker
Cult

Hitched

Carnival

Forgotten (the last in the series coming 2025)

Writing as Ally Adams:

The Saints team (contemporary romance):

Team Lucas

Team Tomas

Team Niklas

Team Alex

Stand-alone titles:

The House on Findlater Lane (mystery/romance paranormal)

The Forgotten House (historical romance)

Three Parts Truth (mystery suspense)

Morphers (middle grade fiction)

With journalist Chris Adams:

The Grave Tales series (non-fiction) x 9 titles:

Grave Tales: Brisbane Vol.1

Grave Tales: Great Ocean Road – Geelong to Port Fairy

Grave Tales: Sydney Vol.1

Grave Tales: Bruce Highway

Grave Tales: True Crime Vol.1

Grave Tales: Queensland's Great South West

Grave Tales: Melbourne Vol.1

Grave Tales: Queensland's Scenic Rim & Surrounds

Grave Tales: Tasmania.

Grave Tales: Cold Cases (an amalgamation of stories from existing titles)

ABOUT THE AUTHOR

ELEN IS A HYBRID-PUBLISHED, Amazon best-selling author. After studying English Literature, Media, and Communications at universities in Queensland, Australia, and obtaining a Counselling Diploma, Helen has worked as a journalist, producer and marketer in print, TV, radio and public relations. Born in Toowoomba, she has made her home in Logan Village, Australia, with her journalist husband, Chris, and Boxer dog, Baxter. She is published by Next Chapter and her own imprint, Atlas Productions.

Connect with Helen:

Website: www.helengoltz.com

BookBub:www.bookbub.com/authors/helen-goltz

Facebook: www.facebook.com/HelenGoltz.Author

Instagram: https://www.instagram.com/helengoltz1/